Praise for

"A great and unique story."

"Ingenious twists in the plot and lively characterisation make this a most enjoyable page turning read".

"The premise was really interesting, and I was intrigued to discover what was going on in the house. It was hard to tell whether it was going to be a crime story, thriller, or horror. And in the end, it was none of those, occupying its own genre."

"Full of vibrant, complex characters with surprises and twists throughout. I liked the way it commented on society through the characters and had a good sense of the changes I have experienced in my lifetime. I could really visualize the characters, smell and taste and feel the world they inhabited."

Ghost Train

Emily Tellwright

 Castle Sefton Press

A Note from the Author

In the summer of 1952 62-year-old Alice Wiltshaw was beaten
to death at her home, Estoril House, in the village of Barlaston
in north Staffordshire in one of Britain's most brutal murders.
The house went on to become part of the Wedgwood
Memorial College and now stands empty and derelict.

These events gave me the idea for this book, but do not relate
to it directly. This is entirely a work of fiction – fantasy, in fact
– and any resemblance to persons, living or dead, or events
other than a building where a murder took place later
becoming a college, is entirely coincidental.

Most of the names, including those of the Class 47s, are
fictitious, but any books mentioned, other than those written
by characters in the novel, are real.

Chapter One

IT WAS A BALMY EVENING, breathless and just short of
stuffy, such as now arrived in the Midlands most summers.
Clyde Tranter opened the great sash windows – floor-length
onto the stone balcony – then turned towards the dressing
room to change. He came out again shortly, his toned figure
snappy in the expensive casuals, ready to pick up his wife from
the station and take her to dinner.

He stood in front of the windows to close them and
looked down through the spindly trees and the dusky cross-
hatch of fencing to the railway line below, and to the charming
small station with its model buildings. One expected to see a
polished wooden-doll station master on the platform. No train
had stopped there in nearly twenty years, although this was the
main line and services passed through regularly. As a new
member of the community, Clyde had put his name to the
campaign to reinstate local services, which would after all be
very convenient for Lucinda and him.

They had lived in London throughout their successful
careers, but a time had come when they had thought of
cashing in the value of their home in the capital and moving

out somewhere. Clyde's work, like that of so many others, was mostly done at home now, but property prices had soared and country bargains in reach of the metropolis were hard to find.

So they had looked further afield. In the charming North Midlands village of Burnton, part way between the degenerate industrial city of Greater Blocton and the insignificant county town of Slackford, Clyde had found a derelict Victorian villa set in two acres of gardens and woodland. Slackford's fast train service to London made it a distinct possibility. The fact that the house was being sold for a song by the desperate Greater Blocton Council – it had been a municipally run residential college since the early 1960s – made it a bargain too good to miss.

Clyde had project-managed the restoration and remodelling while Lucinda had designed and chosen the interiors. Having sold their apartment in the capital, she spent work nights in the studio flat above her chic London art gallery *Endeavour*, whilst Clyde had had one of the villa's outbuildings converted into a habitable annex from which to supervise the necessary work on the house.

Of course, it had been a stressful and expensive process, even with the bargain price of the building and site, and had taken longer than forecast. He had finally moved into the main building now. Lucinda came up when she was free, or for meetings about her new work in the local area that would lead to it becoming her permanent base.

The villa was a welcoming, though slightly heavy, red-brick building of angles, gables and bays. The high oak-lined drawing room, with huge stone-mullioned bay windows that opened onto the sunny, sheltered lawns, had been knocked together with the former dining room in the days of the college, suiting the modern fashion for open-plan spaces. Lucinda had, with her characteristic taste and judgement, struck a happy balance of style between period and practical:

modern sofas, statement art, large television and other technology together with well-chosen rugs and plants served to lighten the weighty architecture. Perhaps she had picked up an inherent lightness of mood that lingered even in the most darkly panelled corners; the building imposed its own steady calm.

All the rooms were enormous. Attics and bedrooms alike had been mini-dormitories, all swept with trade magnolia emulsion and brown industrial gloss to neutralise their original hierarchy. They remained shabbily welcoming, but the surviving bathroom and toilet facilities had been sparse and basic enough to be repellent to those of the Tranters' generation and background. They filled Lucinda with disgust, despite the lingering impression of scrubbed cleanliness on the scratched enamel and stained porcelain.

The upper levels had been unsafe in places where the elements had worked their relentless entropy through a leaking roof and badly boarded windows. Luckily, there had been no vandalism, as the desperate Blocton Council had spent a small fortune on resident security, fences, lights, dogs, cameras and alarms. No wonder they were so anxious to get rid of a place with such high overheads. Clyde had wondered in passing if it wouldn't have made more sense to have spent the money maintaining and using the building.

The restoration was now done: a magnificent master bedroom suite, guest accommodation, Clyde's library, Lucinda's studio, a superb kitchen-diner, a gym, spacious garages and storage. Clyde would be supervising the final landscaping over the next week: maintenance and assessment of the woodland, restoration and improvement of the lawns, paths and flowerbeds, completion of the swimming pool. Only the lodge cottage at the main entrance gate remained to be rescued.

The band of woodland was thinnest on the slope that fell away from one side of the house to the railway line, and it was through this scrub that Clyde's eyes were rather blankly directed as he pushed down the huge, pricey modern sashes. There was a gentle whirring noise, and a bar of shadow drew across his line of vision; a train was passing. But wait. Now he paid attention, it wasn't passing; it had stopped. He was mildly curious, wondering what the hold-up could be, but a flurry of clicks and bangs followed and the locomotive moved off. Clyde relaxed, about to turn away, when he saw figures appear on the platform behind the retreating carriages.

Passengers! Had the local service been restarted? He wondered when it had been decided, but of course, he had been so stretched with the completion of the house and his work together that he had not had much time to keep up with local events.

Lucinda can travel from London straight to her own gate next time, he thought as he got out his car to go and pick her up.

As he waited on the platform at Slackford a short while later, he was cornered by a bored member of station staff determined to pass the time chatting to his captive audience. Unable to escape, Clyde asked about trains stopping at Burnton.

"There's no local service running up the line from here," said the employee, looking puzzled. "I've been here twelve years and there's never trains to Burnton.

"Mind you," he continued conversationally, "it wouldn't be our company. This station is West Coast Express and the stopping trains are London North Midland. But then LNM have been running replacement buses on that section recently, so I don't see how ... They'd know in the ticket office, of course, but it's closed now. Why don't you look on the internet?"

At that moment, Lucinda's train came in and action ensued. Clyde decided he'd look into the new local train service as soon as the final week of work on the garden was finished.

Arriving home later after their meal, Lucinda kicked off her shoes, threw down her bag and went over to the un-curtained drawing-room window to open the glass doors. Here, the original floor-length sashes had been just too impractical. The concentrated smell of dry summer garden drifted in as she went over to pour herself a drink.

"Want one?" she asked Clyde as he drifted into the room.

"Yes, please. Seems I'd left a light on in the kitchen. There's a really odd smell in there, savoury and smoky, as if we'd been cooking."

"Have you been cooking today?"

"No. When would I have had time to cook with workmen here and another ridiculous Teams meeting this afternoon?" He took a breath to calm down. "I thought I might tomorrow, though, make something nice for us when there's time to relax and enjoy the process. It would be good to really use the kitchen at last and start to settle in."

Lucinda vaguely acquiesced; cooking didn't interest her.

"Did the wine arrive?"

"Yesterday. We can open some of the Gewürztraminer tomorrow if the weather stays like this."

"Mmm, it will be perfect. Shame the pool's not ready."

"I've chased them. They're starting Monday and it should be finished when you come next weekend."

"Let's hope this weather holds."

Conversation remained desultory and slightly impersonal; the long periods of separation recently had tipped the balance of their relationship away from that of a unified couple towards two individuals, and it always took them a while to adjust to each other again.

Lucinda got up.

"I'm going to bed," she declared drowsily, "you coming?"

"Okay."

She went to close the windows; Clyde took the glasses into the kitchen. "That smell's still lingering," he called, but she ignored such trivia.

"When's the woman from the cleaning company coming? Whatever they're called ..." She gestured to him with a loose hand as they crossed the hall.

"Wednesday, I think," he replied, starting up the stairs. "Probably be a while before they can find us anyone, she said, with labour shortages ..."

"Well, we might be able to outbid the competition," said his wife. "They probably charge less here than we're used to paying."

"Probably." As a newly adopted local, Clyde was less keen on cutting out his neighbours by an unfriendly gesture; Lucinda was still in London ways. "Hey, I don't think I told you that they've started the trains again. The ones that stop here, I mean."

"Really? You sure?"

"I saw one. It stopped and people got off. But it could have been a special service or a trial or something, I suppose. I'll have to find out ..."

By this time they were undressed and getting into bed. Lucinda touched him lightly.

"Tomorrow," she said, brushing him with a kiss, and fell asleep immediately.

In his brief half-sleep, Clyde thought he heard a burst of running water, but it was not enough to keep him awake.

Lucinda returned to London early Monday morning, leaving Clyde alone in his new work environment. He had taken his laptop out to the veranda and settled himself with a coffee, but found it impossible to get a Wi-Fi signal. To his surprise, he found he didn't really care, the company he worked for had recently been taken over, since when he seemed to have very little work to do.

He took a breath, relaxing ground-ward in the grace of gravity, lifted his face to the early sun and stretched his neck away from the newly heavy limbs. The fresh, bright air of the summer morning brought his skin to life in an abundance of unknowable sensations. Another breath. It must be something about this place that meant, despite the work and stresses of the renovation, that old workhorse, his nervous system, had ceased its constant enervation.

As he opened his eyes, a bullish little pink-and-black bird alighted on the birdfeeder just ahead of him with his statuesque sandstone-coloured partner. His beady black eye looked solidly into the washy blue of Clyde's, holding them together in a fraction of suspended time. When the tiny passerine took once more to the wing, Clyde was left with a new awareness of his existence.

The sound of a van drawing up nearby roused him, and he wandered round the side of the house to see the swimming-pool team.

"Morning, Clyde. Good weather for getting the job done!"

"Hi, Sean." Clyde was uncharacteristically vague and looking straight through the very solid Sean to the shrubbery beyond. There was an awkward pause. "What are your lads doing over there?" he asked.

"These are my lads," said Sean, gesturing to the group behind him, busily unloading the van. "Is there someone over there?" He turned to follow Clyde's puzzled gaze and his lads grouped around him, ready to do some mild taking-on if needed. Clyde drifted back, shaking his head.

"Sounded like female laughter," he said. "Don't want people getting into the grounds."

"I thought your security was pretty tight – we certainly had to use the code to get in. Are you feeling alright, Clyde? Only we're going to be making a bit of noise here today ..."

"What? Oh, yeah, I'm okay. I just ..." Clyde's phone rang and as he took it out of his pocket, everyone heard it shout,

"Clyde! Where the fuck are you? Our meeting started ten minutes ago!"

"Shit!" said Clyde, running back towards his laptop, waving behind himself at the workmen as he went. "Teething troubles with the Wi-Fi ..."

"I don't give a shit! Get yourself in front of that fucking screen and let's get on with it!"

The phone relaxed as the call was cut off. Clyde grabbed his laptop and went inside.

By the time Clyde removed his headphones at the end of the meeting, the workmen were indeed making a lot of noise outside, so he decided to stroll down to the village pub for lunch. The majestic dark cedars sponged up the hazy warmth, casting their own quiet over the drive. His mind drifting in the heady atmosphere, Clyde was shaken awake on hitting the cool patch of deep shade at the bend of the drive, and as his eyes focussed once more on his surroundings, they caught a red bicycle nipping through the gates, pedalled hard by a crouched form. Now fully alert, he jogged the last stretch, but when he arrived at the roadside, the black metal railings were shut across the majestic stone posts.

"But I saw it go through!" he blurted out to no one. It was dingy in the deep shade on a bright day and he might have been mistaken. He shrugged and keyed in the code to open the gates.

It was fairly quiet in the pub, and Clyde sat at the bar chatting to the owner.

"Are you still thinking of reviving the kitchen garden at your place?"

"Well, yes ... it's just a matter of getting the other stuff done first. Luce is very keen on the pool as a focus for parties – entertaining all her art and business contacts and so on. I had the idea of opening the walled garden as a business: getting someone in to do the growing part, selling the produce, running courses, school visits even. I could do a bit of training and get involved with the grubby end myself."

"I'd be interested in taking some of your produce if it happens."

"Great. I'll start planning and looking for a garden manager."

"So, will Lucinda be moving up permanently soon?"

"Ha," Clyde gave a hard sigh, "I dunno really. I don't know if she's ready to cut away from London altogether. Don't get me wrong, she loves it here, loves the house ..." *Loves me*, he almost said, but couldn't quite. "I just don't think she's ready to make it full time. And after all, her work is more dependent on being in London than mine."

Clyde's meal was ready and their conversation was cut short by his being shown to a table. The only other early luncher was also a man eating alone. He had unnaturally chestnut hair sitting thickly on top of his head, a wide, podgy, sallow face, yellow metal spectacles over his little khaki eyes, and wore a shirt in wide crossing lines of orange, yellow and brown.

Clyde began his meal.

"Excuse me," the man called over after a few moments, "but aren't you Mr Tranter from Valencia House?" Clyde looked up and nodded, his mouth full. "My name is Melrose Burke," said the man, getting up and approaching Clyde's table, "local historian and president of the Burnton Historical Society. Perhaps you've read some of my publications?"

"Er, no," said Clyde, hastily swallowing, "Afraid not. Not really been here long, you know ..."

"Of course, of course." Melrose Burke waved his hands and grinned, showing a small mouth full of very large teeth. "May I?" And he sat down.

Clyde carried on eating.

"A beautiful villa, Valencia House," Melrose opened expansively, his squeaky voice achieving an unctuous quality. "Built in 1871 by the Skeratt family, wealthy industrialists from Nettleton, and a fine example of its type. Of course, there were many such houses across the country, but of those that survive, few still have the grounds and outbuildings. I don't know why it's not listed; we have *tried*. Still, I think late Victorian is finally beginning to be appreciated after being a victim of neglect and snobbery – particularly *Georgian* snobbery, the dear Georgians, so dull and *symmetrical* – for so long, don't you?"

"Yes, I think you're probably right," mumbled Clyde vaguely through his salad. "Where's Nettleton?"

"It's one of the five towns that make up the city of Greater Blocton, my dear boy." *I didn't know anyone really said that*, thought Clyde. "It's not a proper city, you know, just a few towns that ran together."

"I didn't know. I've only been there a couple of times."

"Ah, you have so much to learn!" Melrose grinned juicily, patting Clyde's leg like an elderly roué who has cornered an ingénue. "But of course, you know all about *the murders*. They're what makes your house *famous*." He cast a beady sideways eye at Clyde.

"Murders?" This time, Clyde spluttered and put his cutlery down. "In *our house*?"

"You didn't know? My dear boy, it was a *notorious* case. I

must tell you all about it! Oh, but don't worry," he gave another expansive hand-wave, "it was a long time ago – 1950s, not long after the war."

"I thought it had been a college," stammered Clyde.

"Oh, it was, it was. Afterwards. I mean, no one wanted to live in it *then*. Now it's quite different, *of course*." He patted Clyde's arm. "Though some believe it's haunted. That must be nonsense, though, mustn't it?"

"Haunted?" echoed Clyde, still too shocked by the revelation of the murders to find it amusing.

"Oh, don't worry about *that*." Melrose Burke was now positively avuncular. "Let's have a drink and I'll tell you all about it. Coffee?" As Clyde nodded, Burke waved a flabby paw in the direction of the waitress. "Sandra ... Sally ... er, Sarah – whatever your name is – I'm joining Mr Tranter. We'll have coffee for two and a couple of large brandies ..." He cocked an eye at Clyde, who agreed wanly, then added, "Make it the good stuff, that special Napoleon," before settling himself down like a roosting hen. "Now, my dear boy, let's begin at the beginning as you're a stranger to the area.

"Before the war, one of the oldest and largest manufacturers in Greater Blocton built a new expanded factory on greenfield land just outside the village here, a model estate for their workers, and the 'new' railway station, now sadly out of use—"

"I thought ..." interrupted Clyde, thinking of the twilight scene a few nights earlier. But Melrose was in an irrepressible mood.

"The railway made the village easily accessible to well-off folks with business in town, and when the last of the Skeratts was killed in the war, Woodlands, as it was then, was bought by a wealthy factory owner, Brian Hassel of Dorfold Ware in Offshaw, another one of the five towns. He remodelled it as a home for his wife Berenia and himself, and they renamed it

Valencia House. I believe they had a fondness for southern Spain."

Melrose Burke became confidential and his shrill tones correspondingly more bearable.

"The Hassels had no children, only a niece Sheila who regularly came to stay with them, and there were no staff living in the house; there weren't many resident domestics to be had because no one wanted to do that kind of work anymore. A couple living in the gatehouse cottage, Alf and Janet Baxter, did everything between them, with the assistance of a cleaner and gardener from the village."

"I was thinking of making the cottage a home for one of my garden staff ..." murmured Clyde, but a stern frown on the frog-like face opposite shut him up.

"Brian Hassel was rather typical of his type: complacent, self-satisfied and un-dynamic in business with a tendency to sit back and let things be done the way they always had. He took care of his workers as long as it didn't cost him too much or mean that he had to pay them better wages. By the second half of the 50s, he was reinventing himself in his own mind as a cutting-edge businessman of the age, although all this meant in practice was modern office decor, younger, more glamorous secretaries and a lot of jargon that he didn't fully understand.

"Berenia had been a pretty enough girl from a decent background, but her real attraction was that her father, a builder, had made a killing between the wars and become both extremely wealthy and important in local politics. By the time the Hassels bought Valencia House, his company, in which Berenia had a holding, was cashing in on the post-war building boom and making everyone involved a lot more money. Berenia had become a stout and pleasant, but spoiled and thoroughly silly middle-aged woman whose main interests were extravagant hats, expensive jewellery and luxury holidays. Her niece Sheila, Berenia's sister's daughter, was of a similar mind, and the two spent a good deal of time together on shopping trips, lunching out and taking holidays 'for Berenia's health'.

"On the 25th of October 1958, Brian Hassel came home from work expecting to find Berenia and Sheila at home. Normally, Alf Baxter, who acted as chauffeur, would have collected him from work, but that day there were problems with the large saloon car, so Alf had stayed at home to get it fixed while Brian had taken the train.

"When Brian entered the house that night, he found Sheila's body lying in the hall, her throat cut from behind. His wife was in a chair in the drawing room, shot in the chest, dead. Brian ran down to the lodge to find the body of Janet Baxter in the kitchen, shot through the head, and that of Alf hanging in the hall, a cut-throat razor in his pocket and a service revolver lying at his feet."

Clyde gasped. The man certainly had his full attention now.

"Alf Baxter had been wounded and lost for several days during the later stages of the war. He was badly shell-shocked and physically weakened. A mild-mannered, popular man originally, he became taciturn and surly for spells that grew longer and more noticeable. Still, he and his wife had been valuable to the Hassels – Janet was an excellent cook and housekeeper, it seems – who were therefore prepared to be sympathetic.

"Evidence showed that Alf had murdered Janet, Sheila and Berenia before killing himself, but some of Berenia's jewellery was missing and was never found."

Clyde was quite speechless. He didn't feel himself to be overly sensitive or superstitious, so this news probably wouldn't affect his feelings about the house, but it was still a shock.

"I can see that you're having trouble taking it in." Melrose

13

was ebullient and hand-waving once more. "No wonder, my dear boy, *no wonder.*" He patted Clyde's arm. "The council should have told you, of course – you can't trust *anyone* nowadays – but probably there was no legal obligation so they could get away with not mentioning it. Or perhaps some young ignoramus did not even *know.* It has *cachet,* though, you can't deny it. Everyone loves a murder, and the mystery of the jewellery has kept the theories alive even now.

"I'll call round and bring you a copy of my book, *The Burnton Murders: Whose Victims?* I think as the new owner of Valencia House, you'll soon find that you want to know everything you can, and mine is the *definitive* work. Quite free of charge to you, my dear boy, *of course,*" he added oilily. With one last pat of the arm, Melrose was up and waddling out of the pub.

Clyde finished his drink, then paid the bill. He noticed that he was paying for Melrose's lunch as well as his brandy.

Chapter Two

"DARLING, THAT'S WONDERFUL!" It was a Friday and Clyde had phoned to tell Lucinda that the pool area was complete. "I can't wait to see it. We must organise a party right away ... see you later, darling. At 6.12 – I'm getting away early today."

Clyde was bored. He was gradually being side-lined at work, despite his still generous remuneration, and it was not as if it interested him anyway. He'd gone into the business to make money, not because he liked it, and he had. He knew it was time for a change, but there was always one more assignment, however insignificant. The reluctance to let him go might be flattering, but he didn't believe his skills were that valuable; maybe it was cheaper to keep him on, or perhaps the new controlling interests were just keeping their options open. But this was it, he decided. His current project was definitely going to be his last.

On arriving home, Lucinda rushed round the back of the house to the pool area while Clyde parked the car. There were still no local trains advertised, and he hadn't found anyone who knew about the one that had stopped at the old station the previous week. It must have been some kind of private service, if such things still existed.

"Champagne!" Lucinda was at her sparkling best, sailing through the French windows into the kitchen as Clyde unlocked them. She grabbed glasses from a cupboard on her way and a bottle from the wine fridge, and soon had the crystal flutes overflowing with an effervescence that matched her own. "Clyde, they've done a wonderful job, doesn't it look perfect? We must have a party and invite *everyone*!"

"All *your* friends, you mean." Clyde smiled to soften his words. He didn't have many friends, only a couple of old university acquaintances.

The freshwater pool was silky in the late summer evening light. An hour that would have still felt like daytime a couple of weeks ago now suggested cocktails and canapés on the terrace and the stirring of wild creatures beyond. He wished they had canapés and hoped they had wild creatures. A frisson of excitement passed through him in response to the strange-ness of nature, the unknowable life hidden in the rustling dusk, and he felt suddenly sickened by the tame plasticity of his previous existence.

"No, darling, *everyone*! My friends, of course, a few contacts I need to soften up, Craig and Jim, but locals too. You've made friends, haven't you? Some of them might be useful. People it will be worth getting to know if we're going to settle here."

I believed we had settled – I have, thought Clyde, but he said, "I haven't really made friends. A few acquaintances at the tennis club, Blair and Tracey at the pub, Chelsea ... oh, and a really comical historian called Melrose Burke, president of the local history society."

"Chelsea?" queried Lucinda.

"The cleaning lady, or rather person ... the cleaner, I suppose I should say."

"Oh yes. I haven't met her, have I? Is she any good?"

"Yes, very – I mean, take a look round inside. I didn't do it all myself," he smiled, "even if I'm not very busy. She's a smart girl, actually. Used to have some kind of office job, got married to someone else in the office, then they decided to quit and set up a cleaning business. Better money and more independence, apparently."

"Did you mention a local history society?"

"Yes! I must tell you about Melrose Burke. A real stunner. It was him who told me about the murders."

"D'you know, I've been thinking about that – the murders, I mean. A notorious house could be a *thing*. I could make it a theme for a series of new works, or even a whole exhibition. Let's invite the history society to the party."

Clyde knew Lucinda well enough not to expect any sensitivity over something detached by time and lack of personal connection. He still felt entirely comfortable in the house, but couldn't help staring at a couple of spots occasionally where he imagined the bodies must have been found.

"What, all of them?" he exclaimed in surprise.

"Well, just the important ones, the committee or whatever. And obviously this Melrose person."

"You might not feel so sure about inviting Melrose Burke if you'd met him. He'll probably drink us dry and drive all the other guests away by being alternately rude, boring and obsequious. And he'll either come in a Hawaiian shirt or a 1970s maroon velvet dinner suit, I expect."

"He sounds like just the sort of character that the London crowd will enjoy," insisted Lucinda. "I'll feel like lady of the manor for the evening."

"Yes, you'd have been rather good at it," said Clyde, beaming, drawing her towards him and kissing her indulgently. "I'd better get dinner on before I get too pissed."

. . .

"You say you saw a train stop at the station, Clyde? Last month? That's very odd. Let's get George over here. If anyone knows what's going on, George will. Here, George, excuse me, but can you spare us a moment? Mr Tranter saw a train stop at our station just recently ..."

It was the following Saturday and Lucinda's party was in full swing. Along with members of the history society, Clyde had invited some of the organisers of the campaign to reopen the local station.

"Hello, Bernard. What's that you say, a train stopped at our station? Good evening, Mr Tranter. Good of you to invite us. Very nice to see Valencia House back in use."

"Clyde, please, and I'm glad you like it."

"This is George Timmins, Clyde. He's a great expert on all forms of transport, but especially trains." George drew himself up and beamed proudly. "George has been spotting trains since he was so high, haven't you, George?" continued Bernard, holding out a hand just above his knee. "You've probably seen him at STAB meetings."

"STAB?" queried Clyde.

"Save Trains at Burnton," explained George. "And strictly speaking, I'm not a trainspotter," he frowned at Bernard, "I'm a Transport Enthusiast. Now, you say you've seen a train stopping at Burnton Station one evening?"

"Yes, one Friday at the beginning of July around 8pm," said Clyde. "People got off."

"People got off?" Bernard was clearly surprised. "But ..."

"How many people?" asked George curtly.

"About five or six, I think."

"It's very strange that I should know nothing about it. Unless," George considered, "was it a Class 47? There are a few of them running charters. It could have been the *Princess*

Alice 47579, and I'm pretty sure they also use the *Dover Castle 47568*. What livery was it, Intercity or British Rail Green?"

Clyde stared at him quizzically.

"The engine," said George, slowly and loudly as if Clyde were an idiot. "Did the number begin with 47 and what colour was it?"

"It didn't have an engine," replied Clyde equally slowly. He actually was an idiot in the world of transport enthusiasm. "It was an ordinary local-type electric train with the driver's compartment in the front carriage."

"What?" spluttered George. "An *electric*? It's unheard of! I'm going to have to phone Mike at HETS – Heritage Electric Trains Society – and find out what's going on. Still, it explains the stopping at Burnton, the big charters don't do that. Excuse me, Clyde." He hurried off, reaching for his phone.

"Well!" Clyde sighed. "Fancy another drink, Bernard?"

"That would be very nice, thank you, Clyde. Mine's a Martini Rosso on the rocks," said Bernard, following him to the bar. "It's no wonder poor George is upset. I'm not so much of a transport man myself, it's more the historic buildings for me. Preserving them, you know, and if possible keeping them in use. That's why I was so surprised, you see, Clyde, when you mentioned passengers getting off at the station. STAB volunteers have been looking after the buildings at Burnton – with the proper permissions, of course – for some time now. We're responsible for the site, which is naturally well secured, and hasn't, as far as I know, been opened to anyone recently."

"It's all a great mystery," said Clyde lightly, helping himself to another drink as he resupplied Bernard, "and if I wasn't certain I'd seen people on the platform, I'd think I'd been mistaken about the train stopping at all."

Leaving the bar, he felt a heavy hand on his arm. "My dear boy!" Melrose Burke was in an effusive – indeed, slightly inebriated – mood. "So kind, so kind of you to think of me, my dear boy. And very wise to get in with the *hoi polloi*." He rolled his hands at the assembled company, then tapped one side of his nose with a finger and winked suggestively. "Often useful information to be gleaned. My book!" He produced it from nowhere with a flourish. "This one is dedicated *specially* to *you*, but I do have *others* with me. The *Londoners*, you know, *influential* people in the arts scene. It's all about making contacts, dear boy. Time for a schmooze round the room."

He waddled off conspicuously – he was indeed wearing a lime-green Hawaiian shirt and velvet trousers – just as Lucinda arrived at the bar.

"Have we got any Campari? Jules wants a Negroni."

"I think so, let me have a look. I was just going to introduce you to the great Melrose."

"The one like a frog in fancy dress? I've met him. Well, sort of; I held out my hand and introduced myself, he made a weird rumbling gurgle in his throat, then toddled off without saying a word. One of the other historians, a Miss somebody – Agnes, I think she said – was telling me that he has a problem with women and that's what ended his career as a lecturer."

Lucinda had had a few drinks herself, which tended to bring her opinions out forcefully. "A problem with women, for fuck's sake! That's half the fucking population. How does he cope? Anyway, he'd better not have his problems anywhere near me, the pathetic old fart, or I'll have him on everything I can get him on."

Clyde handed her a Negroni for Jules. "He's off schmoozing your London friends. Want one yourself?"

"No thanks, I've got one somewhere ...Ha, well, he's in for a shock when he finds out at least half of them are female. Stupid old twat will probably have some kind of fit. The food looks good, considering it's local. We should probably get started on it soon."

Clyde's friends Craig and Jim hadn't been able to make it to the party, and he felt rather outside the core social activity. He decided to have a chat to the caterers to see if the food was ready.

"It's almost ready, Mr Tranter," said the very efficient lady in charge as he wandered into the kitchen, either keen to reassure her client or wanting to get him out from under her feet. "The hot food's in the ovens and will only be a few more minutes."

"Great, thanks, er, Marina," he said. He found it uncomfortably feudal to be addressed as Mr, but now was clearly not the time to remonstrate. "I'll start shepherding everyone to the dining room."

"Some of the staff should be in there waiting," she called after him as he headed for the door. "Just let them know the onslaught is coming."

Clyde smiled weakly. He cut a sorry figure, he felt, alone at his own party and redundant in his kitchen. His confident, busy, sociable life had been nothing but a veneer, a shiny swirl of noise to distract him from spending time with himself; it had fallen away instantly and without a single lasting connection as soon as he had left London, the office and Lucinda's world behind. But Lucinda had not left her world behind; she'd brought it with her. If he no longer joined in, it was because he had given up the fatuous game of pretending to be interested when there were so many more important things to think about, such as his garden, his library, cooking and the mysteries of life at Valencia House.

The building seemed to have an existence independent of him with a plethora of resident sights, sounds and smells on which he seemed to be constantly intruding. There was never the chill emptiness of sole occupancy even when he was alone. At this moment, a very old-fashioned aroma was permeating the passageway; delicious, meaty and deeply savoury with over-tones of baking and no hint of exotic spice. It was an English kitchen smell remembered from his young days, such as had been borne in clouds of wet cabbage steam from the better school and hospital kitchens and college halls. The damp air muffled the clatter of dishes, trolleys and voices behind him; it sounded like a far busier kitchen than he had witnessed.

In dreamy alcohol-enhanced puzzlement, he drifted in through the French windows of the dining room. Several figures in black-and-white were pottering around.

"I've spoken to Marina, and I'm going to call the guests in," he announced generally – and rather unevenly. There was a murmur of polite assent and the monochrome figures moved to action stations.

"Can I help?" said a deep gravelly voice at his side. He turned to see a short, toughly built man with rather leathery skin and very lively bright eyes. His lantern jaw was softened with an impressive grey-tinged beard that wagged roguishly. With his white steward's jacket, he gave the effect of a gnome butler. "I'm Zeno, the service manager."

"Oh, I ... oh," said Clyde, who had thought Marina was in charge. Perhaps she was. Then he gave up thinking about it. "Er, yes ... no, thanks, er, nice to meet you, that is, Zeno." He collected himself. "I'll call the guests over, you marshal them round. How about that?"

The man twinkled. "Yes, of course."

"The food looks wonderful."

Zeno became genuinely animated. "Oh yes, Mrs Allerton is a very good cook and modern British food is so varied, isn't it? We're like culinary magpies picking out the shiny jewels from all the great cuisines."

Clyde was impressed by this vivid image, visualising pies full of rubies.

"But there's still a place for plain English cooking celebrating a very good ingredient simply prepared," the sparkly little man was continuing seriously. "All these special diets make things so difficult, though. I'm glad I don't have to deal with them."

"Ah," Clyde nodded politely.

"It's all ready, Mr Tranter, if you are."

"Oh yes, of course," mumbled Clyde, his mind returning from the image of a magpie diving kingfisher-like to retrieve a diamond from a vat of stew. "And it's Clyde, you know. Clyde." Off he went towards the crowd, still dazed.

Soon, everyone was eating and milling around, making muffled chat with full mouths over precariously balanced plates. Clyde, feeling more sober after some solid food, found himself in the impressive hall nibbling a superb spicy potato patty and chatting to a neat, slightly mannish elderly lady. It was Agnes Beresford, the historian whom Lucinda had mentioned to him earlier.

"I must thank you, Mr Tranter, for inviting me, and indeed my fellow members of the Society. The food is delicious." She smiled and took a delicate bite of Thai crab cake. "You're interested in local history, then, I suppose?"

"Well ..." Clyde considered. "Yes. I hadn't thought about it before, but when you take on a place like this, which *has* a history, you have to take an interest because it's there all around you. And as I'm new to the area, local history is a way of getting to know it, although I hadn't done anything about it until I came across Melrose Burke. He told me about the murders. Before that, I'd had no idea of any such thing."

"Ah, the murders." Miss Beresford shook her head with a sad smile. "There is so much more to the history of Burnton than the murders. Though it was a terrible thing at the time, I remember it well."

"You remember the murders?"

"Oh yes, I was ten. We lived at Rose Villa just off the green. A lovely house, but far too big to manage once my father died and my brother moved away. Mother and I moved to one of the more modern cottages on the other side, which is where I still am. My father was head of the Blocton City Libraries and Museums Service. It was an exciting time of development and expansion. He was involved in establishing the college here too."

She took another morsel of crab. "But the murders ... it's natural that you should want to know about them, living here. I can't tell you what a shock it was to us in those days. A crime like that would be shocking even now, but such violence was quite unheard of then in such an out-of-the-way place as this. Scotland Yard came, and newspaper men from London, it was an enormous sensation. But the Hassels, of whom I have only a vague impression, were not greatly involved in the local community, and so, although everyone was naturally very sorry, there wasn't a deep sense of personal tragedy in the village."

She paused and chewed delicately for a few seconds, collecting her thoughts.

"Perhaps people felt more for the Baxters, I'm not sure. Janet Baxter was a pleasant, quiet, ordinary woman – the sort we saw about and said hello to. It's Alf I remember most of all because he was strange, and it was a kind of strangeness particularly frightening to a child. He was fond of sweets and always had a bag in his coat pocket, perhaps because he'd given up smoking as his lungs were bad after the war. You'd often see him going down to the garage in the village or Butt's the iron-mongers, and he'd always dip his hand in his pocket, grinning, and bring out a bag to offer to you. Then gradually, there were more and more times when he didn't offer you a sweet, or smile, or even recognise you, and would push past, staring and

24

muttering in a low growl. He would sometimes look right through you as if he couldn't see you, but if you stopped and stared at him and he did take notice, he would point and shout. If that happened to you, you would never approach him again.

"That was really what made the crime so shocking. It was not just the brutality – that was bad, of course – but the location, a quiet country backwater, and the fact that the crime was rooted in the past, a lingering consequence of the terrible violence of the war. This wasn't a youth crime – delinquents or Teddy Boys – or a gangster job; it was the ugly face of our brave and glorious victory, of the sacrifices made by the ordinary man that had never been paid back, of the damage done by the country to its own that had never been properly acknowledged. As the war retreated to some well-remembered finest hour, an example of the greatness of our nation that was, once again, to flower in those 'never had it so good' years, the Burnton murders were an unwanted sharp reminder of the truth."

Clyde was charmed by this erudite speech from one clearly used to giving lectures, and fascinated by her point of view of the murders. He wanted to prolong their conversation, and yet felt rather out of practice at the academic style. He spoke sincerely before she could escape.

"That's fascinating, thank you. I would love to hear what you find to be the most interesting aspect of Burnton history. I know so little." He sounded rather prim, he felt, but Miss Beresford was happy to rise to the bait.

"I am an expert on the pottery industries of North Slackfordshire in the eighteenth century, specialising particularly in the life and work of Samuel Shaftacre."

"Samuel Shaftacre?"

"The pioneer industrial potter of Arcadia, anti-slavery campaigner and enlightenment figure."

"Really," said Clyde, "I had no idea. And he's connected to the Shaftacre factory here in Burnton, presumably?"

"*He* had no connection, but the family firm built a more modern factory here in the 1930s, as I'm sure you know. Samuel Shaftacre's Arcadia Works – just outside Ridgley in Greater Blocton – was phased out and closed in 1950. It's a UNESCO World Heritage Site now, and you must visit it! I was involved in the application myself when I was at the museum in Ridgley. So fortunate that we managed to save it; it had declined into a state of advanced dereliction and there had been an unsuccessful attempt at arson. The city council had plans to replace it with a dual carriageway and a retail park, and it was really only through the help of some wealthy and influential figures, and a good deal of luck, that we succeeded. Of course," she bristled, "they're only too happy to crow about it now it's famous and brings in huge amounts of tourist revenue for the city. I'm sure half of them don't know who Samuel Shaftacre was!"

Clyde looked appropriately contemptuous of such ignoramuses, even though he had been one of them.

"Of course, this house has connections with the industry too. The Skeratts owned the Talbot Works in Nettleton, but by the mid-nineteenth century, the nearby colliery had made the site of their original mansion very unattractive – dangerous even, given there were signs of subsidence – and they moved here. Abel Skeratt was still very much involved in the running of the business, and the coming of the railway made this a practical location as well as an attractive one. I think the grounds may have been somewhat larger then, although I am not certain.

"By the time the last of the Skeratts died in the war, the factory had been absorbed by Royal Charlton. Brian Hassel was director of Dorfold Ware, of course, and that was quite a different matter; by then, they were producing cheap earthenware in modern designs for the upwardly mobile fashion-conscious housewife, and they did very well extending that trend into the 1960s. So well that they were bought out by Shire Potteries in 1970. I think Brian Hassel made a lot of money, but of course it could never make up for what happened."

Clyde frowned slightly. He had a vision of fat, prosperous Brian Hassel, having rid himself of his fat, prosperous and rather silly wife, retiring to the Caribbean with a blonde secretary twenty years younger than him. Could he have been involved in the crime? He shook his attention away from this groundless fantasy back to Agnes Beresford. He had definitely watched too much *Columbo* in his youth.

"I would like to ask you, Mr Tranter," the lady was continuing, "if members of the history society could have a tour of the house? At your convenience, of course," she added, hedging her imperious enthusiasm with politeness. "I don't know anyone who remembers the interior of the house as a private residence now, though when I was young, I knew old Mrs Baker who had been the Skeratts' cook before the war. We all remember it as the Shaftacre Memorial College, in fact, I gave lectures here a few times myself. But I have talked quite long enough and that is a story for another day!"

"Oh yes, the college," said Clyde, feeling that he had got into the mood of the conversation at last. "To be honest, I don't know much about that either. By the time we bought the property, most of the fittings had been stripped out, let alone the furniture, and the annexe at the back had been demolished. I think we always saw it in our minds as a house, and it was hard to imagine it as a college. There were a couple of rather primitive bathrooms left on the top floor – Lucinda was horrified by them – and a lot of brown gloss paint on the woodwork. There were sections of fat, thickly painted pipes around the place, no longer connected to anything, a couple of fire-exit notices, and this." He drew something out of a drawer in the hall table. It was a strip of dirty brushed metal with the inscription 'P Hutchinson, Principal' picked out in black.

"Patrick Hutchinson, yes, I remember the name," said Miss Beresford coolly. "I think he was here at the end. A management type rather than an educator. Some thought he was brought in to turn the college around and some thought to finish it off ...Will you excuse me if I get a little more to eat? The food is excellent."

"Of course," said Clyde politely, realising he would like some more himself. "Once everyone has finished, I'll be happy to show you all round the house so you can see the interior at least."

"Really? That's very kind of you, Mr Tranter. I'm sure everyone will be delighted to take you up on it." She smiled broadly before heading briskly back to the buffet.

"Excuse me!" A piping voice accosted Clyde from behind. A young woman in a smart shirt and trousers was looking up at him from her seat on the bottom of the stairs. "It is Clyde, isn't it?" She seemed a little nervous. "Mattie. Mattie Greville. We met at the last launch party at *Endeavour*, the Sigby Jacobson exhibition." She rose and shook his hand with her damp, limp fingers in an expression of old-fashioned formality that rather surprised him. He was not used to being noticed as an individual by Lucinda's friends and colleagues.

"I remember," he burst out with relief, "from *The Green Door* bookshop next door to the gallery."

"That's right." She grinned, her teeth pearly and perfect. Her white skin was so translucent that Clyde felt embarrassed at the view of the mechanics beneath. She had a coyness of manner which he found unattractive and a very odd expression in her pale amber eyes. "I've been reading this." She brandished a copy of Melrose Burke's book with its red cover in self-published gloss. "Very exciting. Do you think this is the exact spot?" The strange eyes glittered as she held the book open at a page showing an illustration of the body of a woman lying on the hall rug. "Such a shame there are no photographs. Apparently, they disappeared from the records. It's very disappointing!"

Clyde, who remembered Mattie as irritating and clingy, began to find her unsettling as well. The pitch of her enthusiasm was unsavoury.

"I don't suppose this is the original rug? No, it wouldn't be, of course, because of the bloodstains." Clyde didn't have a chance to explain before she went on, "Could we possibly look in the drawing room? I heard you say you would be showing some other people around, but I just want to see where the murders happened. There's a plan." She flicked through the book as Clyde led her into the large room, both majestic and comfortable. She paced around muttering, studying the plan and looking up at intervals. Finally, she focussed on a spot and said, "Okay if I take a few pictures?"

"Okay," said Clyde reluctantly, "but I don't want to see them on Instagram or TikTok, or anywhere else for public view, is that understood?"

"No, that's fine," she nodded conspiratorially. "They'll just be for my private files."

Clyde raised an eyebrow behind her back and was relieved when she had finished and could be shown out of the room. She asked about seeing the lodge, and he explained that he and Lucinda hadn't renovated it yet and it wouldn't be safe to visit for a while, but she eventually pressed him into agreeing to allow her in once it was ready.

"It's such a shame about those photos," she kept saying. "I can't believe *all* copies were lost. I bet they're out there somewhere ..." Her eyes glittered again and her bubbling enthusiasm returned. "I can't believe I'd never heard of these murders. And to know the owners of the place where they

Emily Tellwright

happened … what could be more perfect? Thanks so much, Clyde."

Relieved to get away from Mattie, Clyde realised that he had quite lost his appetite. He felt like a drink.

As he headed for the bar, he noticed a slight, elegant woman, her dark hair in a perfect French pleat, admiring some of the pictures.

"Good evening, Mr Tranter," she said in a formal tone. "My name is Frances Harvey and I'm the librarian. It's a lovely party."

Chapter Three

A COUPLE OF DAYS LATER, Lucinda was in her new studio setting up. She'd been interested to learn from Agnes Beresford that it had probably once been a morning room, facing east and north as it did, but that it had been extended in the time of the college to form the main art room. There had been traces of large benches and pipework for sinks, as well as walls thickly coated in shiny washable white paint. In a large storeroom at one end had been a gas supply and a special electrical connection that Miss Beresford opined had connected to the pottery kilns. Lucinda had no interest in making ceramics and had had the whole cupboard removed to make a modern matte-white space. North-facing roof-lights had been added, along with blackout shutters to the existing windows, to give complete control over the natural light. She'd managed to wangle some kind of regional fund money towards this on the pretext that she was moving part of her art business out of London.

She was surrounded by half-emptied packing cases containing various media, but was at that moment carefully unwrapping several of her completed works to inspect them before taking them on to the Greater Blocton Museum and Art Gallery – the same one where Miss Beresford had spent much of her career – where she was to have a small permanent exhibition space as a condition of the fund. Slackford County Hall Gallery was also having two works to add to its permanent collection as a result of the complex and fractured relationship between the unitary authority and its county that she neither understood nor wished to contemplate.

There were some other commitments involved – workshops, ambassadorships, video diaries, competition judging and so on – in her becoming the kind of 'local' artist conditional to the payments, but she also had to keep up her London gallery and work to maintain her profile. The very existence of the fund acknowledged that London was the prestigious and happening hub of artistic activity and she needed to maintain her presence there so as to have some kudos to transfer to the region. Besides, it was still what mattered to her most; she could not contemplate, and never truly had, a provincial life.

Clyde stuck his head round the door. "Want a coffee?" he asked laconically.

"Great, thanks, I could just do with one." She looked at him. "You at a loose end again?" Her voice expressed a mixture of concern – her work was central to her life and she could not imagine existing without it – and a faint whiff of censure.

"Nothing to do until a meeting at three," replied Clyde dejectedly. His work was not central to his life and he was realising more and more clearly how many others things he would rather be doing; he was also deeply uneasy in the current situation. It was impossible to stand the long periods of inactivity without doing *something*, but he was very uncomfortable doing his own thing when he was being paid to work for someone else. As a result, he did everything half-heartedly. It was a ridiculous quandary and he resolved – again! – to end it once and for all. If only he could get in touch with his boss ... "I've been starting a catalogue in the library and making a list of desirable acquisitions. I don't want to buy more books until I've reminded myself what I've got. I'm going to wander down to the village library in a bit and have a word with the librarian there. She offered to advise me on ways of organising the collection when we met at the party."

"Librarian? What was her name? I don't think I remember her. Was she one of the history lot?" Lucinda's voice was muffled by her having her head in a crate.

"Frances, what was it? Began with an H ... quite a common name. Not a common woman, though. Got that real vintage chic. I'm surprised you didn't notice her. I think she came with the general invitation to the tennis club."

"Vintage chic?" This caught Lucinda's attention and her head popped up. "What sort exactly?"

"Oh, shift dress, sixties style, hair up, super neat, that kind of thing. Just stood out as not being of this era somehow. I think it's something to do with the tailoring ..."

"You're right, I am surprised I didn't notice her. But then it was a busy evening." She smiled at various pleasant recollections and moved over to Clyde. "Just like you to be fascinated by a sexy old-fashioned librarian," she teased, putting her long, slender arms around his neck and kissing him.

Clyde embraced her indulgently. "Don't be silly," he replied, laughing with a flush of embarrassment. "And anyway, I never said she was sexy."

"No, you didn't need to." She looked into his eyes, minx-like. "Don't get carried away in the wrong direction, darling. I know you're bored and I'm busy. Being interested in attractive libraries is healthy; being interested in attractive librarians, unwise."

She beamed and kissed him again. Clyde almost giggled nervously. Lucinda was tantalising and fascinating to him.

33

"Harvey!" he exclaimed. "That was her name."

"Really. Well, I didn't meet her. If she's an expert on the Dewey Decimal System or whatever they use nowadays, all well and good. Just be careful, that's all I'm saying. Why don't you look into the murders? That would be something interesting to pass the time; history with a connection to your home and a mystery thrown in."

"There's nothing to look into. It was all solved at the time – years ago. I skimmed through Melrose's book and there seems little more to discover."

Clyde moved away towards the kitchen. Lucinda snorted slightly at the mention of Melrose.

"That's not what Mattie thinks," she called after him. "She's set up one of her 'files' on the case and has her nose to the ground, bloodhound style ..."

Re-energised by coffee, Clyde strolled down to the library. It was a wide, flat 1970s building with large metal windows and a slightly incongruous tiled roof that had been stuck on at a later date. Maroon industrial carpet softened the floors in a corridor hallway that led to a big, bright square room filled with metal shelving and the magic of books.

He approached the counter, trying to catch the attention of the stooping elderly person behind it across the sea of leaflets and notices that littered the top.

"Morning," said Clyde.

"Hello," said the old man, looking up. He was thin with long grey hair and random clothes, bright but tatty. His well-lined features looked sour, curdled by time. A former hippie, perhaps, thought Clyde. But his speech was of an astonishing and long-expired impeccability, Clyde wondered if he was witnessing the famous Oxford accent. "Can I help you?"

"I was looking for Frances, Frances Harvey," said Clyde. "I

met her recently and she offered to give me some tips on cataloguing and organising my books. She's probably busy," he added hastily, "but if I could just leave her my details so she can get in touch ..."

The eccentric pensioner stared over the top of his half-moon glasses. "Frances Harvey? I don't think I know her. Why were you expecting to find her in the library?"

"She's the librarian, or at least that's what I understood ..."

"Tcha! There's no librarian here now. It's all run by volunteers. I'm the nearest thing we've got; I'm a *retired* librarian." He emphasised the word ironically, then drew himself up. "I was, for many years, senior librarian at The New Left Library."

"That's strange," said Clyde, ignoring the irrelevant reference, "I met her at a party at our house – Valencia House, just up the road, you know – a couple of days ago, and I understood she was the librarian here in Burnton. I must have misunderstood."

A gamut of expressions crossed the ex-librarian's countenance. It was possible that youngish people with sufficient money to renovate houses built by Victorian capitalists and throw lavish parties in them did not sit well with his retrograde political beliefs, or perhaps he was simply miffed not to have been invited. His face finally settled into as charming a frame as it could manage.

"Perhaps I could help? I have a good deal of experience of the things you're interested in. It's a quiet morning and I could show you the system we use here and compare it to a version that might be better for your smaller *private*," he slightly spat the word, "collection." Clyde agreed with alacrity, and the deeply hunched expert shuffled out from behind the counter and across the floor with Clyde maintaining a tactful position behind him.

His guide suddenly stopped and turned precariously. "You

know, I *did* know a Frances Harvey. Years ago. She was librarian at the College of Education when I first worked at the Technical College. She was quite a senior figure even then, although still young. One of those ambitious career women, became a high-flyer in the County Library Service. I don't know what happened to her because I moved on, but I expect she did well for herself. Not being of the same *persuasion*, I never saw much of her outside work ..."

"Quite a coincidence," said Clyde. "Of course, it couldn't be the same person; the woman I spoke to was much younger, more my age."

"Ah," said the old man, and proceeded on his unsteady way.

Walking home with some local tomatoes for lunch, Clyde paused at the gates of the house to look at the lodge cottage. They – he – must really get on with it. The plans for the renovation were largely in place and just needed a few details to be agreed upon. Thank goodness Melrose Burke hadn't managed to get the place listed! Clyde didn't know if they could have stretched to the extra money, work or stress that would have inevitably involved.

The cottage had been made structurally safe and water-tight, and necessary planning permissions obtained. It was secured and alarmed, but the best defence against future theft and vandalism would be for it to be occupied. Clyde decided to get Lucinda down here after lunch – there would just be time before his meeting – and settle things so work could go ahead. If they didn't, the contractor might move on to another job.

As he turned back to the gate to input the code, a figure popped up beside him like Rumpelstiltskin. It was Zeno, the service manager for the party caterers.

"Oh!"

"Excuse me, Mr Tranter," said the dancing-eyed man in a humble tone, "I was just coming to see you. I wondered if ..."

"Yes?" said Clyde pleasantly. "And it's Clyde, please."

"Clyde," Zeno smiled widely and held out his hand to shake. "Thank you. I wondered if you were planning to employ someone to run the house and grounds at all, and if so, if you would consider me for the job?"

"Aren't you happy with Marina?" Clyde had been caught by surprise and still had his hand on the keypad. He typed in the number and said, "Come in. We can walk up to the house together."

"Catering for events is only occasional work," replied Zeno obliquely. "I want full-time hours. I have a lot of domestic management experience, and I actually know the property as I worked at the college here."

"Happy memories, I hope," said Clyde, preoccupied and only half listening.

"Yes, very." The man radiated such warmth at the recollection that he got Clyde's full attention. "Of course, I know things will be different now," he added hastily.

"How do you feel about a residential post?" Clyde burst out on a whim. "We are just about to start making the lodge cottage habitable, and it will need a tenant. We don't have children or pets – yet – so the domestic duties will be quite light, but there will be Lucinda's entertaining to cater for, and I have been vaguely planning an educational market-gardening business in the walled garden."

Zeno beamed. "That's an excellent idea. And yes, I would be delighted to take up your offer. It would suit me perfectly. I can provide a CV and references, and the necessary checks."

"Look," said Clyde, "I've got an important online meeting this afternoon, and I'll need to speak to Lucinda about this role, but give me your number and I'll call you to arrange an informal interview to discuss details and see if we'll suit each other."

"I'm sure we will, Mr Tranter ... Clyde." He smiled broadly, but with a hint of something that Clyde could not quite determine, something undisclosed. He wondered how old the man was; his face, neither ugly nor handsome, had so much character and such strong features that, together with the hint of avuncularity, it made him seem older than he probably was.

"All my details are here. Look forward to hearing from you." Zeno handed over an envelope and was gone, disappearing into the shadows as swiftly as he had come. Clyde was left blinking after him.

He went to lunch satisfied – he had some ideas for his library, and he was pleased to have found Zeno, who he thought would be a real asset to the household – but also worried. Why was he worried? He examined himself thoughtfully. It was the uncertainty. Since they had moved into Valencia House, life no longer seemed to flow in a sensible way. Natural causality was shaken; he was repeatedly surprised and constantly confused. It had started with that train – the train no one knew about that had disgorged passengers to exit from a locked station and vanish into the night.

Then there were the noises. All houses had noises, of course, especially large, old ones, but these were not creaks, snaps or draughts. Water ran in places where there was no plumbing, chatter echoed on the landing and shadows moved in the bushes. Lights turned themselves on. The smells were even more mysterious: baking, cabbage, fried onions and fish when no one had been in the house. What was going on?

Now there was the non-existent librarian. He hadn't been mistaken, she had said she was a librarian here. Was she a gate-crasher? A burglar 'casing the joint'? Neither seemed likely, although he supposed that was how they got away with it. The sooner someone moved into the lodge, the better.

But – and this came as a further surprise – though he was worried, he was neither uncomfortable nor afraid. The house still felt homely and welcoming and he was considerably calmer and less angry since he had moved out of the unsupportable city. He felt settled, and the place stimulated his interests, renewing his old loves of cooking, books and literature with a fresh emphasis on history and a developing curiosity about gardening, food production and nature.

His mood, he decided, must be due to so many changes in his life, a symptom of adjustment. He had uprooted himself from one of the world's great cities to an unknown semi-rural nowhere and taken on all the stresses of a renovation project. His work situation alone – long, long days of nothing and then a violent burst of aggressive activity – was enough to cause madness, and his vacillating about giving notice was making more instability for himself. For the first time in his life, he was spending long periods on his own, and they were followed by periods of once more adjusting to living with his wife. It would worry the sanest personality.

He wasn't unhappy alone. In fact, it dawned on him that, while he was still attracted to and interested in his wife, and he enjoyed her company when she was around, he didn't really miss her when she was away. She seemed completely at ease with the situation, so perhaps this was a way of balancing those differences that had grated between them in later London days and of making their relationship work.

In a flash, he remembered the murders. The murders! What if this whole strangeness was to do with them? What if the house *was* haunted, as some people had suggested?

Clyde shook himself back to his external surroundings with this outlandish thought. He'd bought a haunted house. What an idea! He laughed at himself uproariously as he went into the kitchen, but his mind had opened to the possibility. From that moment, it began to plague him with remembrances of every ghost story he had read or watched with annoying persistence.

After some excellent omelettes – Clyde had been perfecting his technique – and a compote made with blackberries from the grounds, Lucinda suggested they go down to the lodge cottage at once and sort things out. Generally, she was a person who liked to get things done there and then, and she wanted to return to her studio and finish setting up as she had a new project to begin before she next went to London.

Clyde had enjoyed several large glasses of wine with his lunch. He did not usually drink during the day, but had somehow felt he needed it, and it was a pleasingly defiant gesture to the little importance his work now had to him or anyone else. As he walked down the drive once more, it dawned on him that he could do it every day, just one glass, and then perhaps another. First there was the gourmand's pleasure of honouring a well-cooked lunch, however light; then came the delightful relaxed euphoria, making him want to dance and sing and run around the garden like a child; next the long dissociation as concerns and constraints retreated along with the edge of clarity, leaving him floating in an expanded form where nothing seemed to matter; and finally the miserable depression of all that nothingness when he could openly and indulgently dwell on his insecurities. He was rapidly reaching this last stage, though holding his senses together through firmness of purpose.

The weather was turning and a strong bluster hit him in the face like a slap, which was just what he needed. Closely gathered clouds so bulky as to resist the wind filled the bleak and heavy sky. The tall trees of the drive had sheltered the couple from the full knowledge of the coming storm, so it was a shock when they emerged in front of the small house into the nascent tempest. In one of those rapid changes so characteristic of the British climate, a dull sky and a strong breeze had developed into much more in the time it took them to walk to the edge of their property.

"Shit!" said Lucinda. "I bet we'll get soaked on the way back." Dust and leaves were now swirling around them in an autumnal fashion eerie for the long, warm days of summer. Clyde looked up to see one of the window boards flapping. "You'd better get that fixed," said Lucinda, following his gaze then letting herself into the cottage.

It was a different kind of darkness inside; a very deep-brown chiaroscuro sort with a thick atmosphere of oldness and dust. Clyde flicked the light switch, and a tiled hall run round on two sides by the solid oak banister of the stairs and landing was revealed in the low-hanging fluorescent bulb. Still tipsy, Clyde could not tell if the bulb was swinging or he was. Presumably there was a draught, but as he squinted at the nauseating glow level with his eye line, it blurred into a larger image, also hanging, also white, but streaked with red and twitching.

"Aagh!" he shouted and jerked his head away. "This is where it happened."

"I know," replied Lucinda, unmoved, "but it was a long time ago. The college groundsman and his family have lived here since then. There's nothing to see, no bloodstains or anything."

"I know. It's just ..."

"What's the matter, darling? Seen a ghost? That's what lunchtime drinking does for you." The practical Lucinda laughed lightly with just a drop of scorn and entered the room on the left, checking her iPad as she went.

They strolled around, Lucinda consulting and considering, Clyde recovering. After the reception rooms, they went upstairs, inspected the loft and were coming down again to see the kitchen.

"I think everything's fine and we should just go ahead," said Lucinda, strolling down the stairs. "I can't decide on a final colour scheme until we get some daylight in, of course, but that doesn't matter now."

Clyde was ahead of her, rounding the bend under the stairs. He ducked suddenly.

"There's something that needs doing," he said. "I'll have to get onto it." Lucinda looked up at a dull grey tube of metal crossing below the ceiling beneath the landing. She was not as tall as the willowy Clyde.

"I'd forgotten that," she said. "It's not on the plans." It was an old pipe that had served the gaslights. "Won't the builders deal with it?"

"No, I already asked. I have to get someone CORGI registered to take it out, even though it can't be connected to anything as there's no gas here now."

"How silly. Let's lift a floorboard and see if it *is* connected to anything."

"What, now?"

"Why not? There's a screwdriver here." She reached over to a few odd tools left on the window-ledge.

Clyde felt increasingly oppressed by the battened-down atmosphere in the place and wanted to get on, but Lucinda had already picked up the implement and was marching upstairs. He trudged behind reluctantly.

"I've got my meeting at three."

"There's plenty of time. It won't take a minute to look. If it's safe, we can take it out ourselves and save a lot of fuss and delay." Lucinda often saw ways around rules that Clyde would have followed without thinking. She soon had a couple of boards up on the landing – they were rather loose anyway –

and could see the sawn-off top of the empty pipe sticking up from the ceiling below.

"Look, it can't possibly be connected to any gas. It must have come through from the downstairs room on this side and gone on upstairs." She hammered the end of the pipe lightly until it fell through with a puff of dust, then went briskly downstairs and pulled it hard out of the wall at the other end.

"You should be wearing a mask." Clyde coughed through the dust. "You don't know what's in this stuff."

"A little bit won't hurt," she dismissed him briskly, "and the job's done now. I'll just put those boards back and we'll get out into the kitchen." She ran back upstairs, still holding the pipe. As she dragged it slightly behind her, some loose bits fell out of the back end onto the stairs. Lucinda didn't notice, but as the dust settled, Clyde saw them glinting and picked up a yellow metal bracelet set with oblong white stones, two long silver earrings each set with a large red stone and a string of graduated pearls. He stared at them in his hands.

"Lucinda," he said at length over the sound of her tapping a recalcitrant floorboard, "I think you just found Berenia Hassel's missing jewels."

The wind suddenly howled into the house, bringing a lash of rain through the rapidly slamming door.

43

Chapter Four

THE JEWELLERY that Lucinda had uncovered in the lodge had not caused any great sensation. As there was no longer a police station in Burnton, she and Clyde had contacted the force online and eventually someone had come out to collect the items. After innumerable excuses and delays, it was confirmed that it matched the description of the Hassel jewellery that was missing at the time of the murders. What would become of the little hoard now was uncertain; it was not required as evidence because the case was closed, and there didn't seem to be any surviving relations of the Hassels. Clyde believed that ownership should eventually revert to Lucinda and himself, but expected that the issue would remain undealt with and unresolved for long enough for it to be forgotten. And if it was ever remembered again, he wouldn't be surprised to find that such valuable disputed property had once more disappeared without record. He didn't mind; he certainly didn't want it. Lucinda found the items shallow, showy and lacking in taste despite their value (the pearls were best cultured), and for him they were a reminder of their silly owner whose life had ended in such a serious way.

A couple of weeks after their meeting, Clyde invited Zeno to come for an informal interview for the role of general factotum. At first, Lucinda had not been sure about having live-in help; it was not that she minded having things done for her, and she was quite fond of giving orders, but she had the modern attachment to privacy. She was surprised that Clyde had come up with the idea, but considered it to be worth at least seeing the man who had inspired it in her husband.

The intervening days were her first at work in the new studio on one of the fund projects, and her first sustained period living in the house, and Clyde became uncomfortably aware of a change in his wife. She became irritable and dissatisfied with everything she did, snappy with him, restless and uninterested in enjoying any of the pleasures of their new home that he had strived to perfect. After all their time apart, now they had come together for longer, physical intimacy had become slightly awkward. He thought of her condition as 'London withdrawal', but it was starting to look more like 'stir crazy'.

Two nights before Zeno was due to come over, things came to a head. "Can't we go out tonight?" she demanded aggressively on entering the kitchen and seeing Clyde preparing dinner.

He paused in slicing an onion. "Of course. We can go to the pub. If I give them a ring now, I'm sure they can find us a table. This'll keep." He waved his knife at the chopping board. "We can have a couple of drinks first maybe."

"Not the bloody pub! It's so fucking *provincial*."

"Well, I'm not sure there is anywhere else ...How about Slackford? We could have a few drinks around town and then a curry at that new place. Not much use going into Blocton, there's nothing there."

"I don't know any fucker in Slackford! I just want to go

out, meet a few friends and see who's about, but I don't have any friends in this godforsaken hole."

Clyde remained conciliatory. "There's always the tennis club, we know people there."

"Children and geriatrics. It's pathetic."

Her energy was ebbing and Clyde thought it best to stay silent. Mentioning the varied programme of events at the village hall, including the film club, amateur dramatics society and old-time sequence dancing, would, he felt, be like pouring paraffin on the embers of her flare-up. He was quite keen on the film club and was secretly fascinated by the dancing, particularly as he didn't really know what it was, but he didn't think the day would ever come when he could own up to that before his wife.

"Oh, forget it," she said, spent from futility. "You might as well make dinner. I'm going to have a drink. A large one." Lucinda was not normally a boozer, but she held her drink well. That night, though, she was a little the worse for wear.

The following day, she took a long Facetime call.

"Jason Deaville wants me to run a big exhibition for him," she briefed Clyde afterwards, "at *The Ginevra*."

"Great," said Clyde helpfully. Jason Deaville was an impresario so big that even he had heard of him.

"It will mean that I have to spend more time in London and I may have to rejig my commitments here." He knew she meant work commitments, not personal, but it would mean 'rejigging' their relationship too. She did seem to have thought of him, though, because her next comment was, "So it will be a good idea to have someone like this Zeno around as company for you. You'll go weird if you spend too long on your own in this place." She almost spat the last words out in contempt. It looked as if even a part-time rural idyll was not for her after all.

Clyde, who felt himself becoming less bizarre and more real the longer he spent in his Burnton life, just said, "Okay, we'll see how it goes tomorrow."

"I'll still be back at intervals and for events, of course," she added.

"Of course," her husband agreed.

Zeno arrived the next day, looking smart and spotless. He cut a dignified figure in his sharp old-fashioned suit, displaying both his physical fitness and confidence in his ability to do the job in question. Clyde and Lucinda invited him into the kitchen where coffee was brewing and settled into a 'good cop/bad cop' routine, with Lucinda assuming the stern demeanour and Clyde as her light-hearted stooge. The candidate, while a model of good behaviour in every way, remained inscrutable. He gave Clyde the impression of finding it all a highly amusing show, and probably one in which he would like to take part.

They learned that Zeno was divorced from a wife with whom he had run a successful club and restaurant, and that he had two grown-up daughters living abroad. Before that he had, as he'd said, worked in this very building when it was a college. He gave them excellent references from Marina, the catering company owner, and a local hotelier.

"It must seem strange to you, seeing the house back as a private residence," said Clyde conversationally when Lucinda excused herself and left the room to take an important call.

"Not as much as you might think," replied Zeno. "It's a matter of atmosphere and intention. You seem to have brought some of the best things from my time here: hospitality, creativity, respect for knowledge and learning. I think Valencia House feels far closer to its early days as a college now than it does to its former days as a private residence. From what I've heard, the Hassels weren't keen on books, art, learning or sharing."

Clyde was touched by the concept of sharing; he didn't know that he and Lucinda were keen on that either, and he wondered why Zeno thought so.

"There was more political awareness then, though," the man went on thoughtfully. "The general consensus was like background radiation; you were immersed in it and absorbing it, even if you didn't believe in it." He smiled. "I don't feel there are any politics here now."

"Long may that continue," Clyde laughed, "although if we wanted to recreate the full retro experience, I bet I know someone local who could help."

"Do you mean Michael, the retired gentleman who volunteers in the library, by any chance?" asked Zeno with a twinkle.

"Yes! Do you know him?"

"Yes. I'm a member of the local amateur dramatics group – the one that puts on plays in the village hall – and Michael's also our librarian. He's the sole member of the Burnton Communist Party and contributes articles to the *Quotidian Worker*."

Clyde was just about to ask about the drama group, which was much more interesting to him than the BCP, when Lucinda returned.

"I'm so sorry about that," she said politely. "I had been waiting for a call back since yesterday. You know how it is these days. Now, where were we?"

"We'd looked at Zeno's CV and references and he'd told us a little about his past experience," replied Clyde.

"Oh yes," said his wife briskly. "So, Zeno, I will outline the duties that this role involves so you can see if it's what you want ..." Clyde looked into the man's bright eyes. Zeno had decided to take the job long before he'd even arrived, indeed, he had approached Clyde, hadn't he? But Lucinda was a great one for the formalities, and he was not a man to interfere. "... laundry, shared shopping and cooking, possibly driving – you can drive, can't you?" She looked down at the paper before her.

"Oh yes," said Zeno happily. "I have a clean licence." Clyde was certain now that he was enjoying the whole performance tremendously.

Lucinda moved on. "Do you have any health issues that may affect your fitness for the role?" In her eyes, the little man seemed positively ancient, and she was slightly sceptical that he would be up to the work she intended for him. "There will be some climbing involved in the cleaning and a lot of time on your feet."

"I am in excellent health, thank you, and am quite fit for what is required." Zeno spoke humbly, as if he believed Lucinda had no concern except for his welfare, then grinned broadly. "I was a local Latin dance champion for many years – until we opened the restaurant and time no longer allowed for it – and I took it up again some years ago." He looked at Clyde with a very straight face. "I appeared on *Come Dancing* three years running."

Clyde spluttered and hurriedly composed himself as Lucinda resumed. "Well then, Zeno, please can you tell us why you think you would be suited to this job and why you want it?" He suddenly felt like laughing madly, hysterically even, at the ridiculousness of it all: a world that reduced the simplest, clearest realities to a bizarre, complex fiction. But his wife fixed him for a fraction of a second with an icy sideways glare, and he was instantly calm.

Eventually they came to the end of the charade and Lucinda, having covered salary and the terms of the tenancy of the cottage, summed up. "We're delighted to have you at Valencia House, Zeno, and we hope you'll be happy working here. I think it's all worked out very well." Her imperiousness was both magnificent and entirely misplaced, Clyde reflected, and he found it correspondingly fascinatingly attractive and tiresome. "You'll be starting on the 25th and staying in the far attic bedroom until the cottage is ready. We, in turn, will see that it is ready as soon as possible. I will have a contract arranged for you to sign." She smiled mechanically, shook his hand and swept from the room, ignoring Clyde. He felt himself relax and turned to Zeno, shaking both his hands warmly.

"Welcome back to Valencia House," he said.

September came and went. As autumn got into its stride, life at Valencia House seemed to settle down. Lucinda was away in London a lot, working on the new exhibition and, it seemed, making new friends and contacts in the exclusive circle of Jason Deaville, while Clyde had finally put in writing his determination to leave his job by Christmas. As there was now less work than ever for him to do – even the pointless meetings had dried up – he had begun studying productive gardening, organic systems, permaculture, no-dig, perennial vegetables and rewilding while outlining draft plans for his business. The change of emphasis and time spent outdoors with his hands in the soil calmed and grounded him, and he liked to sit on a bench watching the jolly garden birds and gradually learning to tell one from another. His friends the bullfinches were often there, and he would sit companionably regarding their sociable munching, frowning at any corvid that dared a venture. This once athletic but highly strung greyhound of a man had shed his temper and anxiety, and filled out in both flesh and humour. He still kept fit by swimming, playing tennis and occasionally jogging across the gentle heathland, but without any desperate urgency.

He had also got used to the oddness: all those smells,

noises and peculiar sightings. He even heard a train stop at the station every so often, although he'd never actually witnessed it a second time. Somehow, the house had become his friend, and these signs of life other than his own were part of its companionship. He felt it was supporting him in his change of career and lifestyle, nurturing his new interests and complicit in his plans for the garden. It was more of a life partner than Lucinda in some ways, as she was bound up in her London concerns and so frequently absent. The calmness of the wildlife in the garden reassured him that nothing could be wrong; nature would have known.

Lately, there had been activity in the library. The books had begun to move – not flying round the room in front of him, Harry-Potter style, but simply being in different places to where he had left them when he next came into the room. And they didn't just move randomly, but gradually reorganised themselves on the shelves. Sometimes, even, a new book appeared, always from his wanted list. He had never seen the mysterious librarian Ms Harvey again, nor managed to find out anything about her, but he was secretly sure that this was *her* hand at work, fulfilling her promise to help him; running his library, in fact. He felt that she shimmered into the room with silent tread when he was elsewhere, doing her job, and he would not have been too shocked if one day she left him a tidy note informing him of a delayed publication or admonishing him for putting his own books back in the wrong places.

Zeno was nicely established and had taken over all the housekeeping duties from the twice-weekly cleaners, though the builders were still at work on the lodge cottage. Clyde already found him invaluable as an assistant and companion. It was like having an erudite and active sprite in the house: when Zeno was in the room with him, he was usually either busy or talkative, displaying his knowledge of and thought on a wide range of subjects, his beard wagging away and those incredible eyes bright as lamps; but once he had left the room, Clyde couldn't feel his presence in the house at all, as if he had rapidly gone a long way away, or never existed at all. Clyde often heard the vacuum cleaner at a distance, but never a footstep or a cough.

He'd never mentioned the unusual life of the house to Zeno, and yet he was sure that Zeno was aware of it, perhaps even part of it. The noises sometimes occurred when Zeno was present and, although he never said anything, Clyde was certain that he'd heard them. There was a complicity between them that was quite different to the detachment of Lucinda, who was blatantly oblivious to it all. Clyde didn't care. He liked Zeno, who was good company and extremely useful. They shared an interest in food and cooking, taking turns in the kitchen and swapping notes.

There had been a short article in the press about the finding of the Hassel jewellery and this had revived interest in the case, with a few chatty weekend columns retelling the story in an entertaining style quite inappropriate to the grotesque reality. Clyde felt sure it would end there as there was neither mystery as to the perpetrator, nor troubled investigation to recount, and not even a trial to report on.

He had, however, reckoned without the ambitions of Melrose Burke, energised by an enthusiastic new associate.

It was a dark day in October of bone-chilling wetness and layers of mud when nature seemed sure that it would never, ever be dry again. Nevertheless, the ambient temperature in the state-of-the-art insulated house was agreeable and unseasonably free from draughts. Clyde would still light the stoves in the evening; he'd found the glow of the fire compensated for the endless gloom of the English autumn season, bringing a bright end to all those days when you longed to be able to turn up the sun. With his rather solitary life and unsettled feelings, the fire was a comfort and sometimes, he felt, company in a day of dim white skies.

He was grinding through his final project at work and was glad to be interrupted by the gate intercom. It was Melrose Burke, and though Clyde generally regarded him as a cadging old nuisance, today he was a welcome diversion. Clyde listened for the doorbell, then bounded to the door, only to stare wide-eyed in astonishment at Melrose and Mattie together on the doorstep, their hair wild in the wind. He expected Mattie to be in London, but it was seeing her in such an unlikely pairing that caused the stare.

"My dear boy," said Melrose, handing Clyde his coat in the hall.

"Clyde, we've got *so* much to tell you!" spluttered Mattie, effervescent with excitement and putting her hand on his arm in a gesture that might have been acquired from her companion. "*Melrose*," she spoke with comical reverence, "has a *theory*. And we're going to *investigate*. Isn't it exciting?"

Clyde uttered some kind of noise in response as Zeno made an exploratory appearance. The latter raised a bushy eyebrow at his employer.

"I was about to make some coffee?" he said, his voice rising quizzically.

"Good idea," said Clyde. "Want a hand?"

Zeno shook his head, gave a faint twinkle, and swiftly disappeared.

Clyde shepherded the wandering Melrose and bouncing Mattie into the great conservatory, which was feeling the warmth from a briefly emerged sun, and they sat around a glass-topped coffee table in huge old-fashioned basket-chairs against the backdrop of the early stages of Clyde's tender plant collection. He felt that the deep green life together with the trapped warmth had a calming effect. Besides, if he had taken them into the drawing room, he would have felt exactly as if he were in a three-act farce.

"My dear boy," began Melrose once more, smiling and slippery, "in the light of your *most incredible* find, the Burnton murders are once again in the news." Clyde did not bother to contradict him, and tried hard not to stare at Mattie, who looked desperate to speak, as if she were about to burst.

Melrose continued, "I feel it my *duty*, as a widely read and published author, and the foremost expert on this case," he paused for a second as if expecting applause, "to reconsider it in the light of this *extremely interesting* new evidence. I think you will agree, my dear boy, that this places an entirely *new light* on the events of that fateful day.

"Why would Alf Baxter, a seriously disturbed, possibly schizophrenic man, steal and hide those jewels before committing suicide? It makes no sense. Baxter never showed the least sign of interest in material wealth. We have witness statements taken at the time from people who knew him. Even though they had been extremely hard up before the Hassels took pity on them, once installed here at Valencia House, the Baxters were reasonably financially secure.

"And then there is the physical evidence. The police did not find Baxter's fingerprints on Berenia Hassel's jewellery box, nor anywhere upstairs. Alf had no reason to go upstairs in the main house, except on the rare occasions when there was some repair to do, and that had not happened for some time. He did not wear gloves for the murders, as his fingerprints were everywhere downstairs in both houses, sometimes in blood, and on both weapons. So he cannot have taken that jewellery."

At this point, Zeno appeared Jeeves-like from the palm fronds, bearing a tray of hot coffee and milk with homemade biscuits.

"Ah, delicious," said Melrose, beaming.

"A recipe of my ex-wife's," said Zeno, laying down the tray. "That woman was a damned nuisance, but she was a great cook." He departed, leaving behind him a shattered image of the perfect butler.

Clyde poured the coffee and relaxed back with a biscuit. He was still puzzled by the presence of Mattie. Although hanging on to every word of the great historian, she seemed to be invisible to him. Clyde wondered if she'd noticed and how such a collaboration was going to work. As to the jewellery, who knew what Alf Baxter, a man who was tragically disturbed, might have done and why? It was certainly in vain to attempt any reasoning about his behaviour. But Clyde was quite prepared to enjoy Melrose's verbose and egocentric efforts to that effect.

"To proceed," said that hero of academia, swallowing a crumby mouthful, "it is *my contention* that Alf Baxter was no more responsible for the murders than I am. If he didn't take the jewellery, someone else must have been involved with the crime. Who could that be? Someone who knew about that most ingenious hiding place in the lodge cottage, someone with a motive for removing one or more of the victims; in short, Brian Hassel himself!"

Clyde realised that he was meant to be amazed and impressed, and that pointing out the logical fallacy of this argument – there was no reason why the hiding of the jewellery could not be a separate event to the murders – would fall on deaf ears. But he was thoroughly entertained by the whole farrago and so to keep things going, he assumed a suitably surprised look.

"But what about the other evidence?" he asked. "Surely that conclusively shows that Alf Baxter did the actual killing."

"It seems likely, indeed," responded Melrose, putting on his most serious expression and attempting to lower his voice a tone or two, "but who knows? He could have been *framed*.

Although that is a possibility I shall consider at some length, it is far more likely that the poor disturbed man – victim, we may call him – was under duress: some kind of drug, suggestion, or, as my thesis will show, most probably *hypnotism*.

"That would be a very clever way of using a vulnerable person to rid oneself of a wealthy but *tiresome* wife and the young relative to whom she had left a large bequest, whilst giving oneself a perfect alibi and destroying the one person who could tell what truly happened; the poor soul who was forced, through his own weakness and delinquency, into committing these horrific crimes. *Evil*, pure *evil*!"

"He married his glamorous secretary and retired to Spain, you know," Mattie exploded into the conversation at last. Melrose took another biscuit and seemed to acquiesce to the takeover without acknowledging it. "Hardly the grief-stricken husband, was he?"

"How long after?"

"Oh, a few years. They'd been having an affair for some time, but they had to keep up appearances, didn't they?"

"Ah," said Clyde, thinking that he was not the only one to be influenced by *Columbo*, or was this perhaps more Edgar Wallace? "I see."

"I've put Melrose in touch with Warren Bannister – you know, the agent – and he's going to get some articles out there to stimulate interest in the new edition of the book. We'll be hosting the launch at *The Green Door*, of course. I've also made contact with Dr Melanie Azoff, the American criminal psychiatrist, and Colin Shah, the hypnotism expert. We're working on a deal to get their contributions on the way Hassel might have coerced Alf Baxter. Warren thinks there could be a telly series in it – he's got contacts at Channel 5."

It was clear now why Melrose was willing to tolerate association with Mattie. Clyde was rather surprised that the woman whom he had always thought of as a weird drip was so capable and well connected.

"If we really put a favourable spin on Alf, who knows? The *children* might come out of the woodwork for us."

Having dismissed the substance of the discussion as ridiculous, Clyde was moueing inwardly with distaste at the prospect of this circus-to-come, though he knew with complete clarity that nothing he could say or do would stop it. Then he fully realised what he had just heard.

"Children?" he burst out, putting his coffee down with a clatter. "What children?"

"The Baxters' children, dear boy." Melrose took up the narrative seamlessly, though still without any sign that he was aware of Mattie's existence. They'd turned out to be a strangely effective double act. "There were two, a boy and a girl, Keith and, er ..."

"Eileen," supplied Mattie.

"Eileen. Eight and ten at the time. Their names were changed and they were sent to Australia; the two things combined make them very difficult to find."

"Presumably, that was the idea," said Clyde with stern sarcasm. "I'd no idea! They're not mentioned in your book – although I can see why you'd want to protect them. Dear God! The poor things. How would you ever get over something like that?"

"They were not in my *book*," Melrose replied with equal sternness, "because they were not involved in the *crime*. They were both rather sickly children, I believe, and Mr and Mrs Hassel had arranged for them to spend two weeks by the sea at the time of the murders. I agree that it was a blessing they were not present, but an *historian* must deliver *the facts*, and I would not have omitted mentioning them from *sentiment*."

He paused to make his point. "Of course," he deepened

his voice again, and slowed his pace to give weight to the punchline, "there is another significance to their absence."

"It was arranged by Brian Hassel so they would be out of the way, which shows he was in on it," Mattie blurted out.

Melrose gave Clyde a look of resigned exasperation worthy of Oliver Hardy. 'You see what I have to put up with from this *person*', he seemed to be telegraphing, but he said, so slowly and loudly that he almost boomed, "Being a person of *some* intelligence, my dear boy, you will no doubt realise that Mr Hassel getting the children out of the way suggests that he knew something was going to happen. IT SHOWS HE WAS IN ON IT."

Clyde's frustration with these two increasingly dangerous nitwits forced him to speak his mind. "That's not at all logical," he said to them both. "I agree that the absence of the children may have been a factor: if Alf Baxter did the crime alone, the presence of the children might have hindered him, or prevented the trigger that set him off; if someone else was involved, they might have chosen that time because they knew the children would be away, and their presence would have meant either leaving two witnesses or persuading Alf to murder his own children, which he might not have been able to do. But it does not mean that sending the children away was part of a plan. It could simply have been kindness on the Hassels' part. It could have been Mrs Hassel's idea. If Brian Hassel arranged the murders, he would probably have arranged for the children to be absent, but the converse simply does not follow."

Mattie gazed open-mouthed.

"I'm afraid, my dear boy, that you do not have my experience in these matters," returned Melrose in his most unctuous manner. For the first time, Clyde thought that he might be after something more than free biscuits and an audience. "It is *circumstantial,* it's true, but highly *suggestive.* The kind of details that one uses to build *a case.*"

Clyde sighed. Let them dig their own graves, or rather make their own awful television programme. "Were you hoping I'd get involved in some way?"

"My dear boy, *you* are the owner of the scene of the crime."

"Lucinda *and* I are the owners."

"Of course, of course. You *know* what I mean. We were hoping for some photos for the new edition of the book, and possibly some TV footage if things go our way."

"As there are no pictures of the crime scene from the time," put in Mattie. "If you remember, the coroner said they were too disturbing to show to the jury, and they've since disappeared."

"Hmm. I'm not promising," said Clyde, thinking that he might cooperate and use his agreement as leverage to keep things within reasonable bounds. "I don't want people hanging around outside the gates to take pictures, or trying to get into the grounds to have a look."

"Oh, I *quite* understand, my dear boy," said Melrose genially. "We shall take all *precautions.* It will all be highly *professional* and only of the *interior,* so that the *hoi polloi* will not recognise the place." Clyde knew from his experience of television through Lucinda's work that Melrose was in no position to guarantee what the hypothetical producer would do. Whatever they agreed to, the television people would be out to get what they wanted regardless.

"I can't agree to the TV," he said, "but photos for the book will be okay, I think, though I'll have to check with Lucinda. There will be conditions, though. I'm not getting involved with anything gratuitously sensational."

Melrose and Mattie were simultaneously indignant.

Emily Tellwright

"My dear boy, I'm an *historian*!"

"But, Clyde, this will be a major work of true crime!"

"As long as we're clear on that," said Clyde, and helped himself to another biscuit.

Chapter Five

THAT FRIDAY WAS A STORMY NIGHT. A great wind roared around the house, surging beyond the point where it gave one a lovely cosy feeling to sit by the fire, to the level when one began to wonder whether the roof was really as secure as one hoped. Clyde stood in the bedroom, looking out from the great sash windows, watching the upper reaches of the enormous trees sway more wildly than seemed possible for things deeply rooted in the ground.

He wasn't enjoying the storm. Lucinda had booked a taxi from the station to save him going out on such a night, and so he had decided to use the uninterrupted evening to prepare a special meal. There was a time when this would have been deeply enjoyable: the warmth and glow of the kitchen in action, busy but unhurried; the comforting noise, a symphony of so many sounds blended with the faint strains of the radio; the ever-changing aromas as the meal progressed; the pleasurable anticipation of presenting something enjoyable to Lucinda, and of sharing its relish as a reestablishment of their relationship; the simple sense of the heart of home and hospitality that had become essential to him.

But this evening he was restless. The wild energy abroad made him feel his life was tame and dull. There was certainly no essence of such excitement in his attitude to the arrival of his wife. They had planned this new life together; the finding and restoration of the house had been a joint project, even if Clyde had done the hands-on supervision, and as such had brought them closer together. Before then, Clyde was tired of his job and London life, whereas Lucinda relished both and was going from success to success. She'd still dazzled him, but he could feel his stagnating career dimming his attraction for her, could sometimes see a moue of distaste at his pathetic decline. The 'moving to the country' project had ended this; he hadn't been in pathetic decline after all, just transitioning to a luxuriously extended way of life for them both.

It wasn't, though. It was an extension for her, a new back-drop and setting, plus new markets for her work and extra features in her way of life (and even those were becoming more occasional); he really had left the old life behind and started something new, even if he didn't quite know what it was yet. All it had done in the end was to deepen the division and, he was beginning to feel, accelerate the collapse of their relation-ship. When he thought of the evening ahead, which would once have been a cause of excitement, he realised he would probably rather share a bottle of wine and a game of cards with Zeno. (He always won, the jammy sod. Clyde was not a bad player, but Zeno had the devil's own luck.)

Clyde's fascination with and physical passion for Lucinda had mutated into an awkward politeness which made sex virtually impossible, as if a force field kept them from touch-ing. And, bottom line, he just didn't want to sleep with her anymore. Her presence in his life seemed to put him off and dim his drive, although he occasionally thought about the mysterious chic librarian. If he met her again, he might be tempted ...

He and Lucinda were still nominally together, though, and he hadn't got as far as considering the financial implications of separation, which would be difficult. They could stay in a locked cupboard of his mind until he was ready to look at them, ready to say to himself, full in the face, that his marriage was over. Or until Lucinda called time. Not that *she* would do that without considering her position. He wondered, quite without jealousy or ire, if she was up to anything. She had a lot of glamorous friends and was universally flirtatious in a rather lovey arty way, but her essential iciness made a natural boundary to anything progressing; or it had until now. With him, she had been, he decided, in love with being in love, with having a high-earning husband from outside her circle, both things that were fashionable at the time, and things that she might have wanted to experience. She liked experiences to feed her work, and he felt that was a good and natural thing for her. If the particular experience between them was drawing to a close, there was nothing wrong with that and she would probably generate a whole exhibition from the difficulties of their separation. She might also be experimenting with someone new for just the same reason; on balance, probably not, but although the thought of it would once have driven him to violent jealousy, now it didn't matter either way. She was an artist, a natural translator of the ups and downs of life into – in her case – physical objects to enrich the experience of all who encountered them.

He felt much better towards Lucinda having put her into this perspective, but he realised that he was still empty and depressed, hollow and without impetus to live compared to the wonders of the raging gale. It was not the loss of his wife he was feeling – she was still a presence – but the loss of the passion and desire he had once had for her; and without it, it was as if the pilot light of his life had been extinguished. He looked out once more, to where the bank fell steeply away to the railway line, and could feel himself heavy and cold like a stone; a stone that would fall out of the window and down, down, down, untouched by the glorious life force of the wind and weather, dead to the ground below.

At that moment, a whirring sound brought action across the scene of that ground, and a local electric train, jolly with lights, pulled into the station. Clyde's attention was arrested; the 'ghost train' again! This time, he even heard the whistle and the damp-ened metallic slam of the doors along the wind. He watched automaton-like as the little collection of carriages clattered away, revealing the toy station master he'd imagined, next to a feminine figure in wide jeans and a deep brown coat. A vibrant print scarf cascaded in breezy ripples over the shaggy-sheep collar, a sugges-tion of bright hair escaping in between, and a big, flat oblong suit-case of a kind Clyde hadn't seen for many years stood at her feet. As the station master walked away, she picked up her suitcase and in doing so, turned towards the house, looked up, and waved.

When Lucinda arrived, windswept and slightly irritable, Clyde was still sitting upstairs, looking out into the night. He came to when she called him, and rushed downstairs.

"Oh, there you are! God, what a shitty journey. Delays everywhere – tree down or something – and by the time I got to Slackford, the taxi bloke had gone off on another job. Still, good to be here." She didn't sound like she meant it, but she embraced him lightly. "I'll just go up and change."

"Of course, darling, go ahead. I'll get you a drink, shall I?" said Clyde meekly to her back.

"Yes please. A large one!"

Clyde turned away to see Zeno hovering in the hall. "Oh, hello," he said foolishly.

"I've got drinks ready in the lounge by the fire," said Zeno calmly, "and I've kept an eye on the dinner. *You* seem to have forgotten about it."

"Thanks," said Clyde warmly. "Zeno, you're great. What would I do without you?"

"I couldn't let that lovely leg of lamb spoil, I've been looking forward to it! And the roast roots need to go in the oven ..."

"Fancy a drink?"

"I have poured myself a small aperitif, a warming vermouth. Unadulterated by *gin*," he added firmly.

Clyde grinned. "Well, gin does seem a little chilly for a night like this," he said. "Will you be alright to finish dinner off?"

"I'll let you know when it's ready and serve it to you in the dining room," said Zeno. "The fires are going nicely."

"Once you've moved into the cottage, I'll be lost." Clyde was sheepish.

"I dare say I can be around to keep an eye on things," replied Zeno drily, with just a hint of his familiar twinkle as he returned to the kitchen.

Lucinda was soon down, and she and Clyde sat almost companionably by the fire in the drawing room, exchanging everyday news.

"By the way," said Clyde casually, "I love your new work. The one on the easel in the studio. Is it finished?"

"New work? I haven't got anything in the studio here at present; I sent the completed stuff on to the Regional Enterprise people. You know, they're distributing it around local galleries as part of the funding arrangement."

"It's there now," said Clyde. "I was looking at it this afternoon. Quite a different colour palette from your more recent stuff, and a wonderful lucid translucency. Reminded me of Helen Frankenthaler."

"What are you on about?" Lucinda's irritation resurfaced and, businesslike as ever, she marched out, drink in hand, to see for herself. Clyde scurried to keep up, wishing he had kept his mouth shut.

They arrived in the studio, restlessly shadowy in the storm light, and Lucinda smacked on the main lights. Resplendent before them, displayed on the large easel, was a mounted sheet of white paper bearing the abstract of colours that Clyde had described. It was slightly rumpled, but nevertheless beguiling.

"That's not mine," said Lucinda.

Clyde opened his mouth, then said nothing.

"It's nothing *like* my work," she continued. "It's dated in style and technique, and whoever's done it has an incomplete mastery of the advanced school that they are imitating." She pointed, the critic at work. "These runs are intentional, but this bulging is not. I don't recognise the material. Is it ink?" Her brow furrowed, then she took a step back. "It does have some quality, though," she added thoughtfully, her natural fairness and love of art shining through. "The person who attempted it certainly has *some* knowledge, and some potential as an artist."

"I thought so," said Clyde very quietly, for he now had an idea what was going on.

"But the point is," Lucinda was irritated once more, and forceful with it, "what's it doing here?" She turned and stared at Clyde accusingly. He looked steadily, if unconvincingly, back at her, like a naughty little boy confronted by a teacher.

"I can't imagine," he lied.

From then on, they had a rather tense and uneasy weekend. On the surface, everything was good: they took a long walk in the suddenly fine weather on the Saturday, and in the evening were joined for dinner by some of the major local stakeholders in Lucinda's funding package. Zeno had reluctantly prepared a vegetarian banquet, Italian in style, although Clyde privately wondered if all the ingredients – cheese, wine, etc – would pass scrutiny. Everyone had their prejudices, he reflected, glad that none of the guests were vegan. That might have spurred Zeno into open rebellion.

The company consisted of Victoria Makewell, owner and manager of a well-known local gallery specialising in conceptual art, and her husband Mark; Professor David Garner of the city university art department; and Tom Dale, the cabinet member for arts and culture on the Greater Blocton Council. Clyde would have liked to beef-out the occasion with some local company, but the only people he knew well who were unlikely to be controversial were rarely free on Saturdays. He could hardly invite a phantom librarian. If only he had dared to invite Melrose Burke for entertainment value, but Lucinda would not have borne it. He wanted to ask Zeno to sit down and eat with them, but she would not have borne that either.

In fact, Lucinda was taking the occasion very seriously indeed. She was always focussed where work was concerned, but Clyde knew that her enthusiasm for the local project had waned considerably with the reality of everyday life away from London. Still, she seemed to be working harder than ever to make the event a success; she was even, and he had hardly ever known this before, a little tense. He wondered what could be behind such a mood.

He had met all the guests before, and remembered what he could: Victoria was an energetic and talkative art graduate who had a gift for marketing, funding and networking the local arts scene. Clyde supposed she must have done some art once, but he couldn't ever remember seeing or hearing of any. She had a tendency to parochial self-importance, and her connection with Lucinda seemed to exaggerate this, as if the London link had convinced Victoria that she'd been right about her own sphere being close to the centre of the art universe. He didn't care for the kind of art she specialised in – it meant nothing to him – but it didn't affect his respect for her abilities, and once he got away from the subject of work, he found that she was interested in gardening and food and was quite good company. A plump-ish person, as the night went on and she had more wine, she gave the impression of loosening her stays, and laughed long and heartily.

Her husband Mark, who did something in a company doing something with forklift trucks, didn't seem to have much sense of humour, and showed a tendency to want to talk about investments. Clyde thought that if they stayed long enough, he might have to put on his business face and make up some shit about the markets.

Professor David Garner had a genial manner, a dark beard, long hair tied back and a heavy air of 'cool'. He talked only of art – what it meant, what it should be and what was happening at the university – and as a result, in direct contradiction to the desired effect, appeared to be a big fish in a small outlying pond. He had spent his entire adult life from student days to seniority at the same academic institution, which was bound to result in a certain narrowness of outlook. If only he'd got out more, reflected Clyde sadly, listening to another pompous diatribe. If he let go, he might be quite a decent bloke. Clyde plied him with wine accordingly.

Tom Dale, on the other hand, didn't look old enough to be drinking. It was like having dinner with a school prefect. He was rather out of it, really, in that he clearly had no art education or experience; but he did have a remarkable memory for glib phrases and jargon – Clyde supposed he must have memorised them as they had no discernible meaning – and hence made quite a lot of conversation. The others were clearly willing to meet him more than halfway, as was in their interest, and perhaps after all they knew what the hell he was on about. A long exchange of non sequiturs between the jabbering youth and the tipsily pretentious professor at one stage drove Clyde to distraction and he had to resist the urge to ask the council official if it wasn't past his bedtime.

He had been intrigued to see how Lucinda would play the evening. She was ruthless in her assessments and he didn't feel that any but Ms Makewell would gain much of her good opinion. He found with amusement that she was combining the great artist and beautiful society hostess roles: she was poised, smiling and quiet except when appealed to, when she answered briefly and inscrutably. She was a clever minx, he thought fondly, finding the perfect way to negotiate the evening with tact and tactical advantage, as well as pleasing her guests.

He was concerned, though, about how she would pursue the ghost picture, for he was convinced now that was what it was. As the evening wore on and Mark was maundering about the tactics of his investment club, which he clearly thought to be highly original and cunning, Clyde dwelt on it more and more. He found the presence of an invisible artist deeply soothing, just as he found the helping hand of the invisible librarian a support. His ghostly housemates were so much better – and easier – company than was to be found in social situations like this one, and knowing that they were there to retreat to when the solid people had gone was becoming a prop on which he increasingly relied. He didn't feel the need to know more at present, but Lucinda would not let the matter drop. She would, quite understandably, want an explanation, and where would that end?

He was equally certain that she would never accept what he felt sure was the true solution, that they lived in, or at least he lived in and she part-owned, a haunted house; and he was desperate that she shouldn't take any action that might disturb the ménage that had become more important to him than his marriage. There was trouble ahead.

Mark was now asking what he thought about the futures market and Clyde was roused to tell him that on the whole, it was a very bad idea indeed.

They had both collapsed into bed late, tired, full and mildly inebriated, so they had a reasonable excuse for not wanting sex. Lucinda was up early next morning – always so energetic, thought Clyde – looking elegant in country gear, the only clothes that she actually kept in the house.

She strode in with a coffee for Clyde and chivvied him. "Come on," she gave him a nudge, "we've got to get down to the lodge. Zeno's meeting us there at ten to have a look round, and I want to check the place over before he gets there."

Clyde, looking tousled, got out of bed, wondering if Zeno was happy to be up so early. "I'm making breakfast," shouted Lucinda from the landing, "so don't be long."

A short time later, they were walking down the drive through a thick fog, Lucinda kicking the bright leaves, the only splash of colour in a silver world, with her smooth leather boots.

"It's got to be Zeno," she was saying firmly and insistently. "No one else has access to my studio. Burglars don't, in my experience, come in and create a work of art, and then leave without taking anything. Or are you suggesting that one of the builders popped up from the lodge and did it?"

"Of course not," said Clyde miserably.

"I know he's a great cook and housekeeper," his wife went on relentlessly, "and that you really like him. I like him too," she added as an afterthought. "But there have to be boundaries. That studio is my workplace and I can't have other people using it without permission."

Clyde forbore from pointing out that she hadn't used the place for over a month. "I don't want to upset him," he moaned. "We're planning to set up a micro bakery together." He wished she would keep her voice down; Zeno could be just a couple of paces behind them in this fog.

"I will say he didn't use any of my materials," said Lucinda, "so he's not dishonest. And the place was so clean you wouldn't know anyone had been there. But even so, it can't go on. I don't want him to go – it's not as if he's stolen anything – but I have to draw a line. You do understand that?"

"*If* he did it," said Clyde, who was every bit as uncomfortable with this subject as he'd expected. "I think you should at least ask him before you get too carried away with consequences."

"I intend to!" said his wife.

They had a brief look round the lodge, which was almost finished. It had made an extremely attractive cottage, Clyde thought. Welcoming even when it was cold. They had just got back to the hall when Zeno arrived, smiling his gnomish smile.

"Good morning."

"Good morning, Zeno." Lucinda stepped in front of Clyde. "Zeno, before we look around the cottage, there's something I need to say to you."

"That's fine, Mrs Tranter, of course." He put on a neutral expression.

"Zeno, I cannot have you using my studio without permission. I appreciate that you have neither taken any of my art materials for your own use, nor disturbed my things, but even so I can't allow it. The studio is my creative space and as such it is sacrosanct."

"I'm very sorry, Mrs Tranter." Zeno lowered his eyes,

seemingly with embarrassment, and spoke quietly through his beard.

"I'm prepared to forget about it as long as it never happens again," said Lucinda, magnificently magnanimous.

"Actually, the picture was not done in the studio, just left there to dry," said Zeno humbly. Clyde eyed him suspiciously from behind the iron lady.

"I see. Well, as I say, let's forget all about it as long as it doesn't happen again. You're very good at your job, Zeno, an asset to the household, and we don't want to lose you, but I hope I've made myself clear."

"Oh yes, Mrs Tranter," said the abject Zeno. Clyde hoped the man wasn't going to cry. "Thank you."

"Good," said Lucinda, briskly moving on. "That's settled. Let's start in the kitchen." She strode away, leaving the other two to follow.

"Zeno, you didn't paint that picture, did you?" said Clyde quietly.

"Of course not," said Zeno, grinning. "I never said I did."

"I didn't think art was your thing," said Clyde thoughtfully. "But I don't know how you got into drama, either."

"Why?" asked Zeno, puzzled. "I've been in The Burnton Players for years."

"On the basis of that performance," replied Clyde, "you're a terrible ham. Talk about overacting, I thought I was going to have to lend you a hankie!" And the two men went on into the kitchen, laughing companionably.

Chapter Six

IT WAS NOVEMBER NOW, the greyest, though by no means the bleakest, of months. Clyde was raking leaves in the garden. He had learned a lot about composting over the last month, and had taken delivery of some old pallets to make bays for his compost station, as well as accumulating piles of suitable material to start a heap. But some of the garden waste had been put aside for a bonfire, and he'd taken boyish pleasure in constructing it, wigwam-like, in such a way as to give a good blaze. No effigy was to be burned, though; the symbolic burning of another human being was, it seemed to him, a barbaric tradition which could not be forgotten soon enough.

The only thing that had dampened his excitement was the worry of wildlife being trapped in the burning mound, but the inimitable Zeno had produced the solution in the form of a young woman called Perkie Price and her team of trained ferrets. The animals had clearly enjoyed themselves a great deal, exploring every nook and cranny of the pyre that morning, and as Perkie herself had pointed out, "Nowt wunner nestle in theer wunce ferrets uve scented eet."

He had a few good-quality fireworks safely stored and

homemade burgers – meat and veggie – waiting in the fridge, a quantity of cider for mulling, homemade pumpkin ice-cream at the ready and a couple of daft party games to play. Parkin was maturing in a tin. It was an old recipe but something quite new to Zeno, who had respect for Clyde's culinary taste and was looking forward to trying it; Clyde had been firm that it needed a couple more days before tasting. There had been no further mention between the two men of the unexpected artwork in Lucinda's studio, which had disappeared as quietly as it had come.

It would not be Lucinda's kind of party, but his great friends Craig and Jim were coming and would be staying for a week. Zeno would be there, of course, as well as Mattie, Melrose and quite a few of his local acquaintances. Clyde thought how good it would be to have his own cider to mull in future years and that he must go and look over the few sad fruit trees that were still standing. He wanted to plan the new orchard as a matter of urgency as he had only recently become aware that fruit trees need several years to establish before they crop; like most non-gardeners, he'd just assumed that one stuck them in the ground and the fruit appeared.

At least they had the wonderful mulberry tree, very tall and draping wide in an elegant feathery cone; no need to wait a generation for that to bear fruit. It was highly impractical, of course, requiring ladders to pick from all but the lowest branches and probably a cherry-picker to harvest the full crop. Clyde didn't mind; the enormous grace of the organism and the inaccessibility of the berries made them special, magical prizes to be won by those who dared. And they did not disappoint, bursting to overflow the mouth with a deep-staining crimson juice of unique and delectable flavour.

He must find someone to help and advise him in the garden. With this thought in mind, he began to head back to the house; dusk was falling, so early now, of course.

The previous week, Melrose and Mattie – they always seemed to come as a pair now, she following about a foot behind like a faithful but neglected dog – had been to the house with the publisher's photographer from London, a young man called Faz. His manner of speech seemed to bamboozle Melrose into uncharacteristic silence, and Mattie had come into her own, sorting things out and organising the shoot with reference to the plans showing where the bodies had been found.

"Gross, man," Faz had commented, as she pointed out the exact spot where Sheila Cope had lain in a pool of her own blood. "Must have messed up the rug." Despite his laid-back appearance, he was efficient, extremely competent and had excellent equipment. "We need a focus for the shot," he'd said while trying the lighting, "or else you just get an empty room with a carpet. You should play the corpse, man." He turned to Mattie, who was predictably excited.

"I'll need *blood*," she said with relish. "A big gash across the throat, a thick pool under my head, and spatters all over," indicating her torso. "Rubex Stage Blood is the best."

"*No!*" burst in Melrose. "This is a *history* book, non-fiction, a *factual account*, not *The Rocky Horror Show*. Have you no thought for my credibility? Think of *something else!*"

"How about a stain, man?" Faz was considering. "Tasteful faded stain, muted red, here on the rug. To draw in the eye. Could be creepy done right." At this point Clyde, who'd been watching, intervened firmly, pointing out that it was a very valuable rug.

"C'mon, man," said Faz. "It don't have to be this rug. We can use a set rug. Nice artistic stain all ready, just about here." He walked over and pointed at the spot with his toe. "Okay?" Clyde nodded. "So, all done here. Got everything I need for now." He looked at his notes and said, "Which way to the *drawing room*?" in mock-posh tones.

Clyde had showed them through, and Mattie once more helped the potential set-up, showing Faz where Berenia Hassel had been found.

"What sort of chair was she in?" he'd asked.

"We don't really know," she confessed. "The original crime-scene photos are missing. That's why you're here."

"Hmm. Shame. What we need's one of these high-back efforts with sides." He took hold of one of the fireside wing-back chairs. "I can make it look, well, empty, you know, like someone left it with the damage – bullet holes, blood and stuff. Veronica can sort one, no problem."

"*Who*," asked Melrose sniffily, "is Veronica?"

"She's my missus, man. Set and prop builder. Top, she is, nothing she don't know about that business."

"I could forward her the crime-scene description," put in Mattie keenly. "There are some details about the damage to the chair, position of the body and so on."

"Fine, man," Faz smiled happily. "I'll just check out the lighting here and I'm done. On to this other place, where is it?"

"The lodge cottage at the end of the drive," said Clyde. "Zeno, our personal assistant, is down there decorating, but he's finished the hall, which is the room you want."

They had all headed down to the lodge ("Man, you need a golf buggy," was Faz's comment). In the hall, Zeno had painted the ceiling and mouldings white, and the walls a grey-green. The tiled floor and banister rails were shining with polish, but the single bulb in its low-hanging fitting had not yet been replaced.

"Man, that is *perfect*," sighed Faz admiringly. "We won't need no set dressing here. That bulb swings like a hanging man!" And he had taken his measurements.

They had all returned this morning, Mrs Faz accompanying to assist, and it seemed that satisfactory results were obtained. "Pretty good, man," Faz had said to Melrose when they'd finished. "Wait till they're doctored, then I'll send some previews along." Zeno had accompanied them to the lodge this time, and once Mr and Mrs Faz had departed, Melrose had asked if they could be shown around.

"Of course," said Zeno. "This way."

They went round the ground-floor reception rooms, now just awaiting carpets and furniture, and then upstairs. Zeno was very lively and chatty in his enthusiasm. In the front bedroom, he had described vividly how you used to be able to see the village green before the new school was built; glancing into the bathroom, he remembered when there was only a lavatory in the little outhouse and no bath at all; once back downstairs in the kitchen, he reminisced about the kettle always being boiled on the fire, even though there was a perfectly good electric cooker.

Clyde had been surprised to hear him so talkative. He had not realised Zeno knew so much about the cottage. Thinking back over the last weeks when he had been helping Zeno decorate the lodge, he recalled it had been a friendly, companionable time: singing along to the radio; chatting about food, plans for the bakery and all the exciting fruits and vegetables Clyde was going to grow; discussing detective stories, which they both loved; talking about the local cricket club and whether Clyde should join – he was a medium bowler with the advantage of height – and Zeno's latest role for The Burnton Players. Zeno had seemed very much at home, but that wasn't surprising under the circumstances.

What was it that now felt odd?

Clyde had pondered this on the way back to the main house. Mattie and Melrose had departed, and Zeno had remained behind at the lodge. Clyde tried to recreate the field of emotion while touring the cottage with Zeno. Certainly, there was a sense of returning, of Zeno reminiscing about a place he was coming back to; but it was the wrong reminiscence!

How old was Zeno? Clyde couldn't remember seeing a date of birth on his CV, and it wasn't easy to guess, but the man was surely not more than the middle fifties, and he could be younger. He'd come to work at the college here twenty-five years or so ago, but the school that blocked the view had been built in the 1980s. Also, before the renovation, there had been the remnants of a startling maroon bathroom suite upstairs in the cottage, and Clyde was very sure that would have been there before Zeno took up his employment. That kind of suite hadn't been manufactured for over thirty years. As for the kettle on the fire, that could be true, but Clyde had never seen it done in his lifetime. The cottage had been empty and abandoned as part of the college's long decline years before it closed, yet Zeno had been remembering its heyday, probably twenty years before he was supposed to have been there. He'd spoken with the nostalgia mellowed by temporal distance that only the old have when talking about their youth.

A shiver ran through Clyde. What did it mean? Who had lived in the house? The Baxters, of course. And they had had two children, now of whereabouts and name unknown. *They* would have known all about the view before the trees, the outside lavatory and the kettle boiling in the kitchen; who better? Was Zeno the lost Keith Baxter? Was his father a murderer?

It was ridiculous, of course, because then, the man would have to be about seventy. But Clyde was still feeling the shock of the idea that someone he lived with was not who they seemed when Zeno landed at his side, breathless from jogging to catch up.

"Aagh, it's cold," he said, grimacing. "Come on, let's get back to the kitchen where it's warm and put the kettle on. I've made some pumpkin cake, rich, spiced and warming."

He'd jogged on and Clyde, after a moment's hesitation, had loped after him.

It was dark after tea, and Clyde went round the downstairs to light the stoves and draw the curtains. Most of the great windows were dressed with sumptuous fabrics contrary to the modern fashion, but very much in keeping with the house. Lucinda had intended them as just dressings, because the hugely expensive super-insulated windows did not require covering to keep the heat in, but Clyde found he liked to draw the curtains; when the days were short and dark, it felt right to hunker down, to shut out the inclement elements and retreat into the glow of the inviting fire-lit rooms.

Upstairs it was different: it was wild and daring to lie on the huge bed, gazing out directly at the treetops, level with the birds, hearing the sounds of darkness. At the window, he saw moths, bats, tawny owls ... and trains full of ghosts.

Entering the hall, Clyde switched on the wall lamps, turned and started back. In the centre of the spectacular antique Turkish rug was a large red-brown shadow. He bent down. It was definitely their rug and not the prop that Faz had brought. Anyway, the stain was not pink like the one rigged up by the talented Veronica, but almost terracotta in hue, faint, faded and completely dry. But it was in exactly the spot where they had calculated Sheila's head, with its slashed throat, had lain. If he hadn't stared at that spot so frequently, he might never have noticed the mark, it was so lost in the pattern of the rug.

Could it always have been there? It was an old rug; but no, he'd looked at it too often with the murder in mind. It could be some kind of practical joke, but he didn't think anyone who'd been involved in the shoot would damage valuable property for a bit of fun. It couldn't have been a leak or spillage from the prop rug as the genuine one had been kept a couple of rooms away.

Did he, for the first time, feel uneasy about the active presences on his property? No, but he did wonder whether he *should* be feeling uneasy, whether he had reason to. Especially so soon after the revelations of Zeno. Then he shrugged; that faint staining had probably always been there and he'd just never taken it in before.

He went into the drawing room, walked across to switch on the standard lamp – turned wood with a silk damask shade that had cost more than the lamp itself – on one side of the fireplace, and began to make up the stove. With the lower vent open, he laid a mixture of paper and broken briquettes with a wax firelighter and touched the latter with a match. There was a tremendous roar and the flames burst out, sparking wildly. Soon he and Lucinda would have their own logs, he hoped, but there had not yet been time for any wood cut to season.

He opened the door of the little furnace and placed two dusty cylinders of fuel, watching the temperature gauge rise steadily, then crouched on a footstool, mesmerised, until the fire reached temperature and the burn was established. He shut the lower vent and the noise subsided to a distant whir.

After enjoying the firelight for another minute, he rose to shut the curtains. As he did so, he caught sight of a figure, large as life, in the wing-backed chair behind him. He jumped and fell over the footstool, all the time with the intruder in front of him.

She was a plump-ish elderly lady wearing a lightweight tweed coat and skirt such as were never seen nowadays, a rather frilly blouse and polished brown leather lace-up shoes with square toes. She had curly grey hair, but he could not see much of her face because her head was slumped down on her chest.

This time, Clyde was really frightened. He ran out of the

room and into the kitchen to find Zeno, but there was no one there. He was about to run upstairs to see where he was, but paused to gather his thoughts instead. He calmed his breathing. Then, standing very upright, he stepped defiantly but gingerly back towards the drawing room. He pushed open the door, which was ajar, and on the threshold, before daring to look in, turned on the large ceiling lights.

There was no one in the room.

The fire was making a good rolling burn and he could sense the heat barrier in the cool air some distance from his face. He turned his head around the room stupidly and repeatedly, his hand still on the light switch, then sensed a movement behind him and twitched jerkily.

It was Zeno.

"Are you alright, Clyde?" he said, looking up into Clyde's ashen face.

"Zeno," Clyde said as he put a shaky hand on the shorter man's firm shoulder and leaned slightly, "there was a woman sitting in that chair." He pointed weakly. "I was making the fire, almost in the dark, and when I got up, a body was slumped in the chair."

"A *body*?" Zeno showed surprise for the first time.

"An elderly woman in old-fashioned clothes, like something off the television, slumped in the chair."

"Ohhh," said Zeno.

"But she's gone." Clyde was shrill. "Look, the body's gone."

"Well," said Zeno, with the emphatic calmness of an adult comforting an hysterical child, "I expect you disturbed her. Why don't you come into the kitchen and have a drink while I prepare dinner? We'll eat, and then we can talk about it."

Clyde turned dumbly and trudged towards the kitchen, his spirit broken. Zeno took a quick look around the room, turned out the light and followed him.

. . .

Not too long afterwards, Zeno placed two bowls of steaming pasta on the kitchen table and sat down. Clyde, who had drunk quite a lot of wine rather quickly, drooped over the table. He had the firm grip on his glass of a man who feels the determined need for more drink. He gazed, unfocussed, down at the bowl.

"Try some," said Zeno kindly. "It will do you good. Some wholesome food to ground you. And mop up the wine," he added with a smile.

Clyde waved his fork airily. "But I want to know …"

"Let's eat a little first," said Zeno, "and then we'll talk."

Clyde nibbled half a forkful petulantly, but the pasta was very good, and he was soon wolfing it down. He had eaten about half of it when he suddenly stopped and looked directly at the man opposite.

"What's going on, Zeno?" he said.

"I don't entirely know. But I don't *think* it's anything to worry about. In fact, there's a chance things could work out well …"

"Well? There's a dead woman, murdered in 1958, in the drawing room– oh, except she's disappeared. Or don't you believe me? That's it, isn't it? You think I'm delusional. It will all be fine if I see a neurologist, or a psychologist, or an ophthalmologist. You're humouring me because you think there's something wrong with me."

"I don't think there's anything wrong with you at all; things might be going right with you for a change! You hated your job and were bored; you didn't like city life; you'd completely supressed your personality and interests to make money, and once you'd got it, you didn't know what to do with it; your wife had lost interest in you. Now, you have a home, a community, interests, some meaning to your life, a growing personality, friends and, once the hollow remnants of your marriage dissolve, the chance of finding a loving relationship."

Zeno stopped suddenly and gulped, realising that he may have been too frank.

"*The hollow remnants of my marriage?*" Clyde almost shouted. He was about to burst into violent rage, but it dissipated as quickly as it had ignited. "You're right, of course. I suppose you can't help but notice that she comes here less and less often. And she seems to be spending money on the studio flat above the gallery ...We'll have to sort it out, but I don't want to lose this place."

He paused. "You can see from what I've just said that I no longer mind losing Lucinda," he said, more to himself than Zeno. "I did before, in London, when things were going wrong. That's partly why I took this place on. Something to catch her interest, to bring us together, to make it seem that I still had something to offer her. But whatever spell it was I was under has broken, and now it's this place that matters to me, not her."

"These things can be very messy," said Zeno reflectively. "I speak from experience. But the divorce process is a lot more reasonable than it used to be, I believe."

"It's kind of you to say I have friends," said Clyde, growing sentimental with drink.

"Well, obviously we're friends," replied Zeno briskly. "What do you think? And everyone here likes you, even that colossal berk Melrose." He laughed. "Burke by name and berk by nature."

They both giggled as they finished their dinner.

Chapter Seven

IT WAS the day of the bonfire party and the weather was perfect. An atmospheric mist had cleared, exposing the universal wetness to a jolly but feeble sun, and the clear, faded sky promised a nip of sparkling fairy frost after dark. Clyde was delighted; it was such fun to have a proper cold autumn day for once and to be able to wrap up in the hats and scarves that were used less and less these days.

He had been making bread buns and flatbreads for the burgers and the kitchen smelt wonderful. Zeno had been bustling round the house cleaning and tidying, and was now outside sweeping the terrace and setting up the barbecue. Clyde went out to him.

"I can finish off here, thanks, Zeno. It won't be long till you have to head off to the station."

Zeno consulted his large old-fashioned watch. "Yes, I'd better get off in a moment. The traffic's bound to be awful. I'm looking forward to meeting your friends."

"Leave it to me," said Clyde, shivering slightly.

"Great. I'll sort out the hot drinks when I get back."

Clyde had invested in several large vacuum-flask urns with

taps, and he had a boyish excitement about using them. His phone rang and he went inside as he took it out to answer it.

"I'll just change my shoes and be off, then," called Zeno.

"Hi, darling," said Clyde unconvincingly to the phone. It was Lucinda. Normally she FaceTimed, but not today.

"Clyde, has Zeno set out for the station yet?" she demanded without preamble.

"He's just leaving now."

"Well stop him. You need to tell him I'm not coming. I don't want him waiting about for me and messing the evening up for you all."

Clyde was about to express surprise, and then realised that he wasn't really surprised at all. At heart, he'd known she wouldn't come. It was not the kind of occasion she would attend for pleasure, and there were no longer the bonds between them that would make her come as his partner and hostess in their family home.

"Hang on." He caught Zeno just as he was going through the door. The man said nothing, but gave an understanding nod and left. He still had Clyde's friends Craig and Jim to pick up.

Clyde went back to his phone. "It's sorted," he said.

There was a long pause. He didn't feel like asking her why she wasn't coming. He found it didn't matter very much.

"Clyde," she began again.

"Yes?"

"The reason I'm not coming."

"Mmm?"

"I should have said something before."

"Oh?" He wouldn't have spoken at all, but he felt that on a voice call, a vague response was needed to reassure the other party that you were still there.

"Clyde, I'm spending the weekend with Jason Deaville. He and I – well, since he invited me to curate that big biennial for him, we've spent a lot of time together ... I'm not suited for life outside London. We want to get married."

A relaxing realisation swept over Clyde that this was just the right thing for Lucinda. After a short pause, he said, "That's good. I'm glad."

"Glad?"

"C'mon, Lucinda, you usually go straight to the point without taking prisoners. We haven't been comfortable together for a long time. This place was never right for you, although I'm grateful – and always will be – for the skilled hand of your design in the renovation. And I want you to have a life that's good for you."

Another pause. Perhaps his response was not what she'd been expecting. "Thanks, Clyde," she said at last. "What about you? I mean, what about a life that's good for you?"

"I have it here, in this house," he said.

"Well, we'll have to make the proper arrangements, of course," she said, back to her brusque businesslike style. "Fortunately there's nothing in the house that I need urgently. Enjoy your party, and I'll be in touch about sorting things out."

"Thanks, Lucinda. Have a great weekend."

"Thanks, Clyde, for ... well, for taking it so well. Goodbye." And she was gone.

Clyde felt blank and a little floaty, but perfectly fine. He didn't even want a drink.

Everything was ready by the time Zeno returned with Craig and Jim. They all three stomped in through the front door, smiling and laughing, and Craig and Jim dropped their bags, rubbing their hands warm.

"Clyde!"

"Hey!" Beaming, Clyde came rushing through to hug his

old friends. "It's great to see you both," he said with obvious sincerity.

"And you!" they answered in unison. "But where's Lucinda?" added Jim. "Is she okay?"

"Yeah, she's fine," said Clyde calmly. "We're splitting up. She's found someone else ..."

"Oh God, I'm sorry." This was Craig.

"No, it's a good thing," said Clyde, firmly reassuring his friends. "We've been on the rocks for ages, and we both deserve better than that. I'm happier now it's been decided, like a weight's been lifted off my shoulders. Feel free to tell everyone. It's official."

Craig and Jim both looked concerned, as if they thought this was just a brave coping speech by their friend and he was about to crack up under his unnaturally calm exterior. Zeno, however, stepped forward and shook Clyde's hand with both his own.

"I'm so glad things have worked out for you both," he said, smiling warmly at his employer. "I'm sure it's the start of great things for you." Craig and Jim gave each other quizzical and suspicious looks, but Clyde felt it was time to get into the party spirit.

"C'mon, you two. Let's get your stuff up to your room, then have a quick tour of the house before the others start arriving. You okay to manage things in the meantime, Zeno?"

"I certainly am," said Zeno, his cheerfulness sounding incongruous in his deep, growly voice. "It's going to be a fantastic evening!"

Showing Craig and Jim their room, Clyde looked at them both fondly. They made such a contrasting couple: Craig still skinny-ish in tight jeans, denim jacket and high-heeled boots, with a pale face, cropped hair, fancy moustache and silver jewellery; Jim broad, tall, black and perfectly shaven, wearing a mustard yellow silk shirt and brightly coloured silk tie, formal nut-brown trousers and polished handmade leather shoes of traditional design.

"I haven't lit the bonfire!" Clyde exclaimed. "Make yourselves at home and wrap up warm, you're not in London now. Come down for a drink when you're ready, and then we'll do the tour." He made a movement towards the door.

"Clyde," Craig stopped him, "just a quick word." He and Jim exchanged serious glances.

"What?" said Clyde blithely.

"It's just that, well, this guy, Zeno. Are you sure he's okay?"

"Okay? God, yes! He's an absolute godsend, and a good friend."

"But he's not really a friend, Clyde," put in Jim. "He's an employee. You pay him to be here."

Clyde had nothing to say. This was his old life adjusting to his new, and that was rarely a comfortable fit straight off.

"We're just concerned," continued Jim, "because you're here a lot alone with him, you're talking of starting a business involving him, and now Lucinda's off the scene ..."

"Haven't you thought he might fancy you?" blurted out Craig. "Be in love with you, even?"

"What?" shouted Clyde, and then he laughed.

"Straight men never see these things," said Craig, shaking his head in an aside to Jim. "C'mon, Clyde, you saw how pleased he was when you broke the news about Lucinda."

"Oh, that," said Clyde calmly. "We were talking about it the other night, about how the marriage was over and it was only a matter of time. I mean, he's seen us together enough to work it out."

"Even so, man," said Jim, "you've got to admit that it's not quite the normal relationship under the circumstances."

Clyde was laughing quietly now. "You're right about things not being normal here, Jim," he said. "But they're a lot more strange than anything you're imagining." And with that, he left the room, skipping downstairs to get the fire going.

The fire was just forging its way out of crackling and smoky beginnings, leaving room in the nostrils for the smell of warm cider and charring meat. The alcohol and glowing burn were loosening the newly arrived company into sociable mood, and acquaintances were being made. Bernard and George had advised Clyde on the fireworks and offered to run the display for him. At this moment they were some distance away in the dark, heads bent over a torch and an enormous rocket, deep in technical discussion.

Michael, the pensioner librarian, could be heard talking of "Bourgeois decadence" to Craig and Jim. His repeated invoking of the process of historical materialism had the keener members of the Burnton Historical Society crowding into the increasingly heated conversation. Soon Melrose Burke's squeaky tones rose above the rest, although not loudly enough to block out Michael calling him an old mountebank who understood nothing of historiography, and Agnes Beresford remarking crisply to Clyde that it was all a lot of nonsense from two overgrown schoolboys.

Clyde was flitting about with a lightness born of either a hysterical response to deep emotional shock, as his old friends believed, or a childishly simple enjoyment of satisfaction. Zeno had invited some of the dramatic society and had just introduced Clyde to one of the members, Martina, who he thought might be perfect for the job of garden manager at Valencia House.

"It's great to meet you, Martina," said Clyde hurriedly, "and I'd love to talk, but I need to get these burgers round to pacify the historians. They can't argue with mouths full of food. It's turning into a battle re-enactment!" He felt as he said it that it was a feeble witticism, but the girl – she was probably in her forties, he reflected afterwards, but her air of vulnerability made him think of her that way – smiled nervously and gave a helpful little laugh. She was slim, but looked strong-limbed and had a long, interesting face, intelligent eyes and dark wavy hair piled attractively above her tall neck. Her frailty was not of body but of spirit, an impression that she had taken too many knocks to stay firmly standing.

"I can help," she said with a jarring mixture of confidence and diffidence, and followed Clyde round the barbecue to join him and Zeno dishing out burgers, buns, wraps, relishes and sauces to a mobbing band of lively historians, tennis players, actors and village personalities.

By the time the first round of cooking was served, she'd been carried away happily into the crowd. Never mind, there would be opportunities to discuss future gardening projects another time. Clyde saw Martina talking animatedly over a veggie burger with Mattie some distance away. They made an odd couple – the highly strung, deeply thoughtful woman with the eager, bonkers one – but they seemed to have really hit it off.

Craig and Jim were in front of him now, waiting for something to eat. Zeno was busy at the barbecue and the four of them chatted awkwardly, Craig and Jim not being very subtle about sounding Zeno out. They were joined by a few of the tennis club members, and Craig, an enthusiastic player, was soon involved in a lively chat with them.

Clyde went to ask Bernard and George what they wanted to eat.

"Do you know," he could hear George's voice as he approached, "that they've got a fully restored Leyland D6497 Series B? In full working order!"

Once the hot food was over and more hot drinks, parkin and ice-cream had been distributed around the now-roaring heat of the fire, Craig and Jim helped Clyde to get the hoopla and hook-a-duck underway and stayed to moderate the excesses of the more competitive guests. Drifting away to look for Bernard and George to enquire about the fireworks, Clyde found himself in conversation with Agnes Beresford, something which he always enjoyed. For him, her rather stern schoolmistress manner held no fears; he found her lucid and knowledgeable speech so refreshing.

"Another most enjoyable party, Mr Tranter," she said. "Your arrival in Burnton has been an asset for our social calendar. This occasion is rather more homely than the last one, and none the worse for it." She gave him a gracious smile.

"I'm delighted you were able to come, Miss Beresford," replied Clyde sincerely. There was nothing uncomfortable in using formal address with this lady; it was entirely natural. "I was hoping you could tell me more about the college here."

"About its history? Or my personal reminiscences?"

"I'm sure both would be most interesting."

"Well, let me see. It is really very difficult to convey to anyone who did not experience them, and I am sure you are a little too young," she gave him another of her queenly smiles, "the mood and values of the times. They have changed so drastically and so deeply that even those who *should* remember frequently do not." Her expression became briefly stern before softening into what Clyde was surprised to recognise as rapture as she took herself back in mind and spirit. She emerged in a state of lively and irrepressible excitement that he found mildly alarming.

"There was, of course, the post-war political consensus: ideas of society, public services, standards of living and so on; the general agreement that people and the quality of their lives were important. Education was a large part of the ideology, because *obviously* it's essential to *everything*, and the setting was the exciting renaissance of the arts in Britain, the new age of scientific and technological advance and the developing relationship with our European neighbours. I can't tell you how we felt; the shackles were off and we had the space and freedom to do all the things we had dreamed of and take people *with* us on the journey." She opened her arms and looked skywards, as if to heaven.

Clyde was always deeply impressed by listening to Miss Beresford, but he was astonished by the hippy-ish tone of this last outburst. As if reading his mind, she continued after a little ripple of self-conscious laughter.

"I was much younger then! I have to confess, though, that coming from such a correct background, I did not realise at the time the true value of the hippies, the drop-outs and the art-college scene. Of course, many of them contributed nothing *directly* and were exactly what they seemed, I've no doubt, but that band of laxity in society, a margin or gutter where one could live socially but relatively unrestrained, was not only a rich breeding ground for many creative talents, some of them great, it also supported the atmosphere, the belief that there were so many important things in life that lay outside conventional norms and beyond any kind of monetary value. Education became one of those things. It was part of the backdrop against which evening classes, part-time courses and colleges of all kinds burgeoned and flourished and became fashionable across a wide stratum of society, a huge number of them offering subjects that could serve no economic purpose to the student at all."

She sighed. "It was only when money became God that things changed and everything had to prove its worth in financial terms. Not that money wasn't important before – of course it always was, and we'd had currency, price and wage controls to prove it – but this was different." She suddenly looked directly at Clyde and he saw her eyes were moist. "Once you let money assume an importance of its own, Mr

Tranter, once you cross that line where it becomes more important than humanity, however slightly, there is no going back. Once you have admitted the principle, there is no dishonesty, no cruelty, no atrocity that you cannot approve if it is deemed 'financially necessary'. It makes me feel quite sick to relive the cold-heartedness of that change. Everything worth caring for was declared valueless, a null to be discarded. We've lived with it for so long, that icy inhumanity, that we no longer feel the pain so keenly, only the gnaw of the widespread depression eating away at us." She sniffed, and looked in her bag for a handkerchief to correct her face.

Clyde took her arm. "I think, perhaps, you would like a warm drink, Miss Beresford," he said kindly "Let's both get one," and he drew her, still looking into her handkerchief, away towards the Thermos urns.

As he handed her a steaming mug, she said, "Thank you, Mr Tranter. I won't apologise for my emotional display. There was a time when I would have done so, in accordance with the standards of my upbringing, but I no longer feel that I should apologise for feeling the wrongness of the many outrages perpetrated around us." She sipped her drink and raised her head. "It is those who *do not* feel it who should apologise! But I am afraid I have not really told you anything particular about the college. I only seem to have got as far as setting the scene."

"You did it most effectively." Clyde was deeply moved by her exposition, coming after his finally bringing the worthless materialism of his own work-life fully into consciousness. "I shall look forward to hearing about the college from you another time."

She smiled widely this time; the bright, intelligent eyes were as warm as the mug in her hands. "I shall look forward to that too," she said.

.   .   .

Zeno was near the drinks stand enjoying a late burger and he managed to catch Clyde's eye, pointing urgently to his enormous watch. It was time for the fireworks. Clyde sidled along until he could see Bernard and George, to whom he gave the nod, and they set off to start the display. Meanwhile, Clyde politely shepherded everyone to the darkness in front of the great blaze so they could better enjoy the pyrotechnics, but still have warmth on their backs.

The first rocket had just erupted into a sky now full of magic sparkles when Clyde, who was at one side of the little crowd in the darkest spot, felt a light pressure on his arm. It was Frances Harvey, very elegant in a fur-trimmed coat and hat.

"Hello," she said discreetly. "I thought I'd come over and speak to you."

Clyde was lost in confusion.

"I hope you've been pleased with my work in your library," she continued in her soft, correct voice. "I didn't want to be too intrusive, but I thought I had basically grasped what you wanted, and the best way forward was to make a start and refine the process as we went along. So now you must tell me if you want to make any changes, or feel that there could be any improvements. And we need to formalise the process for new acquisitions and decide if you want to set a budget."

Clyde slowed his breathing to calmness before answering. The chiselled features with their illusive qualities, softly framed by the halo of fur, suddenly held no allure for him; he found the effect slightly chilly.

"And could we discuss who you are, where you're from, and how you come and go in my house?" he said casually.

"That too," she replied, after consideration. "Sometime this week then?"

"I'll look forward to it," said Clyde gallantly, not mentioning that Craig and Jim would be there.

Frances turned towards the crowd and called in a whisper, "Laura!" A yellow haze seemed to stir in the group, and a figure in a dark brown coat, the blonde hair streaming over its shaggy-sheep collar, edged towards them. "Have you met my flat-mate, Laura Clarke?" Frances asked Clyde. The woman turned towards him with a smile, and he realised that this was the figure who had waved to him from the platform; a passenger on a train that didn't exist; a ghost.

"It's nice to meet you," she said.

"And you," he replied, held by her frank blue eyes.

While he stood there, an enormous impact with no physical form bowled over him, and he experienced, in all its heart-bursting conviction, the wonders of a sudden fall into love. Overhead, the night sky broke once more into clouds of coloured stars.

Chapter Eight

THE GUESTS WERE LEAVING. It had, as Zeno predicted, been a great evening enjoyed by all. No one, not even Melrose and a couple of notorious tennis enthusiasts, had been *too* drunk, and there was the convivial atmosphere of new social friendships being formed. Frances was about to go and was looking for Laura. She was just saying goodnight to Clyde when the missing woman appeared, a little breathless, beside them.

"It's okay," she said to the librarian. "You get off. I'll be on my way soon."

Frances looked as if she might comment, but only said, "Alright, Laura, see you later. Bye, Clyde, bye, Zeno, see you soon," and departed.

Laura and Clyde were left standing self-consciously alongside one another. The last few people were saying goodnight and Clyde bustled forward, finding bags and shaking hands. Craig and Jim gave him delighted grins, winking towards Laura, and said they were shattered and heading for bed, but would help clean up in the morning. Clyde thanked Bernard and George particularly for their excellent management of the fireworks as they left. Mattie, who had been offered one of the guestrooms for the weekend, said she was going to sleep over at Martina's.

Finally, once the hall was quiet and empty, Zeno said he would be off to the lodge to bed if Clyde didn't mind. Clyde thanked him warmly and the two friends parted for the night.

Clyde wandered back into the garden where he found Laura waiting awkwardly.

"Hello," he said, lost in her presence.

"I thought we could go for a walk," she said.

"Let's." He took her hand, touching her for the first time. It was all he could do to keep going as far as the woodland, he was so overcome with the resurgence of his sexual desire. The sky was a clear, deep black, fresh with cold. Beneath, sparkles of frost glimmered around them as if fallen from the fireworks. It was very chilly, but the sensation of iciness only enhanced his other physical responses: all his senses were bursting into energetic life, a vibrant aura of which his urgent sexual excitement was the culminating expression. At the same time, and as they were walking and talking, he obsessed about her. Was she feeling it too: the cold, the excitement, the vastness of the night, the overwhelming desire? Wonder suffused him, and the activity of his mind merged with the raging of his body, smothering him in questions: what was she like, what were her tastes, what was her background, had she family, what were her plans for the future, her dreams; what was he like, what were his tastes, what were his dreams and plans, why was he here, what was up there, was he alive, what was life, what did it all mean?

"What made you come here?" she was saying.

"My wife and I were looking for a home in the country, a move away from London. This place offered a lot for a bargain price."

"She's Lucinda Lowe, the artist, isn't she?" Laura asked uncertainly.

"Yes, but we're no longer together. It's over."

She seemed a little confused. "I seem to know her work. Forceful, with a strong classical influence. A great deal of skill."

"Admire, but not like?"

She considered. "Like, but not love. The arts of our times sometimes feel meagre in their dosing of love, don't you think? I like the older, more robust passions; there's no reason why they can't be expressed in modern ways." She had a light voice with a slight unusual accent, giving her frankness the power of charm and surprise.

He struggled to contain himself and stay sane. He gripped her hand more tightly and said, "Do you work as an artist?"

"Oh yes, when I can. I exhibit, give art courses and teach classes in French and Spanish – my mother was French Canadian. I'm good, but I'm not in your wife's league."

They'd reached the trees and she stopped and turned towards him, leaning back against one of the great trunks. It was his first long look at her wide freckled face with its small, neat features. He reached out and caressed it gingerly with his fingertips, pushing the wings of fair hair back from her skin.

"She's no longer my wife in anything but law," he insisted, "and you are certainly not in her league ..."

As soon as they came together, the floodgates opened and they were carried away with mutual urgency. Clyde felt so much he felt nothing and just let himself go with his desire until, pausing to look once more into her face, he shuddered backwards as if stabbed. Into his mind had come the image of another body, that of an old woman slumped in a wing-backed chair, and with it the image of the smiling young woman – this very woman who was standing half-undressed before him – waving from the platform of a station that was permanently locked and where no train ever stopped.

They were part of the same thing! The same hideous freak show of slit throats and hanging men. He recoiled with a gasp of repulsion.

She looked at him steadily. After a long moment, she said, "I'd better go. Don't worry, I'll be quite safe getting home."

Within seconds, she had gathered her dishevelment into some order and vanished into the night.

Clyde ran back to the house, shivering with more than the cold.

It was after midday when Clyde was woken by Craig and Jim sitting on his bed. He still had some of his clothes on. A bottle of brandy and a glass were on the bedside table.

"Hey!" Craig gave him a hard nudge. "Clyde, c'mon, we've got coffee."

Clyde groaned in a feeble effort to lift his heavy head from the pillow, failed, and collapsed back onto the bed.

"How much of this has he had?" Jim picked up the bottle of brandy. "He's never been a spirits man."

"I guess things didn't work out with the lovely Laura," said Craig.

"Shame, just what he needed. Doesn't seem to have had much of this, though – couple of large ones at most. Oi, Clyde, get up, man!" Jim's strong arm gave his friend a vigorous shake and something resembling the body parts of Clyde thrown hastily together rose up from the bed.

"Erugh!" it said.

"Get this down you," boomed Jim's authoritative bass. "You can't be that bad."

Craig shoved the coffee mug into his hand. "So ... what happened?" he asked eagerly.

"Uh?" Clyde forced an eye open.

"Last night, after we went to bed. With that attractive blonde woman, Laura."

"Agh!" Clyde shut his eyes again and turned his head away, spilling coffee on himself and the bed.

"Say no more," Craig whispered to Jim.

Suddenly, Clyde sat upright, both eyes open.

"So, you could see her too?" he demanded.

"What d'you mean? Of course we could see her," said Craig. "Everyone could see her. Very attractive. Fun and nice. Wouldn't you say, Jim?"

"That's right," replied his partner.

"And we could see that she liked you," continued Craig. "Which is why we thought that maybe ..."

Clyde groaned again.

"I need a drink," he said.

"Pull yourself together, man," said Jim sternly, picking up the brandy bottle and moving it to the other side of the room. "Whatever happened, it can't have been that bad, you'd only known the woman five minutes."

"I'm going to bring you some toast," said Craig. "Zeno's down in the kitchen. We've all been clearing up. You were right, Clyde, and we were quite wrong about him. Really nice guy."

He went out leaving Jim to strong-arm Clyde into the shower.

Although Clyde got up and dressed, he didn't feel himself. He showed no interest in talking about the party, the house or his future plans. Zeno made a late lunch for them all, but when they sat down in the kitchen to eat, Clyde didn't acknowledge his presence at all. He didn't touch the food. Only when Craig and Jim had swallowed a few mouthfuls did he pick up his fork and eat a little; and he barely said a word, merely mono-syllabic replies if spoken to.

When the meal was over, Zeno went to the lodge cottage. Craig and Jim found Clyde in the drawing room, helping himself to brandy.

"Clyde, what's going on? We need to sort this out," said Craig. "We can't go on like this for the rest of the week. And you can't go on like this, full stop," he added, looking at the full glass in Clyde's hand.

"If I told you," said Clyde shakily, "you wouldn't believe me."

"Don't be stupid," said Jim. "We're your oldest friends. C'mon, sit down and tell us what's been going on."

"Is it Lucinda?" asked Craig.

Clyde did as Jim had suggested, sipping at the brandy, even though he didn't much like it. "No, no," he assured them hurriedly, "You both know that's been on the cards for a long time. Or at least, she's been finished with me for a long time. I couldn't shake off my fascination somehow, even though it's humiliating to keep chasing someone who has plainly lost interest. This place was a last-ditch attempt to get us back together, but actually it made the final split. I've been so happy and hopeful, full of new plans and ideas since I moved in, it broke Lucinda's spell somehow. So no, it's not that."

"Well," said Craig, a note of impatience creeping into his manner, "if it's not Lucinda, and you've been so happy and optimistic about the future, what the fuck's happened? Because you look like a wreck today, and I've never seen you drink brandy in all the time I've known you."

Clyde finished the drink with a wince; it was cooking brandy and it burned. "I'll tell you everything," he said reluctantly, "because I don't know what else to do. There's nothing wrong, I'm quite happy, and yet everything's wrong, nothing makes sense. I know, I know," he added, seeing their expressions. "If you think I'm cracking up now, it's not going to get better when you hear the rest, but just let me tell you. It's hard piecing it all together. Let me get through the whole thing and then you can call for a straitjacket."

There was an awkward pause. "Let's *all* have a drink," said Craig decisively, and fetched two gins for himself and Jim. Clyde poured himself another dose of the firewater brandy and told his story. He started with the non-existent train, the smells in the kitchen when no one had been cooking and the running water where there were no pipes; then there were the figures in the bushes, the bicycles that passed through solid gates, the disappearing librarian and the self-organising library. He'd already told them about the murder, but now he told them about the stain on the rug and the body in the chair. Then there was Zeno: Zeno who heard the noises, who wasn't worried about the disappearing body and who knew the history of the lodge cottage far too well; Zeno who hadn't painted the ghost picture, but knew what it was.

"But I thought you liked him!" blurted out Craig.

"I do ... I did," Clyde amended his words. "After last night, I don't know what to think."

Craig looked questioningly at him, so he continued, "During the fireworks, I was approached by Frances Harvey, the untraceable librarian. She admitted she's been behind the activity in the library and actually talked to me as if I'd employed her. When I challenged her, she calmly said she'd come and speak to me this week."

"It sounds as if she really *is* a librarian and there's been some kind of misunderstanding," said Jim.

"A librarian I never employed, who comes and goes, sometimes in the middle of the night, without a key or security code?" said Clyde. "A woman who turns up under general invitations to our parties, but is unknown to everyone in the village? She knows Zeno, though. When she left last night, she said goodbye to him and 'See you soon' and he replied with the same. So, you see, Zeno's in on it!"

"In on what?"

"On the hauntings, the murders, the ghosts, whatever the hell's going on. Perhaps he *is* a ghost."

"Don't be ridiculous, the man just cooked us lunch," said Jim firmly. Craig gave him a look and he shut up.

Clyde paused. "Go on," said Craig kindly. "There's something else, isn't there? Something that happened last night?"

"It was Laura," said Clyde. "I know you noticed that we were, well, attracted," he went on diffidently, "and she, well, it kind of blew me away, really, after Lucinda and so on. But I should have known!" He jumped up and paced frantically between them. "I should have known because *Frances* introduced us. Laura came to the party with the invisible librarian, so she must be in on it too. I never thought at the time, I was so, well, carried away. It wasn't until we got down to the woods and I kissed her that the image of the corpse by the fire came back to me, and I remembered that it was Laura whom I'd seen waving to me from the station platform. She was one of the ghost passengers. I was making love to a ghost, something akin to that crumpled old body, a woman with her head half-severed and a hanging madman!"

He collapsed onto the settee and reached for another brandy. Craig and Jim looked at each other, wide-eyed and speechless.

After a moment of pregnant silence, Jim said, "Let's get Zeno in here and have it out with him: whether he's heard the noises, if he knows these women, what he knows about the strange goings-on. And for that matter, a bit more about him. He seems like the suspicious character at the centre of all this odd business."

"He's gone away for six weeks to visit his daughters

abroad," said Clyde glumly into his glass. "He was leaving straight after lunch."

"Six weeks?"

"Yes, they live in Australia. He arranged it when we took him on: one main holiday of six weeks every year so that he could visit his daughters."

"So he's gone. To Australia."

"Yes, *that's the thing*! *Australia*!" Clyde was suddenly filled with the energy of hysteria. "The Baxters' children were taken to Australia and their names were changed. And Zeno knew all about that lodge cottage, exactly as it was years ago. Details that he would only have known if he'd spent quite a bit of time there. What if Zeno is one of the Baxters' children? *What if he's come back to the scene of the crime?*"

"Pull yourself together, Clyde," said Jim sternly. "You're talking rubbish. For a start, the Baxters' children didn't commit any crime and weren't even here when it was committed, according to what you told us. And secondly, the boy – I've forgotten their names – must be at least in his mid-seventies by now, probably older – I'd have to check the dates. Zeno's not that old."

"He could be the ghost of the lost boy," objected Clyde, "or what if he's the ghost of Alf Baxter himself? Then he would be the murderer returning to the scene of the crime!"

"I think you're cracking up," said Jim, "and you've definitely had too much brandy." He reached out and removed the bottle. "Look, some odd things have happened and you've been in the thick of it at a challenging time in your life: change of career, change of scene, end of a relationship etc. Let's step back and look at things objectively. There were several gruesome murders and probably a suicide in or around this house. You have seen a body and bloodstains. This could be someone playing a joke, but I can't see why, unless this guy Zeno is some kind of crook up to something. Well, we can't pursue that angle very far until he gets back. More likely they're genuine, er, whatever-you-call-them, I'd say, even if by that I just mean your imagination working overtime under emotional strain," he added hastily. Jim was a practical man. "Well, there are experts we can consult about that, psychologists and those who deal in ... I don't know what you call it ..."

"The paranormal," Craig put in.

"... and I recommend we get the best people in to sort things out."

"That's a very good idea," agreed Craig. "I know Marcus Wareing goes to that famous psychologist in Harley Street. What's her name? Dr Chandira. She's *very* well thought of. And the obvious ghostbuster would be Anthony Lill. You've probably seen him on Channel 5. I know him slightly."

"Great," said Jim. "So, accepting that there might be either a psychological or supernatural basis to some of the happenings ..."

"You mean either I'm haunted or I'm nuts," interrupted Clyde tipsily. Jim ignored him.

"... we can get experts to deal with the situation. If there proves to be something to it, we might find that it explains some of the other things as well, such as the noises, smells or people seen at a distance. I think we'll find that the things it doesn't clarify, such as the unexpected trains and the mysterious librarian, probably have more prosaic explanations and only seem mysterious in the context of the more sinister events. After all, a ghost would hardly come to a party and be seen by everyone, would she ... he ... it?"

Clyde was silent. Moderately inebriated, he was enjoying feeling someone lift the burden of explaining what the fuck had been going on from his shoulders.

"I think we'll find that this Zeno bloke is at the bottom of it, or at least knows all about these other people," continued Jim, well into his stride. "It might all be fine, and it might not.

But there'll be plenty of time to sort that out later; let's get the weirdness bit done first and put your mind at rest."

Craig, who knew his partner well enough not to interrupt him, said now, "We should get Clyde away for a spell while we sort some appointments out. He could come down to London with us, and then maybe you could come back and stay here with him while he settles down, Jim. I can't get away, but you can work from home easily enough."

"Great idea," Jim said, enthused.

"I ..." Clyde hadn't had any desire to return to London since moving away, "... yes, let's do it." He suddenly realised that he needed a break, a chance to get rest and perspective away from whatever was going on. "But I don't want to leave the house unoccupied: no Clyde, no Lucinda, no Zeno," he continued drunkenly.

"What about that gardening woman from last night?" said Jim. "She was out of work. She could stay in the garden cottage."

"Oh yes, Martina. We met her with Mattie," said Craig. "Great idea, darling." He got up and gave Jim an affectionate peck on the cheek. "Right, here's what we'll do. I'll ring Mattie and see if she's still with this Martina woman, and then check on the trains. Fuck knows, with it being a Sunday. Jim, could you just pack everything up, darling, including some stuff for Clyde, and then turn everything off and lock up etc? Then I think a brisk autumnal walk to calm us all down and sober some of us up, before heading into wherever it is to get a bite to eat before the train. Shit, I'd better book a taxi too. Clyde, have you got any local taxi firms on your phone?"

He turned to the sofa to see Clyde was gently dozing.

By the time Mattie and Martina arrived, Clyde was looking fresher and more awake after being out in the cold air. Craig, who knew Mattie best, took charge and explained the situation.

"I could stay, actually," said Mattie. "I've got the week off. Martina can come over and have a look at the garden and keep me company, then you can decide about giving her the job when you get back, Clyde. Although," she added with a glowing smile at the other woman, "I can't imagine why you wouldn't want her."

"Great," said Clyde, glad to be able to postpone any decision in his current state of mind. "You can stay in the gardener's cottage. That's where Martina will live if she takes the job. I was staying there while the main house was being done."

Jim made coffee while Craig sorted out keys and technicalities with Mattie, so Clyde and Martina were thrown together in conversation. He put any thought of mentioning Zeno out of his mind; coping with all that was for another day. There were occasional flickers of desperation in her eyes, he noticed, and with his current mood, they were drawn together as twin souls; but he didn't want to talk about the murders either, and so quickly began on all his ideas and enthusiasms for the garden. The girl – he couldn't help but think of her that way – sparkled into life, although it was a brittle sparkle that he felt could shatter under the slightest pressure. Being inherently interested in nature, gardening and growing, she had most of the subjects of Clyde's recent study at her fingertips. Her energy of mind was enormous – quite destructive if not well-channelled and balanced, Clyde decided – and the large expressive mouth could hardly keep up with the stream of knowledge, ideas and plans for trial and experiment that overflowed enthusiastically in his direction. He instinctively liked her and knew that he would take her on, but felt drained and relieved when Craig announced that everything was settled and their taxi would be there in a few minutes.

"There are a lot of nature pockets in London these days,"

Martina said to him as the others were drifting back over to them. "Hidden reserves and wild areas. I'm sure there'll be something near where you're staying. It can be very helpful and supportive to lose yourself somewhere like that." She smiled shyly at him, and withdrew as the group re-formed.

Having secured the main building and shown Martina and Mattie to the cottage, Clyde and his friends strolled back around the side of the house. Clyde looked up at it, viewing it as an outsider for the first time since he had moved in. It seemed quite as usual, and there were no signs of life – no lights, no sounds, no open windows, no movement – yet it didn't feel empty. There was a subtle sense of occupation and activity, that the life of the house was carrying on without him.

He turned away and trudged towards the drive with his bags.

"Let's wait for the taxi at the gate," he said.

Chapter Nine

LONDON WAS NOT AGREEING with Clyde. Outwardly he seemed better, as he was initially refreshed by the change of scene. He enjoyed meals with Craig and Jim at a couple of very good restaurants – something that was not so easy to do at home – and mooched round a few of the current exhibitions, vaguely trying to catch up. He just couldn't get into the place, though, and he realised now that he never had; he was always on the outside, an onlooker, somehow never fully involved or accepted. How that could be changed, he hadn't understood, and it must have been one of the barriers between Lucinda and himself as she was so clearly a natural Londoner. He missed his home, designed so much to suit his ways: the steady routine of the days, being surrounded by nature, cooking, the garden, his books, the community, Zeno ...

He blocked home out of his mind. He would not think about it! If he let any thought of Zeno occur, then all the unbearable unexplainables came rushing back and he knew that he would eventually break down. If he let Zeno in, then Laura would follow; the overwhelming, all-encompassing thrill of being with her that occupied his mind, body and emotions was only kept down with a rigid strain that was breaking him. Its most effective tool was alcohol, although at least he had switched from brandy to wine.

Jim was busy with work, getting things ready for a week or two away from the office, but Craig was free to take care of Clyde. He'd made an appointment for him with the renowned Dr Chandira for the following week and was already in touch with Anthony Lill, to whom he'd sent a copy of Melrose Burke's book as background. But he had a struggle keeping his friend occupied. Clyde was only interested in eating, drinking, reading detective stories and staring at the Christmas movie channels. He looked pasty, dull and unhealthily puffy.

"Lucinda wants to see me," announced Clyde one morning from his sprawling position on the sofa in front of the television. He looked down over the top of a cereal bowl at himself with some surprise. "I'd better sort myself out."

"Oh," said Craig, slightly perturbed. "Why? Will you be okay?"

"Divorce. Now we've signed that online thing applying for one, apparently we have to take twenty weeks to 'reflect' before anything happens. She wants to get all the financial stuff sorted while we're waiting."

"Oh," said Craig again.

"I suppose it's better than the old two years," continued Clyde gloomily. "I just wonder what her plan is – because she'll definitely have one – and whether I can afford it."

He pointed a tipsy finger at Craig, but nevertheless got up and washed and dressed.

"I need some fresh air and exercise," he announced once ready. "To pull myself together. Is there anywhere to walk round here?"

"There's the park," said Craig, who wasn't a countryside person. He caught Clyde's expression and added, "Or how about the nature reserve? It isn't far, but I've never been there."

"Okay, let's go." Clyde was already putting his boots on. Craig, deciding that this was probably a positive sign to be encouraged, hurried to get himself ready.

The nature reserve was an extended triangle wedged between, and to some extent underneath, enormous roads, railway lines and fatuous development, and gave the impression of having been boxed in and left behind, although this being London, it would almost certainly have had some earlier stage of use. Reedy pools and marshland stretched at length between banks of trees and scrub crossed by a network of gravel paths and wooden bridges. It was incredibly noisy due to the proximity of the roads, but birds flickered around them as they walked, Clyde striding out at a mindless speed, Craig stuttering along behind trying not to look as uncomfortable as he felt.

After what to Craig seemed an unreasonably long time to have spent in a muddy patch of waste ground, he almost collided with his friend's back, which had stopped unexpectedly before him. Quite suddenly, they had come out upon the lowest point, a deep dip with an expanse of still, viscous water. The fall-off in background noise was almost a shock; then beguiling trills of birdsong called them like the fatal fairy music that leads to the land of no return. Clyde sniffed the air, at once dank and fresh, and a moorhen chugged out of the reeds and across the pond, raising the surface in thick lips around it.

Then, silence.

"Let's go back," said Clyde.

After that, Clyde went alone to the nature reserve every day. There was a wooden hide in the dip by the pool and he spent long periods in there, watching a smart-looking fox on similar duty in the reeds on the opposite side, and the tasteful paint-work of a water rail popping in and out of view on the shore. By the second day, he had acquired a pair of cheap binoculars and let them drift across the reed tops, pausing at every sign of life, vaguely wondering what it was he was looking at. A chat-tering crowd of birds like flashy gangster sparrows, some in black helmets, became his favourite company. The hide wasn't popular in the cold weather and he never saw another human being.

He'd called Lucinda to arrange their meeting that evening. "Don't let's go out," she'd said gently. "Come round to the studio flat and I'll get a takeaway. Better to have quiet and privacy."

"You're right, of course," he'd replied.

"About seven, then?"

"Fine. You will be alone?"

"Of course."

"It's not that I mind, I mean ..." He realised that minding too little might be unflattering. "It would be better if it was just the two of us so we can talk."

"Of course," she'd said again in her most harmonious tones. "I'll see you about seven."

"Will you be okay?" Craig had asked for the umpteenth time once she'd rung off.

"Fine," Clyde had assured him, looking better than he had since the party.

It was a fine night, much warmer in London than it had been at home. Clyde felt renewed at having something constructive to do that didn't involve the insoluble problems he'd left behind. He showered and dressed with care, not because he wanted to impress his wife, but because he felt like it. He hadn't had a drink all day.

He decided to take a train and walk from the station. He had started to enjoy feeling his limbs working. In fact, it was more of a hustle than a walk. He'd become more observant of life, more reflective on his own experience since moving away from the city, so where he'd just blindly put up with things before, now he noticed himself weaving through the forest of bodies, and found it lonely. The maze of enormous buildings, huge on every side, which had once seemed impressive even where they weren't attractive, felt cluttered and irrelevant. Above, he could barely sense the night at all. The huge vistas of echoing blackness that he saw from his garden on the edge of the village felt like outer space compared to this pallid fake daytime of over-lit streets. His home felt equally far away. For a second, he couldn't believe he was on the same planet, let alone in the same country.

Even when he arrived at the gallery, with which he was so familiar, it looked exotic and foreign. At least it was attractive; a tall, thin building, vaguely Dutch in outline. The large ground-floor window was topped with curled grey moulding, and from there the building progressed upward in a series of restrained Baroque conceits of leaden colour. The studio flat occupied the distant attic where two candle-flames of light could be seen glowing under altitudinous gables.

He rang the bell and waited.

Lucinda looked more elegant than ever. She almost glided down the open staircase, so smooth were the movements of her long limbs in the expensive shift dress. Clyde thought that she barely had a torso at all and wondered how he'd ever made love to a bodiless woman. For a second, he remembered the wide, flat softness of Laura's body, but gulped such thoughts firmly down and concentrated on his beautiful and talented wife.

She kissed him lightly on the cheek as she did all her fond or useful acquaintances and he followed her running legs back up the stairs.

"Drink?" she said with barely a change in breath.

Clyde was shocked to find himself a bit puffed, but accepted a cocktail with an attempt at an affable smile.

"Are you alright?" said his wife with concern. "You don't look yourself. I hope it's not because of us."

"No, thanks for asking," said Clyde. "You were right to end things between us, and I'm glad you've found something better for yourself. I've just been a bit, well, out of sorts. A lot of changes all at once, and all this hysteria about the murders ..."

"You always were *sensitive*, weren't you?" she said kindly. "It took me a long time to realise. I'm not, of course – not in that way. I'm observant of detail and alive to ideas, but you take things to heart."

"Like you, for instance." He smiled and she put her hand on his shoulder in half the embrace she used to give.

"I did love you too, you know. You had such charming feyness and self-deprecating humour, and underneath that temper, you were very kind. I suppose we're just on diverging paths."

"Yes, it seems we are," he replied, and after a smiling look through damp eyes, they broke apart and became freshly businesslike. "I don't seem to have much temper anymore."

"You're still kind, though," she said, but the intensity of the moment had passed between them, probably for the last time. She asked about life back in Burnton, and although Clyde remained matter-of-fact and moved the conversation on as quickly as he could, he felt all the scenes and happenings from home breaking through in his mind.

When the food arrived, he became increasingly unsettled. The more he looked at Lucinda, the more he thought of the woman he had encountered so closely the other night. Somehow, being in the company of a woman so blatantly not Laura brought her to mind – and not just mind. Perhaps it was being close to a woman at all that made him feel aroused, having been without a partner for some time; but no. Lucinda was the partner that he'd no longer been able to sleep with, and he still felt nothing for her in that way

His rational mind kept telling him that it was nothing; how could he feel anything for a woman he barely knew, had only met once, in fact? It was a denial of what another part of him knew to be an inexplicable but quite genuine attraction; a type of instant connection that rarely ends there. Close to Lucinda, bathed in her powerful femininity, even though it was of a type that he now found inert, he let his imagination lose itself in a heady haze of sexual desire and romance. He created some kind of divide in his mind, a coping mechanism whereby he could think of Laura in this context completely separately from the unsettling happenings with which logic had connected her. The more he immersed himself in fantasies of love and desire about her, the more he could forget the other stuff, and of course it made him feel good, rather like a drug. He might not need to drink so much now.

While Clyde's inner world had been rearranging itself in this way, they had been casually eating delicate noodles as Lucinda talked with deliberate sensitivity about her future; work, life and marriage. It was easier to keep their attention elsewhere with chopsticks than a fork, Clyde observed; a fork could shovel the food in so fast, one's mind didn't have chance to work at all.

He had been maintaining a suitable expression of compassionate interest – although actually he found that, as long as Lucinda was okay, he didn't give a shit about the details – and the inner churnings of romantic confusion probably helped him exude an emotional involvement that he didn't feel. But

115

she was coming to the end of her narrative, her tale of a career extended abroad rather than to the regions, and her married to the fabulously wealthy and flamboyant Jason rather than the moderately well-off and home-loving Clyde. He had a vision of her on a luxury yacht with her new fiancé, like Jackie Onassis or Diana, Princess of Wales. She was a match for them, he thought admiringly, and more.

"What about the funding for your move to the Midlands?" It was time for a sensible question, he felt. "Will you have to pay it back?"

"Oh no, I don't think that will be an issue," she said confidently. "Firstly, I can claim personal circumstances, the breakdown of our marriage meaning I need to relocate. Secondly, I fulfilled part of the brief; the works and exhibition. Thirdly, Jason thinks I'm likely" – *Jason is going to make sure*, thought Clyde – "to be appointed to a cultural ambassador role that will mean I need to travel extensively and couldn't possibly continue with the regional project. And that in itself will give further value to the work I've already done for them as my profile will be raised worldwide, so I don't think there'll be any question of refunding the money as long as I keep vaguely in touch in a supportive way and make the odd appearance. After all, it wasn't their – the region's – money."

"I see." Clyde did see, only too well, but it was good news for him because it might reduce the settlement he had to pay her for the house.

"Which means," continued Lucinda, now in full management mode, "that it will be much easier to sort things out between us and get the divorce. I assume you want to keep the house." It wasn't even a question.

"Yes," said Clyde.

"Well," Lucinda was about to say something that didn't come easily to her, "we've decided that you can with just a couple of conditions. We want a no-fault divorce as quickly as possible. I know you agree – obviously. You've completed the application, haven't you?"

"Yes," said Clyde, who had and did agree, although she hadn't actually asked him.

"Good. Jason and I want to be able to marry as soon as seems appropriate." Suddenly, Clyde had a desperate curiosity to know exactly how long Jason and Lucinda had been intimate and what had been going on in his wife's mind – he knew something would have been – since they had. There was no way he could ask her or anyone else, though, without seeming jealous, vindictive or victimised, so he said nothing; he just felt the need to find out one day, as a matter of clarifying what had been going on in his own life; the last month had almost certainly not been what it seemed.

His wife was continuing. "So, all we want from you is for you to sign your share of this – the studio, I mean – over to me and to pay all the costs. All the other assets – cash, investments and pensions – are in our own names anyway." She swallowed hard. Financial concessions were unfamiliar to her.

"The studio plus costs in return for the house," summarised Clyde stupidly. He knew he could find the costs with little effort, and that she and Jason would know this, and was inwardly elated at the prospect of his marriage being over so easily. Jason could have bought him up lock, stock and barrel and barely noticed; his wealth was such that he could easily have written the whole thing off with no discernible effect on himself or his new wife, but that was not the way of businessmen anywhere, nor of businesswomen such as his wife. Clyde was glad. He could not have accepted the house for nothing, making him a cat's paw for the great Jason Deaville.

"Taking into account the amount that I put into our flat in London and the investments you made in the gallery business" – he'd forgotten that, but didn't care – "it's fair enough," she said magnanimously, but not sounding completely convinced. "I'm sure you agree."

"I do," said Clyde. "What happens now?"

"We'll be assigned a case number, and then, unfortunately, we have the twenty-week wait before completing more online forms. I should have said that there will be no question of us making financial claims on each other in the future."

"Of course not."

"There's just one more thing," she continued in her most icy detachment. "Our legal advisors think that you need to be seen to be earning. I mean, we know that you have enough capital to live on for now and your investments and so on, but it would make the settlement more acceptable if you had a source, or a potential source, of income. So if you could produce a concrete business plan for your market garden idea, say ..."

"And the bakery."

"Yes, if you like."

"That's no problem at all. You know it's something I was working on anyway, and I think I've found a suitable partner for the garden business."

"Great. I'm glad it's all settled. I'll be in touch about the next stage as soon as the twenty weeks are up." Business over, she became warm and sociable again. "What's he like? The gardener, I mean."

"Oh, it's a girl. A woman, I should say. Martina."

"Ooh." She gave him a teasing smile and he saw a plan forming in her head that would tie up all the loose ends completely and leave her to move on, conscience clear. Not that there was any reason for her not to have a clear conscience in his eyes, but her own vanity might insist that he would never quite get over her; if she settled down with a provincial gardener of what she considered limited attractions, her ego and conscience could both rest easy. He decided to let her keep her beliefs for now and not mention that he thought Martina was more likely to get together with Mattie.

As he walked away from the invitingly lit windows of the gallery, he wished for the fresh cold of the bonfire weekend. It was inclemently mild, a characterless, neutral temperature inexpressive of season that left him feeling too warm at the least exertion. He wasn't ready to think of going home, although he missed it, so instead he dived back into the welcoming dream world of his fantasies about Laura, and stayed there as long as possible.

By the time of his appointment with Dr Chandira, Clyde was outwardly much improved. He was no longer drinking during the day or watching the Christmas movie channels (perhaps it was only the former that made the latter bearable), and was getting up for his daily trip to the nature reserve, even in the rain. Craig had felt safe going back to work.

Inwardly, however, he was feverish and disturbed. He looked better because he had divorced himself from reality by creating an obsessive fantasy world, one where he had conversations with an imaginary Laura, travelled with her, shared interests with her, cooked and tasted delicious food with her and shared a home with her – in addition to the obvious physical pleasures. The only respite he had from this strength-numbing frenzy was reading classic detective stories, of which he got through almost one a day – merely a change of comforting fantasy, and his time in the hide by the pool. There was no need to do anything there but sit, like the surreptitious fox, and be aware of what was around him; there was nothing else he could do amongst creatures who could only be themselves and do the things they did.

It was in this state of disturbed, brittle contentment that he set off for Harley Street for his first therapy session. He had met enough wealthy people to know some who used Harley Street practitioners, and yet he somehow didn't really believe they still existed, his limited experience of the medical profession being associated with stuffy and crowded buildings of the concrete, metal and plastic type. Lucinda had had a private doctor, but he'd never bothered himself.

He supposed if they'd had children, he would have combined all their medical care to one practice, but it was not something they'd ever discussed. He realised with a jolt that he'd got through a good portion of his adult life and marriage without giving children much thought at all. It wasn't that he didn't like children or definitely didn't want any, just that having children was something that happened to other people; something that if it were to come into his own life would be so far in the future as to be currently over the horizon. In so many ways a boyish innocent, he simply didn't feel old enough for such a momentous responsibility.

These thoughts were in his mind as he was ushered into the consulting room of Dr Chandira. "Good morning, Clyde," she smiled broadly and reassuringly. "Lovely to meet you. Please take a seat."

"Hello," said Clyde, feeling shy.

"Your friend, Mr Minter, outlined the situation to me – with your consent, I understand."

"That's right."

"Good. I believe that it's a question of supernatural experiences and psychic phenomena in your house relating to violent events that once happened there."

"That's right." Now he was definitely nervous.

She consulted her notes. "Mr Minter tells me that you are also consulting an expert in such happenings, a Dr, er," she checked, "Lill."

"I didn't know he was a doctor," said Clyde stupidly. He almost giggled.

"Please try to relax, Clyde." She smiled kindly but firmly. "There is nothing to be afraid of. There is nothing *wrong* with you. You are, no doubt, a sensitive person who has been through some great life changes recently and been confronted with a traumatic legacy in your home. In a nature such as yours, such things can cause an imbalance of mind, that's all."

But I saw a dead woman in my drawing room! Clyde wanted to scream. Instead, he smiled weakly.

"I'm not saying," continued the handsome doctor, "that supernatural phenomena do not exist. You may be quite right to consult an expert in such matters." She spoke as one who wholeheartedly approved of consulting experts. "But my clinical experience and practice," Clyde noticed for the first time that she was wearing a white coat over her clothes, "have taught me that it is an imbalance of mind such as anxiety, trauma or even depression – though that's rarer – that opens one to the experience of being what we might refer to as 'haunted'. The phenomena may exist independently, I do not have a professional opinion on that," – *hedging your bets nicely*, thought Clyde – "but only a psychological weakness opens us up to experiencing them. Now, perhaps you could describe the phenomena to me."

Clyde had been enjoying not having to say anything, because his mind was blank with tension. "Oh!" He jumped slightly. "Well, there were noises and smells like running water and cooking."

"Ah, olfactory impressions. Very interesting. Please go on." She was sitting opposite him, making notes as he spoke.

"A few times I thought I saw movement or people in the garden. And then there were the bloodstains on the rug and the body."

"The body?" Her interest was certainly genuine now.

Clyde explained about the murders, Melrose's book, the finding of the jewellery, the photoshoot, and afterwards the real bloodstains and the body in the chair. He made no mention of trains, books, Frances, Laura or Zeno. After all, as Jim had opined, there was probably an unlikely but understandable explanation for them.

"I would like," said Dr Chandira, her eyes very bright, "if you are willing, to use hypnosis. I believe that it will be the quickest and least painful," Clyde winced slightly in spite of himself, "method of accessing your subconscious and releasing whatever wounds are making you sensitive to these suggestions. It may take several sessions, but I am confident of success."

"Okay," agreed Clyde weakly, thinking that she looked rather as if she were going to eat him. But probably the worst that could happen was that he'd become a feature in her next book.

"If you would come over to the couch, then." She rose and guided him towards the back of the high room to a padded adjustable reclining couch. "Please make yourself comfortable." He removed his shoes, lay down and she adjusted the position to suit him. "It helps to keep warm," she said, covering him in a luxuriously thick, soft, fluffy blanket.

"Hypnotism is nothing to be afraid of," she continued as she prepared herself and moved her chair to a suitable position. "You simply listen to the sound of my voice and relax. You will drift off and it will all happen without you knowing you've done anything. No effort at all. I shall ask certain questions while you are asleep and from your answers, I can direct further exploration to the root of the neurosis. It will be over before you know it, and you will have had a restful experience." She smiled confidently as she gave him an eye mask.

Clyde heard a kind of droning music begin in the background. Dr Chandira was speaking slowly and clearly. She had a low, sonorous voice with beautiful enunciation and a faint attractive accent that he couldn't place, but it sounded exotic.

He drifted into a restless somnolence, half-asleep but uneasy after being forced to recall disturbing recent events, and never fully lost awareness of his surroundings. Perhaps he wasn't a good subject.

Dr Chandira asked him what was uppermost in his mind. Without thinking, he told her his last coherent thoughts before nerves had wiped his mind clean: children and why he'd never considered having any. She was clearly delighted by this scent and followed it enthusiastically, asking all kinds of questions about his childhood and marriage. Clyde's mind wandered between answers, for safety's sake taking refuge in his fantasies about Laura. Dr Chandira was talking about adulthood and responsibility and wanting him to see something, but by now he was seeing something quite different, although equally adult. The enforced rest, warmth and semi-sleep state seemed to heighten his sensations and he was feeling the pleasure of the dream intensely until, with a shock, he heard Dr Chandira say that it was time to come back into the room. Jolted fully awake behind his closed eyes, he realised that he was lying on her couch with an erection. As she was progressing gently through the awakening routine, he was flushed with panic, desperately hoping that the blanket would give him sufficient cover while he thought of something violently unappealing. Fear was making his blood rush, which wasn't helping when, in the nick of time, he visualised Melrose Burke with a puffy paw on his arm, saying, 'My dear boy.' That did the trick.

He was still flustered when he removed the eye mask and stood up gingerly, wondering if she'd noticed.

"Take your time," said the doctor, turning towards her desk. "You may need a few minutes to become fully present again." Could he be done for harassment? It wasn't as if he'd been thinking of Dr Chandira. Still, she wasn't showing any signs of being upset or alarmed.

Emily Tellwright

In a state of confusion, he hurriedly put on his shoes and his jacket. At least it was a longish one; he felt safer once it was fastened all the way down.

"That was a very successful session, Clyde," Dr Chandira was saying. "We got to the heart of several important issues. We should leave it at least a week before we continue the therapy." She moved to the door to show him out. "There's no need to feel embarrassed," she said, smiling.

He hoped she was right.

Chapter Ten

WHETHER HER THERAPY had helped or not, Clyde never made another appointment with Dr Chandira because he found that he was coping satisfactorily. When he'd allowed Laura to become a romantic fantasy, he had separated her from the unsettling occurrences at Valencia House in his mind. As it was the shock of unwittingly being intimate with a sinister supernatural entity that had pushed him over the edge, the desperation of his disturbance had subsided.

Craig and Jim seemed pleased to see their friend returning in character; Clyde got up at a normal time, dressed and showered, ate normally and drank only moderately in the evenings. Also, although he still didn't refer to his life at home, he was more focussed on the future, making an appointment with a solicitor in Ridgley about the transfer of ownership of the house, and taking an interest in the forthcoming appointment with Anthony Lill by buying some of his books.

He was still distracted, though, and Craig and Jim often had to repeat themselves to get Clyde's attention. His progress with the Lill books was slow as he had to keep rereading passages when his attention drifted. His thoughts of Laura had saved him by crowding out all other concerns, but in the process had become an obsession. Given the slightest opportunity, he would be safely away in a world of his imagination. In this world, everything was expanded, exciting and full of promise. He was never bored, depressed, rejected or challenged. It was an addictive hormonal high that he rapidly came to depend on, a slave to his own body's drugs. However, the maintenance of this parallel existence depended on absolute secrecy – it was his and his only – and he began to take pleasure in a degree of furtive cunning to mask his new reality from those around him.

By the Saturday of the following week, a fortnight after the bonfire party, Craig was concerned again. Clyde and Jim were due to return to Burnton on the Monday, and so Clyde was cooking a special meal for his friends that evening. While he was busy in the kitchen, Craig and Jim went out in the afternoon for a little time together and stopped for a coffee on the way home.

"How d'you think he's doing?" asked Craig apprehensively as they sat cosily together in a corner of the café.

Jim considered. "Hmm. Well, better, obviously, but not quite right somehow. I don't think the therapy helped. We need to get to the bottom of what's going on in that house, if anything is, and then he can put it behind him or move on for a fresh start. What d'you think? I've been so busy, I haven't seen that much of him."

Craig put his arm comfortably through Jim's and took his coffee in his other hand. "He's certainly better than he was, not at a point of complete breakdown at least. And he's taking an interest in the Lill investigation, which suggests that approach is going to be more successful than the therapy. But I can't get him to talk about going back on Monday. Sometimes I wonder if he even *knows* he's going back on Monday. He's so abstracted all the time I think he may have got better by supressing some of his anxiety, in which case you may have a rough time if he's forced to confront things next week."

"Dr Chandira's prescribed him some tranquilisers for emergencies, hasn't she?"

"Yes, I've got them, and I think you'd better keep hold of them so they're only used when needed."

"I will. I'm hoping to get him going on the garden with that Martina. Something to keep his mind occupied, and a bit of physical work outdoors is the best thing to calm anyone down really."

"Great idea. You might want to have a word with Mattie, though, if she's still around, to keep off the subject of the murders. You will be alright, won't you?" Craig looked into his partner's eyes anxiously. "I wish I could come too."

"Don't worry." Jim smiled and squeezed Craig's hand reassuringly. "If things don't go well, we can just come back here. And in the meantime, I'll FaceTime every evening."

"Okay," said Craig, taking a sip of coffee.

The radio was on and Clyde was enjoying himself, busy externally with something he liked to do and internally with chatting to Laura about the meal he was preparing and the music. His phone rang and rather absentmindedly, he answered it without noticing the unknown London number.

"Hello?"

"Hello. It's Laura." As she spoke, his illusory world fell away in the presence of reality and left him feeling naked and exposed to life. He couldn't reply.

"I got your number from Mattie," explained Laura nervously. "I thought ... I couldn't rest with how we left things after the party. I don't know if you've been feeling the same, but I thought you might be. I'd like to explain a little, and perhaps you could too ... so as I am in London for the weekend, I hoped we could go for lunch tomorrow."

There was a long pause. "Okay," was all Clyde could eventually manage.

"Mattie told me where you're staying," she continued with more confidence, adding hastily, "Not the address, of course. Anyway, I thought somewhere central would be the easiest, so I've booked at the King's Head on the Strand for 12.30 tomorrow. If you want to join me, I'll be in the upstairs dining room. I don't think the food's that good, I'm afraid," a charming friendliness had come into her voice that Clyde found utterly beguiling, "but it's a good place to talk."

"Okay," said Clyde again.

"I'll hope to see you tomorrow."

"You will."

"Good." She rang off.

Craig and Jim returned to a delicious dinner served by a cool and silent Clyde.

"Anything happen while we were out?" Craig asked cautiously.

"Laura rang. I'm meeting her for lunch tomorrow."

"Oh!" Craig and Jim looked at each other across the table, and then continued their meal. After a moment, they resumed general chitchat. Clyde said nothing unless asked. Divested of his crutch of fantasy, he felt completely blank. He finished his dinner and cleared up robotically, then sat in front of the television for the rest of the evening, drinking enough wine to ensure that he could escape the void of his mind in sleep.

The next morning was very much the same. Clyde said little, but got ready efficiently and on time for his date. He was not prepared to think about anything, and he could just about hold out in that position until lunchtime. He didn't know what would happen then, but he had to go. It wasn't a matter of wanting to, there was simply nothing else he could do.

He would take the Tube into town, and then walk. He set out early as he couldn't settle to anything else. As he wandered abstractedly down the showplace thoroughfare, turning his head this way and that, he saw the pub sign ahead; now, his emotions would no longer be suppressed and he felt a hysterically nervous excitement shudder through his system. He was quite shaky by the time he reached the entrance, but as he did so he was brought up short by a figure coming from across the road and touching his arm.

"Hello." Laura smiled broadly, and any strength he had remaining dissipated instantly. "You're early!" She wore the dark coat with the shaggy-sheep collar, wide cord trousers and a dark polo neck with a magnificent silk scarf of jewel-like colours. The bright slash of lustre breaking from the muted tones corresponded to the power of the personality that emanated through her rather shy manner.

"Hello," managed Clyde. He thought he was smiling.

She took both his arms and leaned up to kiss him on the cheek, then kept hold of one arm and led him into the pub at a trot. "C'mon." She jogged energetically up the stairs, found their table and settled herself. There were no signs of trauma in *her*.

Oh God, thought Clyde desperately, *I had this bright, beautiful, lively creature in my arms, and I let her go.*

He too settled himself at the table, sitting opposite her in a corner of the dark panelled room that managed to be dingy even though they were next to the window. The pub was old but without character, just as the food was acceptable but without distinction. All the tables were occupied, but the odd shape of the space forced theirs to be a reasonable distance apart from the others. Clyde rather formally got drinks and, after they had both consulted the menu in silence, returned to the bar to order the food.

The practicalities complete, there was nothing to do but talk until the food arrived. Reluctantly, he looked at her – he had to – and for all his erotic fantasies and her liveliness, kindness was what he most felt in the frank gaze of the clear blue eyes.

She put the back of a hand to her cheek. "I never get used to how warm it is here these days," she said irrelevantly, then reached out and put her hand over his on the table. "I'll go first," she said gently. "I want to help, and there are things that I can tell you."

Suddenly, Clyde wanted to blurt out, "Are you a ghost?" but as she had hold of his hand, it seemed silly.

"I know that some odd things have been happening back at the ... at Valencia House," she began, "and I don't fully understand them myself, although I seem to be caught up in them. So I don't have all the answers, but I have been around the place for longer than you, so I do have a bit more ... *experience*." The wonderful smile illuminated him once again, and he thought he would melt, even though his rigid hand felt like ice in hers. "But I don't understand what upset you so suddenly that night. Can you tell me about it?"

Her brow became expressive and he realised that with the liveliness came a deep, almost childlike seriousness. "Yes," he said carefully. Her implication that the problem was one they shared was a great support. "It began with the trains. I see trains stop at the station and passengers get on and off. *You* were one of them." He started to become agitated, but she squeezed his hand reassuringly. "But no trains that anyone knows of ever do stop at our station anymore, and the station itself is locked and secured at all times. So I knew, you see, that the trains were one of the oddnesses and you were part of them because you'd been on the train." He gulped in initial relief and there was a thoughtful pause.

"I see," she said slowly. "But was that all? Why did you break away so suddenly?"

"Oh no," he was getting into his stride, "I didn't mind all the oddnesses: the cooking smells and noises in the pipes, vanishing figures seen at a distance, phantom librarians, ghost trains and ghost pictures ..."

"Ghost pictures?"

"Yes, a large painting, or it may have been a print, a translucent abstract appeared on the easel in Lucinda's studio. She wasn't too pleased!" He laughed reminiscently, but Laura looked surprised for the first time.

"That's one of mine! At least, I think so. Lots of sea-green shades with this sort of form?" She made lively hand actions in the air.

"Really? Yes, that's it. And it's your work? It's very good," he finished disappointingly, completely failing to find the words to describe the warm attraction he had felt for the piece.

But she was thinking again. "Did you say 'phantom librarian'? That must be Frances." She rolled her eyes. "What has *she* done?"

"Oh, well, she was helping, really. I asked her to help – before I knew she was a ... I mean, before I knew that there was anything wrong ..."

She laughed. "Before you knew she was bossy and interfering?"

"Before I knew she was a ghost," he mumbled sheepishly into his chest. He'd had to say the word.

This time, Laura looked puzzled as well as surprised. "Yes, I can see why you might think that, but she's quite real, you know. If you spent any length of time with her, you'd be in no doubt of it!" Her smile appeared again and she went on, "She's quite as real as me," and then broke off with a look of dismay.

"Oh, is that the problem? You thought I was ... *a ghost*?" For the first time, she looked upset.

"Well, yes, maybe ... that is, I wasn't sure, but that wasn't the problem."

She stared at him, clearly shaken.

"You see, I didn't mind the oddnesses. In fact, I rather liked them. They stopped me from being lonely, made me feel as if I was part of the house's existing community. I love the house, it's my home. And I love you," he said with sudden confidence, reaching out to caress her cheek. "I don't care if you *are* a ghost, it makes no difference. You're real against all the empty illusions of rational society. Like a blackberry growing in the city."

"What?" She laughed through eyes that were brimming with tears.

"Oh, you know. When I was picking blackberries this year, I thought how much more real an occupation it was than anything that went on in my previous world, than my old job ..."

"Darling Clyde ..." She was laughing enough now to stop the tears.

"Darling Laura, I'm so sorry. It was just a shock juxtaposition in my mind between you and the murders. I realise now that they're nothing to do with you." He was smiling, but she had stopped laughing.

"*Murders?*"

"The murders at Valencia House in the 50s – the Baxters and Mrs Hassel and her niece."

"Oh, yes, I did hear something. But why would you think they're anything to do with me?"

"I didn't really. But shortly before the bonfire party, I saw the body of Berenia Hassel in the drawing room, and blood-stains on the rug where Sheila died, and I associated it with the other oddnesses, especially as Zeno seemed to know what was going on. You were part of the other oddnesses, and when we were out in the wood, my mind suddenly linked everything together, and then when I looked at you, I kept thinking of the old lady's corpse."

"I don't understand," she said, thinking hard. "I don't understand. And I don't know anything about the murders, except that there were some before the house became a college. Did you say Zeno knew what was going on?"

"Well, yes, he seemed to. He knows you, doesn't he? And Frances, and he is very familiar with historical details of the lodge cottage that he couldn't possibly know. And he wasn't shocked or worried when the body appeared, only puzzled."

"Wasn't he? Yes, I know Zeno – he and Frances and I used to work together – and of course, he was at the college years ago, so he would be familiar with the site. But he wasn't surprised by the appearance of the ghost corpse?"

"No, he laughed it off."

"Laughed it off? Have you tackled him about it?"

He felt her strength for the first time. "He's in Australia."

"Oh! Visiting the family."

"Yes."

At this point, the food arrived, and they settled down to companionable eating. He knew he was convinced by her, even though she hadn't given him any explanation of the odd circumstances that *did* involve her. The sinister aspects were a mystery that had still to be faced, but they were a mystery to *both* of them and might even be something they could investigate together. He felt enormous relief and the relaxation of his body under it was, for the moment, as much as he could bear; there would be no more questions from him that day.

She had relaxed too, and it was fun to be free of that desperate physical attraction and able to enjoy the flow of their relationship with the excitement of something more to come.

133

They talked generally about art, travel, and naturally, since they were eating, food.

"I love food, but I'm not much of a cook," said Laura, nibbling a chip. "There are a few things I can do well – omelettes, a couple of spaghettis, lamb chops – but I've often been working at places that have really good catering, or I'm travelling. When I was a student, my flatmate was a great cook, and my ex-boyfriend was too."

"You must come over for dinner – when I get home," said Clyde.

"I'd like that," she said, her frankness once again tempered with a tinge of shyness.

"Can I give you a ring next week?"

"Oh … yes, I'll give you my number." She rooted in her handbag and scribbled on a leaf of a tiny notebook, which she tore out and handed across to him. "I haven't got a mobile phone … yet," she said awkwardly, suddenly seeming slightly ill at ease. "I'm not very up on, er, technology."

Clyde smiled, trying to relax her, but it was odd and they both felt a hiatus of mood. He knew people who resisted the smartphone or could not cope with it, but even his elderly Aunty Gwen had a basic mobile for phoning and texting. That a young artist and teacher who travelled for work should be without one at all was bizarre – almost impossible these days, like a travelling salesman without a car.

"I have an answering machine," she said lamely, and then changed the subject. "You're a member of the tennis club, aren't you?"

"Yes, I've always been keen on the game. One of the things that attracted me to the village was the club. Some places are very badly served," he laughed at the involuntary pun, "and you have to drive miles to find somewhere to play. I'm not a great player – I don't practise enough – but my height's an advantage. And it makes you keep fit if you want to keep playing. Do you play? I haven't seen you at the club."

"Oh, I'm a lapsed member." She looked rueful. "I simply haven't had time recently to keep my game up. When I was younger, it was no effort, but now I need to keep fit as well. I hope I'll get back to it because I love the game, it's so competitive and demands a lot of physical versatility and coordination. Though I've never really got used to the modern racquets. They're so light and huge, they seem to require a different set of muscles. I don't feel I've got the same touch somehow."

Clyde murmured assent, although he was not quite sure what she meant; his brain had resolutely shut down all interrogation. Laura had gone on to her love of horses and riding, and knowing little about this, he listened. She had family in Quebec and was telling him about her riding experiences in Canada.

By the time they'd finished the meal, Clyde was explaining about his job. Though an English graduate, he'd been keen on money and motivated solely by that. He wasn't sure why now, although it was useful that he had been. Perhaps it was having so little family – no brothers and sisters, and rather distant separated parents, both of whom had since died – that had made him feel such a need to stand on his own two feet, financially secure and independent. He'd been lucky to get started at a time of huge expansion and rewards, and it had been stimulating up to a point, learning new things and keeping his wits sharp in a competitive arena; but having got the hang of things, he'd stagnated. New developments became just the latest version of the same thing, and day-to-day work was simply maintaining the status quo. He was frantically, impossibly busy for short periods, and then left with nothing to do for long intervals, and it was during these that he began to think of another kind of life.

"What about your job?" he asked with polite, though

genuine reciprocal interest. "I know it's art and languages and that's an interesting combination, but I don't know where you work. Is it a university?"

She suddenly looked at her watch with alarm. "I'm sorry, I've got to dash!" She slipped her arms into her coat and stood up hurriedly, putting herself straight and gathering her bag. "I'll speak to you next week, then." The shyness was back with a charming downbeat of the long brown lashes. He rose, and as she looked up, they kissed briefly but decisively.

"See you soon," said Clyde.

"Bye," she replied, and walked away. For a minute or so, he wondered how he could possibly cope until he saw her again.

Chapter Eleven

ALTHOUGH THE CRISIS of Clyde's condition was over, and Laura had ceased, on his developing a relationship with the real person, to be a drug-like fantasy, he was still in the dangerously floaty, ungrounded state that can come with what is known as falling in love. Laura had given him energy and enthusiasm for the future once more, and he was full of plans for life back at Valencia House; he had put the murders and the sinister sightings associated with them out of his mind once he felt confident that they didn't involve her. Now he had to go back and deal with them.

Jim broached the subject over tea on the Sunday afternoon.

"I've been in touch with Mattie. She's still there. I think she might have packed her job in ..." He was digressing and returned to the point. "Anyway, she's opened up the house ready for us tomorrow and got a few supplies in. Martina's got some ideas for the garden she wants to discuss with you."

"Great," said Clyde.

"Anthony Lill's coming on Tuesday morning, remember,"

continued Jim. "Are you going to be alright with the whole, er, 'ghostbuster' thing?"

"Yes!" Clyde was firm, emphasising his feelings with an expansive hand gesture. "I want to get it all out of the way."

"You're not afraid anymore? There's no guarantee that we'll find out what's going on, let alone resolve it."

"No! Laura says the murders are nothing to do with her, and so they're not really anything to do with me. I'm sorry for what happened, but I'm not *involved*. If the late Mrs Hassel wants to pop up in the armchair by the fire, it's a minor inconvenience, that's all. Mind you, I hope the niece doesn't turn up. I wouldn't like to have to keep walking past a vision of severed arteries."

"You make it sound almost fun!"

"I wouldn't go that far," said Clyde thoughtfully, "not like the great Melrose. Or Mattie, for that matter. She's absolutely ghoulish with enthusiasm for gory details. Odd, because she's always seemed quite harmless and is fond of animals. It's nice to have a home with a history, though, even if I would prefer it to be something less tragic. I suppose it makes me feel I have background, not having much sense of family."

"So you're not going to collapse into hysteria or depression or a breakdown or something when we get there," said Jim firmly.

"No," Clyde laughed, "my neurotic phase is definitely over!"

"Thank fuck for that," replied Jim with enormous relief and, in an unusually demonstrative gesture, got up and gave his friend a half-hug.

By Monday evening, Clyde, Jim, Mattie and Martina were all comfortably settled at Valencia House. Mattie had served up an excellent vegetarian chilli with polenta and salad greens on the big kitchen table, and afterwards they remained there in the cosy warmth, sharing coffee and chocolate walnut buckwheat cookies that Clyde had made over the weekend. The fragile Martina was robust with enthusiasm when discussing the fruit and nut orchard, restoring one of the old glasshouses and going on a no-dig gardening course in the New Year. She amazed them with the revelation that she and Mattie had been swimming in the pool – "Exhilarating! Made me feel quite alive!" – and Clyde noticed that they were holding hands a lot of the time under the table.

As for Mattie, she had indeed given up her job to move in – if Clyde gave his permission – with Martina, and was full of plans to open a village bookshop – "New stuff and old, we could even do a kind of book exchange, and hopefully a coffee shop too. We thought you and Zeno could do the cakes, Clyde" – as well as hopefully starting a true crime club to discuss and investigate doubtful and unsolved crimes from the past.

"I might even do a book myself," she enthused. "*Murder in the Midlands* maybe, or *Treachery in Slackfordshire.*"

"Melrose won't like that." Clyde laughed, putting to the back of his mind any thought of Zeno, who was a problem still to be dealt with.

"I wouldn't impinge on his territory," said Mattie primly, "and if I referred to his work, it would be properly referenced, of course."

"As an *historian* would expect," mimicked Clyde, still laughing, "though I think Melrose would be just as cross if you impinged on his *income.*"

"It would probably boost sales of his own book if Mattie referred to it," said Martina loyally, "and the true crime club would be a boon for him. I mean, he could be chairman or something."

"Good idea," said Mattie, and they beamed at each other.

"This murder business has made me think about local history," Clyde said. "What I mean is, there's so much more to the history of this house, and the history of Burnton, than just the murders. That lady from the history society was telling me a little about it and I'd like to know more. What *is* her name? It won't come to me ..." He put it generally to the table.

"Did I meet her?" asked Jim, puzzled, and the others shook their heads uncertainly.

"It's on the tip of my tongue ..." said Clyde, frustrated. "Emily ... Amelia ... Agnes, yes, Agnes! Agnes ... what was her last name? It's on my phone. I'll just go and get it or it will drive me mad." He rose and left the bright halo of the kitchen for the shadowy drawing room where only the stove burned. As he entered, he flicked on the bright ceiling lights and leaned over to get his phone from the coffee table. On straightening up, he saw the body of a plump-ish elderly lady, this time wearing an emerald green cardigan, slumped forward in the wingback chair by the fire. With barely a pause, he turned, extinguished the light and left the room for the kitchen.

On sitting back down at the table, he said, "Well, Mr Lill should be in for a good time tomorrow. Old Mrs Hassel's just put in an appearance."

Jim looked hard at him, and the others gasped. Although Craig had, with Clyde's permission, filled Mattie and Martina in on the strange happenings before Clyde's return, this was still a shock to them. Mattie made as if to jump up and see for herself, but Martina's hand on her leg restrained her.

"Leave it till tomorrow," she whispered.

Clyde was looking at his phone. "Agnes Beresford," he announced with satisfaction. "Let's invite her over to dinner. Anyone want another cookie?" he asked, passing round the plate.

· · ·

The following morning Anthony Lill, renowned paranormal investigator, author of *The Truth about Ghosts* and other works, and who had his own show on Channel 5, arrived accompanied by his personal assistant and his driver. It was a windy day and Clyde, Jim and Mattie huddled a little back from a window, watching them nervously. Martina was hesitating at the far door. They all turned and Mattie went over to her.

"I thought you didn't want to get into all the murder stuff," she said gently. "It's quite alright, everyone understands." She looked round at the others who murmured assent.

"I don't," said the pale woman, "I really don't want to go through it, but at the same time, I need to know. If I'm going to live here," she glanced at Clyde, "I need to know what's happening and be involved. However much I don't want to." She trembled, almost a shiver.

Clyde felt a wave of sympathy for the white and shaking waif, who had intelligence and strength of character to match her unexpectedly wiry limbs. After all, he felt very much the same. He was no longer worried by the apparitions, and didn't truly want to delve more deeply into the detailed troubles of long-dead strangers, but this was his home and he needed to deal with the events in some way, just as he would have dealt with a blocked gutter or a broken window. He gave Martina a reassuring smile before going to answer the insistent doorbell, the others hot on his heels.

The man who strode rapidly in as soon as the door was opened – only turning to make contact with the opener as an afterthought – was reasonably tall with shining skin and close-cropped hair. He had strong, pronounced features and his figure, rather solid beneath the black polo neck and jacket, looked artificially slimmed in the necessary places. Clyde wondered if he was wearing Spanx.

141

"Ah," he pointed at Clyde. "*I* am Anthony Lill here on investigation, to see the owner of the house."

"I'm afraid," said Clyde with a face that was very straight from supressing a desire to giggle, "that the butler is away. I'm Clyde Tranter, owner of Valencia House." He held out a hand and Anthony Lill shook it without interest.

"I see," he said and started to look around the room. Clyde turned to the entourage.

"I'm Fiona Bullock, Anthony's assistant," said the smoothly groomed woman, shaking hands blankly, "and this is Devon." The tall moustachioed black man in uniform was the one who had driven the car. He didn't offer a job description and just nodded to Clyde.

"Anthony won't be socialising much," continued Fiona, "and he won't be taking any refreshment, as he needs to fully concentrate all his energies into his work. It takes a great deal of sensitivity to pick up the signals." Clyde was in a confused state between amusement, ridicule and discomfiture at these rude people – for that was what Anthony Lill's professional attitude amounted to – invading his home. He was already feeling supportive of any ghost that might want to appear and rather hoping that they gave Anthony a run for his money.

Fiona was just consulting her iPad and reminding Anthony of the details of the case when there was another ring at the bell and Clyde opened the door to a particularly dishevelled Melrose Burke, his preposterous hair flopping forward over his eyes.

"My dear boy," he said whilst reassembling himself on the doormat, "thank you so much for inviting me to this most, er," he raised an eyebrow at Clyde, "interesting occasion." In fact it was Mattie, who was still collaborating with Melrose, who had asked Clyde if he could be present.

Anthony Lill showed no sign of being aware of another arrival and was still pacing the hall impressively. Clyde suddenly felt a wave of affection for Melrose, who, he considered, was going to come out low on the scale of mountebanks compared to Mr Lill. And Melrose himself showed his awareness of the fact by merging into the crowd and not competing for a star part in an audition he could not win.

"So," said Anthony Lill to Clyde at last in a baritone that could have easily played to the back of the upper circle, "*this* is the stain?" He stretched out an authoritative finger at the brown haze in the centre of the rug.

Shame for him that melodrama went out of fashion, thought Clyde, but he said blandly, "Yes, that's it. Once it appeared, it's stayed, like a real stain."

"Hm," grunted Anthony Lill. "And this is the drawing room," he gestured to the door, "where the human apparition is witnessed?"

"Yes, she was there again last night," said Clyde.

"Devon!" shouted Anthony Lill imperiously. "Geiger counter!"

As the large, silent man stepped forward to follow Anthony Lill through the door, Clyde noticed that he was carrying a case. They all followed breathlessly to see Devon opening the case on the coffee table and removing and assembling various pieces of sophisticated-looking equipment. Anthony Lill was pacing again. Clearly, he didn't rely only on that amazing personal sensitivity. Melrose tutted discreetly and dug Clyde in the ribs. Martina whimpered a supressed laugh. Devon was waving a box about that was clicking and flashing, and as he approached the ghostly old lady's chair, the signals became faster and more condensed.

"Aha!" said Anthony Lill. "Record those last readings, Fiona!" He was looking up, arms outstretched, to the ceiling above the haunted armchair. Fiona was typing at a laptop in the case. No one else dared catch anyone's eye.

Anthony Lill leaned over his assistant perfunctorily and

flicked through the results. "Hmm," he said. "Please be seated." He waved to his audience and Clyde was enjoying the performance far too much to interrupt it by pointing out that he was the host. They all sat or perched, blank-faced, in an arc around the table, looking up at the ridiculous figure of authority.

"My preliminary investigations are concluded," said the great man, displaying his aquiline profile around the room, "unless anyone has new information to add."

"I thought you would be using EMF meters and infra-red cameras and setting traps," said Clyde.

"This is the 21st century!" snapped Anthony Lill waspishly. "And this is science, not superstition." He almost spat the last word. "Did you expect me to bring a crucifix and a bible and exorcise demons too?"

Clyde thought that it wouldn't have surprised him, but he said, "I'm sorry. Please go on."

"Thank you!" Anthony Lill became calm and spoke in his resonant voice as if into the distance of posterity. "The *toys* that you mention are the discredited apparatus of primitive times. Today, we know that paranormal phenomena are a feature of quantum physics and represent discontinuities in the space-time continuum. Put *simply*," he smiled in odious condescension and held his large hands out in front of him, "parallel realities run alongside like this, until a disturbance – which could be, amongst other things, an act of violence – causes sufficient instability for the timelines to touch." He stretched his fingers back and allowed the insides of his knuckles to brush together. "Like so. In some cases, the disturbance can be so extreme that the lines will cross or become intertwined." He elegantly crossed his hands like a ballerina dancing *The Dying Swan*. "But then we should see *moving* phenomena. For example, in this case, I would have expected to see the murderer – what was his name, Baxter? – perhaps in the frenzy of his crimes, or even his suicide. But that has not been the case. The passive tableaux that have materialised are merely expressions of a touching of the timelines forming slight lesions. Given the absence of activity, they are quite harmless.

"My readings suggest that movement of the timelines has now ceased and that the lesions are healing. It is possible that the occupation of the building once more has provided an opposing impetus to the original disturbance, I cannot be sure. There should not be any new phenomena from now on, but the stain and the apparition of the murdered woman will, I fear, remain. It would be dangerous for me to attempt to fully separate the timelines once the wounds have healed as, even with *my* experience, this is a very unpredictable process, and could lead to unforeseen movement and further – and more active – crossings of timelines. I shall not attempt something so irresponsible. I can only assure you that the phenomena in your house are quite minor and benign. In fact, of very little importance at all." He sniffed and for the first time looked directly at Clyde.

Clyde, in his turn, stood up. He felt like a chairman responding to an inaugural address. "Well, Mr Lill, er, Anthony," he said, getting into the spirit of the role, "it only remains for me to thank you, on behalf of us all," he waved a hand at the still blank faces looking up at him, "for using your considerable expertise," he suppressed a splutter, "and experience to put our minds at rest. I'm sure we would all like to show our appreciation." Everyone nodded. "And if there's anything we can do ..."

"Thank you, no," cut in Anthony Lill, nodding regally around his audience. "Your apparitions are not of a quality to merit further research or inclusion in my forthcoming book, *Other Worlds Among Us*. Not at all suitable for television," he added. "Not sufficiently sensational." And with that, he turned and left, Fiona rushing ahead of him to open the doors.

"I'll email an invoice for immediate settlement," she called to Clyde by way of goodbye. Devon followed on after a nod, carrying the case.

Clyde accompanied them to the front door with the others behind him. As soon as the car pulled away, they unanimously and simultaneously collapsed with relief into frantic giggles, and then laughed until they cried.

Clyde no longer drank during the day, but after such an uproarious morning, he felt it was appropriate to open and serve some calming red wine with lunch. A pumpkin and feta pie stood on the table and next to it, he was slicing a home-boiled ham. Two bowls of beautiful bejewelled salad – red cabbage, carrot, parsley and roasted peppers – piquant with mustard, vinegar and capers graced the spread to which Mattie in oven gloves was adding scalding plates of baked potato wedges. It was everything that Clyde loved about food: pleasing to the eye, delicious and nutritious, sociably shared among friends; celebratory and stylish without ever straying into formality.

As everyone began to eat, the murmur of conversation died out as it always does at the start of a good meal. There were occasional complimentary comments and approving noises. It was only once second helpings were mooted that talk began to revive.

"Is there pudding?" asked Mattie cautiously when asked if she would like more.

"Dorset apple cake and cream," said Clyde with a twinkle. She beamed.

"I'll wait."

Melrose accepted a further portion with alacrity and

refilled his glass. Clyde noticed that Jim was knocking back the wine uncharacteristically quickly and felt a pang of regret for the stress and trouble he had caused his friends. He must try to make it up to them in some way.

As the extended meal drew to a close, dusk was falling and Melrose, Jim and even the girls, as Mattie and Martina were becoming generally known, showed some signs of wear.

"My dear boy," slurred Melrose, closing his fat fingers round Jim's arm, "I understand that we have you to thank for that highly entertaining, and totally spurious," – he paused for a silent burp – "exhibition this morning. How on earth did you come to get hold of such a person?"

"Agh," said Jim to the table. He was gently drunk now, Clyde noticed. "Well, it was really my partner, Craig. You've met him," he said accusingly to Melrose.

"Charming man, my dear boy, remember him well," Melrose was swift to counter.

"Well," Jim made an effort to be coherent and became exaggeratedly confidential with it, "Craig knew Anthony Lill way back ... when he was Antonia!" He splurted a grin around the table.

"But that's not a problem these days," objected Clyde, who was sober. "Why would he mind people knowing?"

"No, it's not a problem these days, thank God!" agreed Jim, suddenly vehement. "But it isn't that he doesn't want the public to know ... er, rather the opposite, really." He chuckled to himself. "You see, Anthony has been planning a big publicity campaign, blowing the gaffe, as it were: 'My Story by Famous Ghost Hunter'; 'How I Resolved My Own Tangled Timelines and Found Happiness as a Man'; and so on. You get the idea. I think he's just been waiting until he was sufficiently famous to get the most out of it."

He paused to collect himself. "What Mr Lill is most afraid of is that someone who knows him from the old days might cash in first. Make a bit of dosh for themselves and ruin his big scoop, as it were. That's why he's *always* happy to do a favour for an old friend in return for their discretion."

Jim tapped his nose in an exaggerated gesture and paused, looking at Melrose.

"I shouldn't have told you that," he said at length.

"My *dear* boy!" Melrose was effusive. "You can *rely* on me," and he patted Jim's arm reassuringly.

Yes, I bet you can, thought Clyde, *but to do what exactly?* He was not in the mood for the drowsy and desultory conversation that was winding down around the table. He felt restless and in need of exercise, but the wind was now beating rain hard against the windows, making outdoors very unattractive. Instead, he wandered around the house in his usual evening routine of drawing curtains and lighting the fires.

When he entered the drawing room, he turned on a lamp and saw the familiar figure in the chair by the fire. He was no longer disturbed and certainly not surprised, so for the first time, he studied the inert form for a moment. She looked so comfortable and peaceful, with no feeling of violence or distress. Clyde wondered if Berenia Hassel just missed her old home. Her presence seemed somehow to have nothing to do with the crime. But what did he know about such things? He smiled to himself. At least as much as Anthony Lill, which was very little indeed.

His mind echoed what Laura had said of herself; she didn't understand what was happening around her, but it was nothing to do with the murders. He suddenly ached with longing at the thought of her and decided to ring her the next day.

Chapter Twelve

WHEN CLYDE DID FINALLY TRY Laura's number late the following morning, it was the answerphone that spoke to him, and indeed every time he mustered the courage to contact her that day, it was the same. Then he remembered that she had mentioned travelling for work and realised that she must be away. He would have to keep busy with other things.

One of those things was Christmas. It was already getting late for making all the deep-flavoured foods celebratory of the dark, barren days – such as mincemeat and rich fruit cake – that were some of the last culinary links with centuries past. And he hadn't even ordered the turkey. He had no idea who would be there on Christmas Day, and realised the need for a household conference to settle arrangements. Coffee in hand, he went to stocktake in the pantry and see what seasonal ingredients he had in. But he could not feel his usual enthusiasm.

Clyde loved Christmas, which was entirely natural in a person who enjoyed home, cooking and company, but this year his rampant innocence, which delighted in colour, fun, presents, games and laughter, was so much more to the fore that he had been expecting to revel in the season. Of course, more than any other, it was not the time of year to be alone, but the cool and sophisticated Lucinda shared so few of his festive delights that her absence would not be a hindrance, particularly if there were others around.

No, it was Laura again. It was Laura with whom he longed to spend the festive season and share every delight: the silly, the sensual, the magical and the spiritual. But he had no idea if he would see her over the holidays; he was only moderately confident of seeing her again at all, although the alternative didn't bear thinking about. And now the fantasy was over and he had properly met her, he was uncomfortably aware that she might not share his taste for the festive season.

This woman to whom he was so profoundly and passionately attracted might not fit with him at all, he knew enough about life to realise that love didn't guarantee that, and she certainly wasn't going to solve his problems – finding a fulfilling occupation and meaning to his existence, for example – any more than she had the key to his ghost mystery. Not that the ghosts were so much of a problem now, although Zeno's involvement was still hanging over him. He couldn't even put the man out of his mind anymore as he needed Zeno's involvement to plan for Christmas.

He'd ply everyone with chocolate cake tomorrow, he decided, taking cocoa, dark chocolate and muscovado sugar from the shelves, and get things as settled as possible. He'd better speak to Aunty Gwen, although she was unlikely to want to travel. He smiled to himself.

At least Mrs Hassel can be relied on to be here for Christmas, he thought.

He phoned Agnes Beresford to arrange for her to come to dinner later that week and consulted her as to the acceptability of roast lamb and Apple Charlotte. Accommodating everyone's tastes and requirements was the most difficult part of entertaining, and he thought wryly of Zeno and his robust intolerance of fussy eaters.

The next morning, Clyde found himself in a windy car park on what felt like the escarpment at the end of the world. This might be how the ancient folklorists imagined that place, he thought: level with a blank sky, exposed to the elements; facing the edge of a great nothing off which one could so easily fall. He had, in fact, arrived in Ridgley, which at this end seemed to consist mostly of great gaping spaces around a skeleton of diminutive but proud remnants of a town. There was no feeling of active destruction like a bombsite; the atmosphere was far more passive, as if the place had just crumbled and rotted away. There were one or two of the usual twentieth-century development disasters standing huge and abandoned like petrified dinosaurs, and on his way in, he had passed some fruits of the even more terrible hand of twenty-first century regeneration: meaningless, random and unwanted except by the profiteers, yet plastered all over in patronising lip-service optimism. Such empty lies.

He consulted his phone, crossing the windy top in front of a swaying tower of empty offices that threatened the once-respectable Victorian pub at its feet. Heading downhill, he passed a huge terracotta block of a building and stopped to look at the abandoned structure. It was solid, splendid, provincial and a bit tatty, and exuded a rather likeable character, like a disreputable friend.

"For Sale, Former Town Hall," said the sign, and on closer inspection, Clyde saw that it was indeed forsaken, with its ornate façade blackened with dirt and opulent mullions boarded up. He imagined the heavy door open to a flood of community life, as it must once have been, and thought what echoes of humanity were now resonating around those deserted corridors.

He tore himself away from the melancholy prospect, rounding the building's corner beneath its shabby scroll-work and crossing to a small cul-de-sac of late Georgian cottages. Looking down it, he once more had the sensation of being about to fall off the edge of reality. What was it about this relict of a town that felt so much like a portal to the unknown? Beneath its awfulness, there was powerful magic, perhaps even revealed by the destruction. He wondered about its ancient history, imagining a Stonehenge atop its windy brow.

The street was called Adventure Place, and smiling wryly at this, he found No 4, the offices of Lemon, Rex, Shuttle-worth & Shuttleworth, and buzzed the intercom.

Clyde had an appointment with Neville Lemon, a solicitor specialising in conveyancing, to arrange the transfer of his and Lucinda's ownership of each other's property. In the tiny, shabby downstairs office, he was asked to wait by a sensible-looking person who might have been an assistant, but could equally have been a Rex or a Shuttleworth. It was clearly an establishment that did not run to minions.

After only a short interval, there appeared a small, dishev-elled, wrinkly man with longish grey hair, thin on top, wearing a tailored pale-grey pinstripe suit that, though old, had once been so well cut that it could only accentuate the odd lie of his body. Clyde wondered if any of his limbs fell off when he wasn't wearing it, but put on his serious face to shake the man's hand, or rather his fingers, the rest being swathed in moth-eaten fingerless gloves.

"I do apologise," said Mr Lemon, looking regretfully at his hands, "but it's rather cold upstairs and my circulation is not as good as it might be. Never mind, I can at least offer you some hot coffee." Clyde followed the elderly lawyer up some narrow rickety stairs to a tiny landing. The multi-paned sash window had metal security bars to the outside, which was just as well as two of the panes were cracked and held together with Sellotape. Once inside Mr Lemon's office, Clyde shut the door, but as it no longer fitted its aperture, an icy draught whistled underneath it, causing the room, which he would not have believed could become any colder, to lower a few degrees more in temperature.

It was impossible to tell if the walls had been intended as white, cream or yellow, as the paint that was not actively peeling was stained a greasy brown; the oily linoleum had worn glassily thin, the rattling sash window seemed little more protection from the weather than a mere hole in the wall, and the plywood blocking the dilapidated fireplace did nothing to expunge a further icy draught. Mr Lemon, after graciously showing his prospective client to a hard and rickety seat, settled himself on top of a cushion in an enormous leather office chair, having first put on his overcoat and scarf. A tiny radiant electric fire burned resolutely in one corner, sending out ineffectual scalding beams from a socket that Clyde surmised might have been considered perfectly safe in about 1950.

"Coffee?" said Neville Lemon in his best legal interrogative. "I should if I were you. It will at least keep your fingers warm." At Clyde's polite nod, he unscrewed – with some difficulty as his hands were rather blue – the white plastic top from an enormous shiny red flask and filled a discoloured and crazed Silver Jubilee mug with what looked like dry ice.

"You must excuse the state of the place," said Mr Lemon frankly, waving a juddery arm generally around the room. "Landlord, you know. Getting us out of here when the lease ends next year and won't spend a sou on the place in the meantime. They were hoping to force us out sooner, of course, as they no doubt have some nefarious development scheme in mind, but I ask you, Mr, er ..." he put on a pair of heavy-framed black glasses to look at Clyde's name on the manila folder in front of him, "... Tranter, why would I go? I intend to retire next year anyway – there are only Mrs Taylor and myself left now – and if they think a little cold and discomfort is anything to a person of my generation," Clyde wondered just how old Mr Lemon might be, "they are very much mistaken.

"There's no money in the law now," continued the ante-diluvian, as Clyde sipped the scalding coffee and enjoyed feeling the steam melt what he imagined must be ice on the tip of his nose. "Not unless you're one of these corporate people." He pulled a sour face. "No money, and no authority; if you have enough funds and the right backing, you can do what you like and have a good chance of getting away with it. Which makes the rest of it a pointless bureaucratic exercise."

He sighed. "I shan't be sad to go. I have my dahlias, and at least they have come back into fashion. Now, you have a bit of conveyancing business for me, I understand, relating to a divorce. Though we are not acting for you in that matter," he added wistfully.

"No," said Clyde, getting a word in for the first time, "we're having one of the new no-fault divorces through an online service and don't need solicitors as we have agreed on a settlement."

"No money in the law now," Mr Lemon intoned like a chorus. Clyde wondered if he had once had seedy detectives in long macs working for him, getting 'evidence' that would ruin people by scandal. It was not really so long since the divorce process had relied on such a practice: probably more recently than the last testing of those disquieting electrical fittings.

"You are relinquishing your ownership of your wife's art gallery and studio," continued the sage, "in return for *her* relinquishing her ownership of your house in Burnton," he stared at Clyde's letter in his hand, "Valencia House. *Valencia House*? That's the old Shaftacre Memorial College!"

"That's right," said Clyde. "We bought it and renovated it. It had been empty for some time."

"The old college!" Inner sunshine illuminated the man's grey countenance. "Why, my father was one of the governors. Many, many years ago, of course. I'm so glad that you have rescued such an attractive and well-loved place."

Clyde thought of the murders, but only said, "Perhaps you would like to come over to tea one day and I could show you round. We are about to begin renovating the kitchen garden."

"My dear Mr Tranter!" Neville Lemon beamed so warmly that the arctic temperature of his office was momentarily forgotten. "That's most kind. I should be delighted. I'm not too far from Burnton over in Scoyham. Such a shame that the trains no longer stop there."

"Yes," replied Clyde quietly. "Would this Sunday suit you?"

"It would, indeed," said the lawyer with great enthusiasm. "Would 3pm be too early, I wonder, so that I can see the grounds before dusk?"

"Not at all," said Clyde. "I'll be glad to show you round and hear any suggestions that you may have."

"Perhaps you are planning a cutting garden?" said his legal advisor brightly. "I can certainly advise you on dahlias, and perhaps bring a few catalogues. Twenty-seven gold medals, you know." He beamed, tapping his chest. "I can't pretend I'm not proud."

Clyde looked suitably stunned by this impressive record and made appropriate noises.

"Now, don't worry about this bit of business," continued Mr Lemon. "It's a simple matter, soon dealt with. We just need you to do the formalities of identification. On an *app*, you know," he almost winked. "Mrs Taylor will explain when you go down." He rose to show Clyde to the door and asked with a sly look, "Do you have any preferences as to dahlias? Size, shape, colour?"

"To be honest," said Clyde lightly, "I don't know much about them."

"Aha!" cried the ancient solicitor with almost a skip. "You soon will. You have it all to look forward to, Mr Tranter. Until Sunday, then." Behind Clyde, he once again wedged the warped door into its ill-fitting frame.

His business concluded, Clyde found himself glad to be outside, where it felt considerably milder than in the solicitor's office. He was still frozen to the bone, though, and decided a brisk walk followed by a hot drink was in order. He strode through the open space at the end of the mews-like street to a wide boulevard. At one end was the former police station, which he saw was being converted into investment flats. He strode on to the door of the impressive City Library and Archive to find it boarded up with posters of the block of flats it was to become. Next door, however, was the still-functioning City Museum and Art Gallery, to which Lucinda had contributed work.

He resolved to visit it soon.

By Friday night, when Agnes Beresford was due to come for dinner, Clyde had made progress with his Christmas plans and established that Martina, Mattie and presumably Zeno would be there on Christmas Day, and that Jim and Craig would be joining them for New Year. Aunty Gwen would be spending the season with her good friend Gladys as usual and looked forward to seeing him when he visited next year. He had ordered a turkey in the secret hope that Laura might join them too, although he kept telling himself that she would surely have plans with her family and not be available. He also planned to ask the irrepressible Melrose, who he strongly suspected had nowhere to go and was always such good value as entertainment. Somehow it wouldn't seem like a celebration without the old fraud.

He had made a dark brick of a Christmas cake that had barely enough cake to hold the fruit and nuts together – as it should be, in his opinion, and tough on those who didn't like it – and a huge crock of mincemeat rich in walnuts and soused in rum. For the dried fruit haters, he would make shortbread nearer the time and perhaps something Continental. He didn't know much about European Christmas cookery and wished Zeno was there to advise him. He'd have to look into it.

He was now busy with trays of chipped root vegetables, which he planned to roast with garlic and rosemary. The kitchen smelt deliciously sweet, savoury and just slightly smoky from the lamb in the oven, and as Jim bustled in, Clyde was wrestling with a basin lined with slices of buttered bread, trying to fill it with warm apple puree.

"What's that?" asked his friend.

"Apple Charlotte. A bit of a risk, really; sometimes it comes out perfectly for me and sometimes not. Turning it out's the tricky bit. Perhaps you can have a go when the time comes. You're quite dextrous."

"Glad to help," said Jim dubiously, "as long as I don't get the blame if it goes wrong."

"Well, it will still taste delicious, just not look as impressive. Anyway, you've finished early today."

"Yes. Thought I would so that I'll be ready for Miss … remind me of her name again."

"Beresford."

"That's it. So unusual to have to remember a surname these days."

"Perhaps she'll invite us to call her Agnes, but I wouldn't bet on it. Want a drink?"

"Why not? Can I get you one?"

"Yes please. There's a nice Manzanilla in the fridge. A dry sherry seems to go with Miss Beresford somehow, and anyway, it's perfect before the richness of lamb. There are some nuts knocking about somewhere ..."

"Got them," said Jim with his mouth full. "That must be her," he added in response to the doorbell, and "I'll get it," as Mattie and Martina tumbled into the kitchen from the back door.

It was a little awkward at first, as things always are with rather formal people you don't know very well, and one of the disadvantages of doing a roast was that Clyde was busy at the cooker when he should have been playing host. Still, Miss Beresford's correct speech and old-fashioned poise did not make her stand-offish and she was soon in the kitchen, sitting at the table partaking of nuts and sherry. She had brought an enormous armful of tawny chrysanthemums of a quality that Clyde had never seen before.

"I got them from Mr Vickers the retired policeman who lives on the other side of the green. He has an enormous conservatory and is a great enthusiast. So fortunate when someone who has had an all-encompassing profession finds an all-encompassing hobby for retirement."

"Rather like my solicitor, Mr Lemon," said Clyde from the stove, "although I'm not sure how much his profession is occupying him anymore."

"Would that be Neville Lemon of Lemon, Rex, Shuttleworth & Shuttleworth?" asked Miss Beresford with interest. "Very keen on his dahlias?"

"That's right," said Clyde. "Do you know him? He's coming to tea on Sunday as he wants to see the house."

"Oh yes," said Miss Beresford. "His father and mine were friends, and the firm has always been our family's solicitors. Although I suppose once Neville retires, I shall have to find someone else. And probably, once I've found them, they will close or be taken over or move on and I shall have to start all over again. It's very unsettling that no one seems to know anyone anymore."

"He mentioned his father was a governor of the college here." Clyde was indistinct now, as he was juggling hot pans and dishes and had a face full of steam. Mattie helped him to set out the plates and dishes while he carved the juicy, pink flesh from its bone.

Conversation became desultory as everyone was absorbed in their food, but it gradually developed in a general way, with Miss Beresford gently getting to know Jim, Mattie and Martina. Clyde learned a few things himself: Martina had a degree in geography, had had an academic job and done a spell as a teacher at a private school before retraining herself in horticulture, and Mattie's degree in sociology and psychology specialised in crime. Miss Beresford seemed to regard them as promising schoolgirls and gave them characteristically imperious encouragement and interest. Jim's natural reserve charmed her completely, however, and Clyde was surprised to find that Miss Beresford, who must surely have had to struggle to assert herself against many authoritarian men, starting with her revered father, loved male company. Clyde thought of people as just that regardless of gender, but he realised that the divisions must have been more clearly delineated in Miss Beresford's day.

The Charlotte had turned out beautifully crisp and utterly delicious, worth the enormous quantity of butter, thought Clyde. Miss Beresford, though keeping her portions small, enjoyed the meal heartily and complimented him on his cooking, again he felt in a way that she would not have spoken to a woman. A man who was a success in the kitchen was a phenomenon – or a professional – something to be celebrated, not an uninteresting domestic drudge.

He suggested that they move to the drawing room for coffee, where the fire was rolling enticingly and there was – he had checked – no sign of Mrs Berenia Hassel, it being long past her usual hour for haunting. In fact, Miss Beresford took the ghost's chair, coffee at her side and a tiny crystal glass of viscous Cointreau in her hand. There was a gentle silence as everyone relaxed and pondered the flames.

"Sitting here," pronounced Miss Beresford to her audience, "I am reminded of old times at the college. This is the room that has changed the least, although," she smiled graciously at Clyde, "the furniture is very much more comfortable."

He regarded her with encouraging interest.

"Yes, I remember evenings sitting just here – it was an open fire in those days – talking to students after supper. The food was rather good, of the simple but well-done home-cooking variety. The mood was a lot more political then, and there was often heated and passionate debate." She smiled reminiscently. "It was an era when theory was still thought to have something to offer; in fact, to be a possible saviour of the human race. The only question was, of course, which theory?" She gave a little laugh. "It may seem hopelessly naive now, but it usually had the right spirit behind it, and stimulated a great deal of education and intellectual development. And really, the question of how, as a society, or even a species, we should live our lives has not gone away and never will as long as we survive."

The others sipped their drinks and absorbed this new form of entertainment along with the heat of the fire. It did seem unexpectedly appropriate, and Miss Beresford was, as ever, effortlessly engaging.

"The other main subjects were art and languages," she continued, "Hubert Ball, the Greater Blocton mayor who was so influential in the founding of the place, being a believer in the European ideal. It all seems so distant." She sighed.

"Did people study for qualifications?" asked Jim.

"No," said Miss Beresford firmly, "and that's just what makes it all seem so impossible now. There were no exams, no certificates and no profits to be made – the fees merely contributed to the expenses of your stay. I sometimes speak to young people now about education for its own sake and they simply cannot understand what I mean; it all has to be for results, leading to jobs, leading to money. And teachers are even worse, poor things, so brainwashed by the system that is killing them. There is talk of providing a value-for-money service! We thought about living our lives, improving the world, enjoying ourselves – having the full human experience, if you like, and making that available to as many people as wanted it."

"Didn't that make the standard of teaching rather lax?" said Jim, now devil's advocate.

"That's very astute of you." Miss Beresford smiled on her favourite dinner companion. "It could have done. And there was a great deal of nonsense in education in those days, as there was in art and many other fields as people broke away from the old constraints." She held up a finger waggishly to Jim. "Ah, you may think I'm old-fashioned now," she grinned, "but it needed doing! There remained enough of us who believed that academic – or artistic – integrity was important. I'm not saying it was perfect at all," she beamed this concession over him. "It is the attitude, the atmosphere, the belief in learning and creativity as ends in themselves that I find it so hard to be without."

"What sort of art courses did the college do?" asked Clyde.

"Oh," said Miss Beresford, coming down to earth, "ceramics, of course. Basic drawing, oils and watercolours, landscape and life classes. Quite traditional. There was Henry Parry who had worked for the Shaftacres and was an excellent tutor of classical drawing, watercolours and ceramic techniques, and ... let me see ... a young woman, I can't remember her name. She taught languages as well, and her own work was rather abstract, but she was quite sound on basic drawing and oil painting techniques. At one time, the college thought of offering music courses, but in the end, that was taken up elsewhere."

Something was niggling at the back of Clyde's mind, but before he could focus on it, the conversation moved swiftly on to music and concerts, and eventually to the village amateur dramatics society. All except Jim, they had tickets for the December performance.

"Doesn't your assistant Mr Padchurch usually appear with them?" Miss Beresford asked Clyde.

He started slightly as he was so unfamiliar with Zeno's surname. "Yes," he said with a smile, "but he's away at present visiting his daughters in Australia, and so I expect he won't be in this performance."

"He's excellent at character parts and quite good in comedy."

"I'm looking forward to seeing him on stage," Clyde said blandly, hiding a queasy turn at the thought of Zeno and mysteries still to be resolved. The longer it went on, the more he became afraid that the man was taking advantage of him, or even making a fool of him in some way. Zeno had definitely taken on a sinister air in his absence.

Miss Beresford felt it was time to take her leave and Jim went to the hall for her coat. "Give my regards to Neville Lemon," she said as she rose from the haunted seat. Clyde smiled at the thought that she had kept the chair fully occupied and the apparition simply did not have the presence or personality to displace her. "I haven't seen him for quite some time."

"I shall certainly mention you, Miss Beresford."

"I have no doubt he'll bore you to death about dahlias," she smiled, "but he does know what he's talking about. Come to think of it, he used to be very keen on the theatre and amateur dramatics himself when he was young, but his father didn't think it was appropriate for a solicitor, who needed to command respect in the community and purvey a reassuring attitude of rectitude and sobriety."

"I'm not sure even bishops manage that, these days," quipped Jim as he helped her into her coat. She laughed and wished the girls a warm goodnight with some last pieces of encouragement for their future endeavours. She then shook Jim and Clyde by the hand.

"Goodnight, Miss Beresford," said Clyde, "and thank you for a most enjoyable evening."

"Thank *you*," she replied, releasing him from her cool, bony hands. "My friends," she beamed at him and Jim, with the first touch of self-consciousness that Clyde had ever witnessed in her, "I would like you to call me Agnes." And with this grand and surprising announcement, she turned and walked away into the darkness of the drive.

Chapter Thirteen

CLYDE AND JIM were enjoying pottering about on the Saturday morning after a stressful work week for Jim made harder by his not being in the office. Clyde was just reflecting that at least one problem had been lifted from Jim, as he was safe and secure in his mind and his home once more, when Mattie burst in through the back door in a wild state of excitement.

"Clyde! Jim! Come quickly!" she shouted, slipping off her muddy shoes and running into the house. "Look at this!"

Clyde and Jim duly followed her. "What is it?" asked Clyde anxiously.

"It's about the murders," she replied breathlessly. "I've had a response to all the feelers I put out online looking for the Baxter family, or people who knew them or the Hassels."

"And one of the Baxters got in touch?" Clyde was astonished and disappointed. He was reconciled to the murders as a part of the history of the house, albeit an unpleasant one, but he did not want to bring them into the present by meeting long-lost survivors.

"Oh no, sorry," said Mattie sympathetically, misunderstanding his reaction, "the person who's got in touch is John Eastley. He's the grandson of Superintendent Geoffrey Eastley who was in charge of the murder case. And he's sent the photos. Look!" She held out some printed sheets. Clyde took them and glanced at them, while Jim was asking what photos they were.

"They're the missing crime scene photos," said Mattie impatiently, watching Clyde. "Remember they were so horrific that they were not shown at the inquest, and when the files were released under Freedom of Information years later, they had disappeared. That's why we took those current set-ups with that man Faz," she added. "Well, this senior policeman in charge must have kept a copy for some reason, perhaps when he was ordered to remove them from the files. Who knows? His grandson found them among his papers and had no idea what they were until he came across my appeal. After all, the murders aren't very famous these days."

She looked at Clyde, who was staring at the images on the sheets in his hand. "Those are just rough prints," she explained, "but he says he'll let Melrose use them in his book. For a consideration, I suppose."

Clyde was still staring and Jim was looking at him.

"They *are* really gory. It's a massacre," Mattie continued happily, but added after seeing Clyde's face go white, "Perhaps I should have warned you first. After all, I'm used to looking at that sort of thing ..."

But Clyde held most of the sheaf of bloody corpse shots unseen in his left hand and was gazing in wonder at just one picture. It was that of a middle-aged woman slumped in a tall armchair, a ragged visceral hole imposed violently on her rather fussy frock.

He shook his head. "No, you don't understand," he said slowly. "It's not that at all. *This is not the woman I see sitting by the fire in the drawing room.*"

. . .

It was later that morning that Clyde, Jim, Mattie and Melrose Burke sat by the drawing-room fire in conference. Mattie had phoned an eager Melrose soon after showing the pictures to Clyde, and was busy negotiating a quid pro quo involving her new bookshop with the great man, who was endeavouring to hold his own. Jim was finding the whole thing immensely entertaining, Clyde noticed, and Melrose still could not look Mattie in the eye, being as she was a woman, or fully suppress a slight twitch of – actually, Clyde couldn't decide what it was, but he thought not repulsion or hatred. More terror. What was the man afraid of? Images of domineering mothers, sexual repression and related clichés crossed Clyde's mind before he promptly dismissed his inner – and very amateur – psychologist in response to a direct address from the subject of his analysis.

"So, my dear boy," Melrose was not close enough to paw his arm, "do I understand correctly that the, er, phenomena you have witnessed are *not* in fact related to the murders?"

"Well," said Clyde, "this woman," he pointed to the body of Berenia Hassel in one of the prints laid out on the table, "is certainly not the one that I've seen here." He indicated the chair on one side of the fireplace, and the others jumped slightly in spite of themselves.

"It's a great relief," said Melrose, beaming. "I mean, my dear boy, whilst the supernatural has publicity value, it is hardly a subject for *sound academic research*. It put me in a very difficult position, as, out of respect for your experiences, I could hardly publish my book without at least a passing reference to possible *hauntings,* but to do so would hardly increase the credibility of the work. As it is, the situation is most happily resolved and there is no need to involve *that person*."

"Oh, do you mean Anthony Lill?" Clyde laughed. "Yes, he

was a bit much with his discontinuities in the space-time continuum."

"But you still have them, don't you?" put in Mattie. "I mean, you still see her. And the stain on the rug is still there."

"Yes, but I think I know someone who can explain it," said Clyde calmly.

"Another paranormal investigator?"

"No, just someone who knows what's happening."

He said this with such finality that Mattie probed no further. She changed the subject by addressing Melrose, who gurgled with discomfiture.

"So, Melrose, I've taken that empty shop in the village, and we thought that with a few weeks to go before Christmas, we could have a flash opening – a quick refurb of the front room, a few shelves, stock from Gardners, free refreshments at weekends – to get things going, then do a proper conversion as we go into the New Year. Are you any good at DIY and decorating?"

"Mmmiss *Greville*!" Melrose spluttered and choked slightly over her name, "I can recommend Gary Hargreaves the handyman. *I* do not do that kind of work. No. *No*! I appreciate that I am, well, er, indebted to you for your finding the photographs. A *very desirable* archive source and indeed you are to be congratulated. *However*, that does not mean that I shall be at your beck and call whenever you require *male assistance*."

Clyde was laughing so hard now that he could barely keep it down. Tears came to his eyes and he thought it very naughty of Mattie, even if she had been provoked.

"Now should you require someone to host a *literary event*, perhaps discussing one of their *former publications of local relevance*, I should, of course, be only too happy to oblige. After all, a bookshop is a *worthy venture* and deserves support."

"Oh, that would be wonderful, Melrose," she gushed. "Who better to be the special guest at our launch event?" And, puffed up and smiling graciously, the great historian managed to take his leave of her almost as if she were a man.

"I don't know what you're laughing at," said Mattie in mock sternness as Clyde shut the front door behind Melrose Burke. "After all, you're useless at DIY. Lucinda told me you had to have workmen in to do absolutely everything. You didn't so much as hold a paintbrush."

"Well, that's true," admitted Clyde sheepishly as he, Mattie and Jim walked back across the hall, "but I did help Zeno with the lodge, and I'm happy to have a go at holding a paintbrush in a good cause if someone is there to show me what to do. Zeno will be back soon and I'm sure he'd help, but we could try Handy Gary in the meantime."

"We ..." Mattie broke off and her jaw dropped. They had reached the drawing room doorway, and there before them, in the tall chair by the fire, was the elderly lady, slumped forward as usual. Thrilled, Mattie made a move to approach, but Clyde put a restraining hand on her shoulder.

"Don't go in," he said. "Somehow, I don't want to disturb her." They tiptoed away to the kitchen.

With Zeno away and Jim working, Clyde had got into the habit of having the girls round for meals in the big kitchen. He was happy to be kept busy with the cooking as he was increasingly aware that he needed something to occupy his mind. There was the garden, of course, but he didn't think that would be enough, and still only intended to be a part-time dilettante horticulturalist. He could always employ someone else if it was a success. He needed something mentally challenging, a purpose, and he had no idea what it might be.

Mattie was busy with the new shop, as well as fitting out

her and Martina's home to suit themselves. Martina was outside all day, working hard on the garden. She was currently spreading a load of compost she had had delivered over cardboard to make new vegetable beds. She and Clyde were just finalising the plans for fruit trees so that they could plant the orchard varieties bare-rooted in winter. Clyde remembered their talk about the composting bins and thought that perhaps Mattie had the handy assistant she needed living at home with her. As for Jim, he existed under pressure of work, and that, although he wasn't sure he thought Jim's work at all meaningful anymore, just made Clyde feel even more adrift.

He was contemplating what to make for dinner, pasta with pumpkin and blue cheese, or courgette meatballs, and thinking that he was behind on his Christmas preparations and hadn't given much thought to gifts. What could he give to Laura? It was a shock to him to realise that he already thought of himself and Laura as being together. After all, neither one had said anything, and not much had happened between them; but there it was. He no longer felt single because some deep connection that he could not rationalise had formed between them and it refused to be got over. But, he reminded himself, he still knew nothing of Laura's family and it would be unlikely that she would be free for Christmas.

He hadn't arranged to see her again yet, and suddenly felt a desperate urge to know that it was going to happen soon. He drew a deep, fulfilling warmth from a dream that she would be coming home tonight and every night; that he would be here in the welcoming heart of their own haven, ready to celebrate the day with a hearty meal of his creation. Was it a dream or a premonition? It seemed so real in his mind.

He took out his phone and pressed her name. An old-fashioned ring trilled on his ear.

"Hello, 345737?"

"Laura?"

"Oh, Clyde!" His heart dissolved as her pleasure flowed down the line. "I'm so glad you've phoned."

"Really?"

"Of course. I was hoping we could meet up. I've only just got back from a last-minute language trip to Paris. Did I tell you about it?"

"Sort of. After calling a couple of times, I remembered you were often away."

He thought he could hear her smile. "It was nice of you to call. The trip was all very confusing ... upsetting, even. You see, I got the boat train from Crewe ..."

"Boat train?" Clyde didn't think he'd heard of such a thing outside a novel.

"Oh God, I suppose they don't have them anymore, do they?" she almost wailed. "That was it; I came back by Eurostar, through the tunnel, but I'd never heard of it. How can you be booked to travel on a form of transport you didn't know existed?"

Clyde didn't know what to say, but he knew he was there to help in her distress. "Laura ..." he said urgently.

"Can we meet soon, darling? I need to see you."

"Let's go to the museum in Ridgley. You can show me round. On Monday?"

"Yes, that will be fun. Eleven o'clock in the foyer?"

"Wonderful!"

"I'll see you then."

His stomach hit the floor as contact was broken, but his heart roared because she had called him darling.

Having decided on the pasta, Clyde went back to the kitchen to get started. He could enjoy planning for Christmas now, feeling – quite unjustifiably – that Laura was going to be part of it in some way. He wondered yet again about her family and what she would be doing on Christmas Day, but these were complicated thoughts and he abandoned them to the mood of uplifting warmth left by the knowledge that he would be seeing her soon.

He had just decided on serving some sharply dressed winter salad leaves to temper the richness of the dish, when he noticed how dark it had become and decided to do his nightly ritual of drawing the curtains and lighting the drawing room fire. First, though, he paused and took out his phone to call Mattie.

"Hi, Mattie, are you free to come over a bit early for dinner? Martina too?"

Mattie replied that Martina was still in the bath scrubbing compost from under her nails, but she would come straight away.

"Is there something the matter, Clyde?" She must have heard the urgency in his voice.

"No, but I'm going into the drawing room, and it's usually this time of day that ..."

"I'm coming straight over," she said and rang off.

Clyde called Jim, and then waited for his friends in the drawing room doorway. He had turned on the lamp nearest the door, and sure enough, found himself watching the lifeless figure as usual. Jim sidled up alongside him, and then Mattie joined them, breathless from rushing. Clyde put a restraining hand out and made a sign for silence. Mattie stared wide-eyed at the body whilst trying to ease her heavy panting.

As soon as she was calm, Clyde released his arm and signalled to the others to follow as he tiptoed to the chair and stood in a confronting posture above the dumpy figure. Today, she was wearing a yellow patterned shirt dress in some unfamiliar shiny material and an enormous cabled cardigan that might have been homemade. He bent down to examine the figure, putting his face very close.

"Ugh!" ejaculated the body, and twitched convulsively. They all jumped back, and seeing the corpse settle back into repose, by common consent left the room, trying not to look as if they were rushing. No one said anything, but everyone was glad when Clyde offered them a glass of wine back in the kitchen.

When Clyde arrived in the foyer of the City Museum on Monday morning, Laura was already there. It was mild, wet and windy – the worst kind of British winter weather in Clyde's opinion – and he didn't recognise her straight away covered in boots, trench coat and waterproof hat. As soon as she saw him, she rushed over, snatched off the hat and kissed him. They had once shared better kisses, thought Clyde, but it was a good start.

"How about some coffee?" he asked with a smile. "God, what a day! They do have a café here, don't they?"

The café turned out to be a shiny off-white basement of the most utilitarian kind, but the coffee was hot and reasonably good, and the tables well-spaced enough for conversation. Clyde recounted the visit of Neville Lemon the afternoon before and the superfluity of shapes, sizes and colour of dahlia in the catalogues he had left behind.

"He's quite an amusing old chap, really. He was very keen on amateur dramatics when he was young, but the family didn't approve of such things for a solicitor, so he's immensely chuffed that his great-nephew or second cousin or something, Timothy Lemon, is now a big noise on Netflix. Been in some series about the royal family. I wouldn't know, I never watch that kind of stuff."

"Was someone in his family connected with the college? I'm sure I know the name."

"Yes, that's right, his father. He was one of the governors."

"Oh, good Lord," she laughed, "I remember him now – your Mr Lemon, I mean. He used to come to special functions sometimes, dinners and so on, at the college. Regrettably flamboyant, was how his family regarded him, I think. His father once sent him home from the office for wearing a coloured shirt!" They both laughed heartily and then stopped short at the realisation of a woman in her early thirties reminiscing about something that happened years before she was born.

They gazed directly into each other's eyes for a second. "Let's go and look at the pictures," said Laura to break the impasse, "then we'll talk. I'll tell you everything I know, and hope you can help me."

"I've got something to tell you too," replied Clyde, thinking of the encounter in the drawing room two days earlier.

She smiled and took his arm. "Come on. It's not a very interesting collection of pictures. Just one or two good things, but the ceramics are amazing."

They strolled around the upper floor, and the pictures were indeed, even to Clyde's unprofessional eye, mostly mediocre at best; but he enjoyed hearing Laura talk about them: technique, composition, what she liked and didn't like. Then he suddenly remembered Lucinda's exhibits, and steered Laura away to the ceramics galleries.

They were satiated before they'd got halfway round the overwhelming displays. "We should come with Agnes Beresford," said Clyde, who'd been telling Laura about his dinner guest. "I bet she would bring it to life with her expert knowledge. It's hard to take it all in when it's just one amazing pot after another."

Laura laughed. "They should use that phrase in the publicity," she said. "'Blocton City Museum: One Amazing Pot After Another'. I wonder if she remembers me. Agnes Beresford, I mean." She looked troubled once more.

"She did mention a female art teacher who specialised in abstracts and taught languages, but obviously it was too long ago to have been you ..." He stopped open-mouthed, his conscious mind unable to process the shocking possibility that had just surfaced.

"Oh."

"Hadn't we better have everything out? I can't help you if I don't know, can I? And you know I want to help you if I can. Very much."

They tripped silently down the tatty stairs back to the glaring basement, and ordered salads, they being useful things to pick at in a difficult situation.

"Right," said Clyde. "You first. From the beginning." He touched her hand in what he hoped was a supportive gesture.

She gave a wry smile. "I wish I knew where it started! Well, here goes. I was a young art teacher at the Shaftacre Memorial College. It was the perfect job for me because I was single and got to live in in turn for fairly light caretaking duties, along with Frances Harvey the librarian – we shared a small flat in the main building – the housekeeper and the groundsman. I got to use my French and Spanish too; I think I mentioned my mother was French Canadian, and I'd spent time in Spain as a student. I still had time for my own art practice and had just had quite a successful small exhibition which had attracted the odd favourable notice.

"Life at the college was lots of fun. The people who came were mostly keen to learn and interested in their subject, but often eccentric – always entertaining – and there was a lot of social activity, plus trips abroad sometimes. All in that lovely setting. Looking back, it seems too good to be true.

"At least, it was too good to last. You know – or I suppose you do – how times changed, the mood changed, priorities changed. The college came to be seen not as an asset or an achievement, but an expensive indulgence and a liability. Languages and art were no longer regarded as important – not marketable – and political and economic discourse and independent thought were not encouraged. We carried on our work, but now there were always pressures – targets, results, costings, inspections – and the fun seemed to die with them.

"And that's when things started to get weird for the resident staff. Arthur Colclough the groundsman had died suddenly and never been replaced; his family left and the lodge cottage remained empty. After that, council workers came in to keep the outside just about tidy and do any essential maintenance. That left Frances, myself and the housekeeper, Zeno Padchurch. That's how Zeno will know the lodge cottage so well, he was great friends with Arthur. They used to play cards together. Anyway, we were told that the college could no longer support residential staff and was going to be shut up at nights and only run day courses. It was a blow to us all; Frances had lived there for years and felt the library was her home as much as the flat, and my long engagement had just ended in a break-up, leaving me feeling very dependent on communal life.

"In fact, we never left. None of us knew how it happened, but we just carried on. No one challenged us. And gradually, we slipped backwards to better times and younger days, but without losing the memory of our lived experience. It wasn't so dramatic really because not that long had passed. New people came to the courses – God knows where from – and I still travelled abroad. There were changes and developments, of course, but we were somehow in a different version of time. I don't know how else to describe it.

"At least, that's how it was for Frances and me. Zeno ... well, Zeno managed to come and go. He left for a while when it all started to, er, slip, and got married and ran a restaurant. But later, when that broke down, he came back and just slotted in. I don't know how he did that. You'd have to ask him."

"Shit," said Clyde quietly. "A discontinuity in the space-time continuum. What if that conceited idiot Anthony Lill was actually *right*?"

Laura looked at him questioningly, but he shook his head and signalled for her to continue. "So there we were, making the very best of our reality because we'd felt the misery of another kind, when we started to, well, *bleed* back into this." She indicated her surroundings with a gesture. "This present. Now.

"I think it may have been your coming, actually," she smiled bashfully at him. "You made the college a good place to be again."

He smiled half-heartedly, his brain puzzling. "So, you, Frances and the self-organising library, the cooking smells and water noises, the non-existent trains, the strangers in the grounds and the ghost picture ..."

"Yes, that was mine."

"... were all slivers of this prolonged past or alternative timeline you've been living in bleeding into the present? Our present? Now?" He also gesticulated.

"I think so. It's as if the old spirit of the college was ready to merge with the new spirit you brought to the house."

"What about the stains on the rug?"

She looked embarrassed. "I'm so sorry," she said sheepishly. "I could kick myself. I think *I* made that stain. I never thought, when you said *blood*stain. Actually, I was taking a short-cut through the hall and spilled some iron oxide powder – it's used for tinting ceramics. I scrubbed and scrubbed at it, but it left a rust-coloured stain. Why the stain should be on *your* rug and not the one that used to be there, I don't know. It just shows the confusion of past and present mingling that I wanted you to help me with."

"Hang on," said Clyde, almost brusquely, "there's still the body ..."

"I've had a think about that too." She matched his earnestness. "It sounds like Marjorie. Marjorie Barker. If she's slipped through in some way, as we have ..."

"Who's Marjorie Barker?"

She laughed lightly. "Oh, she's really an old nuisance. An elderly widow from one of the cottages at the far end of the green. Comfortably off and not much to do. She came to *all* the courses, first art, and then languages, one after another, and even politics and economics eventually, until she knew the place as well as we did. She just started hanging around being 'useful' and became a fixture. I think she saw herself becoming a governor, but of course, that wasn't going to happen, and it was easier – and kinder – to keep her as a sort of volunteer than get rid of her. She mainly clucks round the place putting people's backs up, cadging free meals and – this is the thing that made me think your apparition might be her – snoozing in a comfy chair by the fire before supper. It's one of her best tactics; it's harder for her to pretend there's anything for her to do in the evenings, so she has a little rest after finishing for the day before going home, then she wakes up and it's just time for supper and so she might as well stay for it ..." They both laughed.

"She should meet Melrose Burke and compare notes on cadging meals," said Clyde. "It does sound like her, and it explains something that I only realised recently didn't make sense; the woman in the chair keeps appearing in different clothes. Perhaps I'd better have a chat with Mrs Barker ..."

"Good luck with that! Once she gets going, you might wish she was a corpse after all."

There was a pause.

"I need your help," said Laura simply. "I don't think I can cope with this alone." He looked questioningly, waiting for more. "I'm here now obviously," she gave a nervous laugh, "but only recently I was back there and the transition is really unnerving."

"A lot's changed. It will be like going to live in a new and different country in a way. But you'll get there."

"It's stranger than that. I know things I don't know about! For example, you phoned me on my home phone, my ordinary telephone plugged into a socket in the wall and connected to a network of wires around the world. It's the only kind of phone I've ever known, but the call came through on *this*," she held out an iPhone, "and I *seem to know how to use it*. Even though I don't remember ever having bought it or used one before. I'd never heard the word internet, and yet when people mention it now, I understand them."

Clyde could only keep looking. He didn't know what to say.

"And there are bigger things. I've just been to Paris with a language group. I took the boat train from Crewe as I always do – it's an old relic of a service, but rather fun – and then the ferry, but when I came back I went straight to London from Paris by Eurostar through the tunnel. I knew that was what I had to do, and I knew how to do it, but I also knew it was different and I'd never heard of it before. Can you imagine how strange that is?"

"No," said Clyde firmly. "I can't. I don't know how you're staying so sane." He thought for a moment. "It sounds," he said, "as if your subconscious has sort-of updated with the time slip, but your conscious mind hasn't, because you haven't actually experienced these new things in any way. Sorry," he added lamely, "I know that's just cod science ..."

"It makes sense, though," she said with satisfaction. "God, I mean, we don't know what the hell's going on, do we, and we're unlikely ever to have a scientific explanation; who'd believe us if we tried to get one? So as long as we have a way of understanding what's happening that works for us – that helps us to live, love, be productive and survive – that's all we need."

He stared at her. It was a revelatory perspective.

"Like art, really," she went on. "There's no objective scientific truth in art, but there needs to be a personal truth if one's work is to have any integrity. A work is your way of conveying how *you* understand and cope with its subject, and of course a few of the people who view your work may get it – feel some knowledge of your experience as the artist – but most people will have their own experience of your work, and so it goes on in a miraculous network of individualities."

There was another pause. "I'm sorry," she said, smiling. "I hope I wasn't boring you."

He shook his head. "No," he said, still stunned by her magnificence. "But you don't seem to me to be very much in need of help."

"Oh, but I am! Look how you just helped me by putting things into that perspective. I need someone to help me adjust, someone who understands what's happening and can be there at the unsteady moments."

"I'll be happy to do that." He smiled, putting his hand on hers. They looked at each other.

"It could lead to some very interesting work," said Laura at last. "This strange experience, I mean. If I can survive it."

"I don't think you're going to have any choice about that. You seem to be made of tough stuff to me."

She smiled a little self-consciously, then said, "I do really need your help, though. Not just in that way, but with something very practical. You see, in this time, the college has turned into your house, so I have nowhere to live, and no job to go to. And it's not as if I have any family left. I'm staying at the pub because I didn't know what else to do. I can't believe the prices! Even though my bank account seems to have adjusted with inflation, it's still *a lot*!"

"Well, that's easily solved. The college was your home and it still can be. Just move back in. God knows, there's plenty of

179

room, and a big, new art studio." He paused, suddenly hearing all the implications and problems in what he'd just said. "I mean, you wouldn't have to ... even if we didn't ... there'd be no conditions attached ... I ..." He gave it up.

She stood up, walked round the table to him, and looked into his eyes before kissing him. "I don't think I've got much choice," she said. "And I don't know why I'd want one."

Chapter Fourteen

By the time they left the museum, the rain had stopped and a hearty wind was breaking the cloud cover. It almost blew them up the funnel of a street leading back to the former town hall. Laura stopped indecisively at the highest point and looked down a level street packed with diminutive shops and pubs on one side facing an enormous edifice fronted in grey stone with columns like a Georgian mansion. 'Post Office' was carved in elegant letters near its apex. It was, of course, long closed and boarded up.

"I haven't got used to this," she said mournfully. "It used to be such a proud, busy town. Everything from the old-fashioned smart shops where they called you 'Madam', to the bustling market hall and the big chains. What are we, four weeks before Christmas? All the shops would be glowing with lights and decorations, and this part of town would be packed with people, rushed and excited, overloaded with bags, fighting through the weather back to the bus station. You can't believe that it was once too busy for comfort or convenience, and that people would plan to get here early or late so they could avoid the queues, can you?"

Clyde looked at the abandoned post office, the enormous chain pub beyond it and the row of gaudy plastic Turkish barbers and betting shops. Some force about her – maybe just her personality, maybe something to do with her exceptional experiences – projected sepia ghosts around him: harassed women with bags holding the hands of small children, lads playing the fool, young women, very smart, men in coats with cigarettes, all bathed in the glow from the enticing little windows, decked to tempt.

He blinked and it was gone.

"I'd better go," said Laura. "There are so few buses now I must catch the next one."

"I can give you a lift," Clyde replied.

"No, thanks. The bus will give me time to collect my thoughts. I found a storage receipt among my papers, and I'm wondering if some of my things are there ..."

"Will you be coming round later?"

"Is tomorrow okay? It will just give me time to sort out my stuff, if it *is* in this storage place."

"See you tomorrow, then."

"Tomorrow."

Turning hastily away from their goodbyes, they went in opposite directions, Clyde striding past the redundant post office. As the town opened out into wider streets and squares, he found it pleasant to be there. It's true that there weren't many shops to interest him, and that there were a number of querulous inebriates of some kind, but to one accustomed to the modern British city, it was refreshingly peaceful. Laura might reminisce about days when it was crowded with shop-pers, but Clyde being used to the gridlocking of anywhere worth visiting – fighting to get there and non-stop pushing and shoving when you did – loved being able to walk freely around and pause, even go into a shop and peruse the wares at leisure. There were enough others around to make the place feel used, and that was just about the maximum concentration of people he felt like dealing with these days.

He'd heard bad things about the town, and indeed it ought to be ugly and depressing with its crumbling edges, defunct public services and community of derelicts, but he couldn't find it so. There was just something about the place, an energy that defied defeat; perhaps it came in on the icy wind. Or, there was a fountain of life somewhere beneath the ground here, a portal to something beyond the reality before his eyes.

As he arrived back at the spot where he'd said goodbye to Laura, almost at the car park, he glanced down to the museum. Black shadows rose before his eyes, an inky sky and clusters of fat wine-bottle chimneys spread wide across the descent into the valley. From sooty enclosure walls traipsed streams of men and women, rolling down the hill and diverging into lines of boxy cottages like balls in a bagatelle.

He shook himself clear of the enchantment and headed home.

Passing through the outskirts of town, Clyde pulled into a petrol station to fill up. As he walked over to pay, he casually glanced at the newspaper headlines and stopped in his tracks. Anthony Lill's secret was out.

Melrose Burke!

Back at home, Clyde prised Jim from his screen for a cup of tea just as the girls burst into the kitchen, asking him if he'd seen the news.

"I take it it's no one here," said Clyde. "No one's let anything slip?"

"Of course not!" said Mattie indignantly.

"Who would I tell?" asked Martina, confused. Jim just gave him a look.

"Melrose!" they all shouted at once.

"It must be," said Clyde. "It's too great a coincidence. Jim lets the secret slip out to the old chancer in his cups, and then, as soon as we hear that the hauntings aren't connected with the murders and won't need to be in Melrose's book – i.e. he won't need to reference Anthony Lill – the story is all over one of the tabloids."

"I saw him yesterday," said Mattie, "and he had a new coat, full-length chocolate leather, and a big, flashy gold watch."

Clyde groaned, but Jim cut in, "Actually, I think it's okay. Craig phoned just before you got in, Clyde, and it seems that all the leak has done is create a market for more details. After all, Melrose didn't know anything but the bare headline – and Mr Lill has his book of revelation pretty much ready to go to print. I think the only thing Anthony's really pissed off about is that he can't get it out in time for Christmas."

"For fuck's sake," said Clyde. "Let's have a cup of tea."

As they were all seated together, Clyde took the chance to tell the others that Laura would be moving in the following day. There were a few cheeky smiles, murmurs and nudges. Blushing, Clyde laughed it off awkwardly and went on to tell them the solution to the house mysteries. That shut them up, at least for a while.

Martina broke the silence. "That's wonderful!" she said. "It's here again. The college, I mean. Things to learn, sociable, fun, a haven. We can have new subjects. Gardening and nature studies."

Clyde stared at her in alarm. "No! That's not what I meant. It's not going to be a college again."

"But it *is*!" insisted Martina. "It already was, because you were going to run gardening courses. Laura does art and languages. You have your library – why not teach English or creative writing? Melrose and Agnes can do local history and Zeno can do the cooking. It will be *fun*!"

Clyde had never seen her so excited. All the difficulties – space, money, people, facilities, paperwork, officialdom and more – crowded into his mind, a whole team of wailing Cassandras.

He opened his mouth and, over the negative cacophony in his head, his voice said, "You're right. Let's do it!"

They talked excitedly over the top of one another for a while through mouthfuls of homemade biscuit. Eventually, Jim said, "Well, one thing's certain; if Laura's moving in tomorrow, it's time I went home."

The girls tittered, and Clyde and his friend smiled at each other. "Thanks for everything," Clyde said from the heart, and hugged Jim. "I hope you'll stay long enough to say hello to her," he added.

"Trains permitting, of course," said Jim.

"Mattie," said Clyde, noticing the time, "do you think the apparition in the drawing room will have put in an appearance yet?"

Mattie consulted her phone. "Possibly," she said. "Shall we ...?"

"Let's go and pay her a visit," said Clyde decidedly. He got up and led the way, the others following nervously behind him, striding up to the fireplace where the somnolent figure was slumped as usual. He bent down, and firmly but gently lifted and shook one of the lifeless arms.

The eyes snapped open and the head jerked up to face Clyde. All the others stepped back, but Clyde held his ground.

"Who are you?" demanded the ghost perfunctorily, and without waiting for an answer, added, "and why hasn't the fire been lit? The fire is always lit by this hour at this time of year. Standards round here are slipping!"

Clyde took some matches from the mantelpiece and silently indicated to Jim to light the stove. "And who are you?" he countered, charming but resolute.

"Me?" The phantom was affronted. "I'm Mrs Barker, of course," it said huffily. "Mrs Marjorie Barker. Everyone knows me. I suppose you're the new owner or manager or principal, whatever they're calling it now, are you, Mr er ...?"

"Tranter, Clyde Tranter." Clyde was starting to enjoy himself. The others watched in awe, huddled round the stove.

"Well, Mr Tranter, I'm pleased to meet you." Marjorie Barker shook herself together and rose, proffering a firm hand. It was a very solid handshake for a ghost, and the robust apparition had more to say. "I don't think," she continued, "that I like the new layout of furniture in this room. Not well organised for social purposes, and simply not enough seats. But I congratulate you on the curtains, which are just right! Beautiful, and on inspection, I found, of excellent quality. Most unusual nowadays and highly commendable. I expect your wife chose them, did she? I'd like to meet *her*."

Clyde opened his mouth to speak, but there was more to come from Marjorie. "I also approve highly of the new stove," she went on, turning to the now glowing fireplace. "I will be the first to admit that I was not at all keen on replacing the old open fire, having been used to one all my life, and nothing is more welcoming or warming in my opinion. Good wholesome flames, not like this stuffy gas. Still, no one can say I'm not fair, and the stove, which at first I thought was an ugly-looking thing, gives out all the beauty and warmth of the fire without the smoke or mess. And there is a lot less draught, which is greatly to be commended. You don't enjoy draughts when you're my age."

Clyde murmured something suitable while Mrs Barker bent down and re-emerged with a handbag big enough to carry the entire luggage of an economy airline passenger. "You'll excuse me if I go and tidy up," she said with a gesture that indicated it was herself she meant to tidy. "I like to have time for a small glass of sherry before supper. It's very warming. I'm glad to have met you, Mr ..."

"Tranter," Clyde reminded her.

"And your secretary ..." She gave a brief nod to Mattie, who was standing nearest to Clyde, waddled stiffly to the door and was gone.

Everyone stepped forward to look at Clyde, but no one could think of anything to say.

The house was a hive of activity the next morning: Jim was packing and anxiously searching for items he'd distributed as he had made himself at home; Clyde was doing some rapid housework that was much needed in the absence of Zeno and making up one of the spare rooms for Laura. Jim asked him what he was doing, being sure no second bedroom would be needed, but if he was amazed at the response, he merely raised an eyebrow and said nothing. Clyde was always so quick to observe others in context, and so slow to acknowledge what was happening to himself.

Laura phoned. She'd found a trunk and two packing cases in a storage unit she didn't know she had and was wondering how to move them.

"There was a time when we could have used the groundsman's van, but ..."

"Yes!" said Clyde, thinking of the college, garden and bookshop projects and having a sudden brainwave. "We need to buy a van!"

"Buy one?"

"Yes."

"Just to move my luggage? Can you get one as quickly as that?"

He pulled himself together. "Oh no, I was thinking of ... Laura, I have so much to tell you! Don't worry about the luggage. I'll give Bernard a ring and ask if we can use the community minibus."

"That would be great. I just want to get home now."

He flushed with pleasure and nerves at the thought of his house being her home.

"I'll sort it out now and get back to you straight away. Can you text?"

"Yes, I like it."

"Send me the address to meet you at then, and I'll confirm when I'm on my way."

"Okay."

"By the way, I'll be cooking dinner tonight. Remind me, do you have any special dietary requirements? Or things you don't like?"

"Special requirements?" For a second, she sounded puzzled. "Oh, you mean am I a vegetarian or allergic to strawberries or something? No. And I really like everything. Except," he could hear her smiling down the phone, "things I have to cook myself!"

"Perfect."

"See you soon, then."

"Yes."

There was a long, nervous pause.

"I'm looking forward to it," he said ridiculously.

"Me too."

"Bye, then."

"Bye."

He rang off, feeling more of a fool than he had ever done in his life.

Mattie and Martina came into the kitchen. "Hi, Clyde," began Mattie awkwardly, "we've been thinking ..."

"Yes?"

"Well, now Laura is moving in ... I mean ... we won't be walking in and out unannounced anymore. Don't worry."

"Oh. Yes." Clyde was discomposed enough to be completely tongue-tied.

"When's she arriving?"

"I need to arrange with Bernard to borrow the minibus so I can go and get her luggage. And her, obviously. And I really need to finish the housework. And Jim's got to get his train ..." Clyde was suddenly in a state of nervous collapse.

Mattie put a kind hand on his arm. "Let's take a coffee break," she said. "I'll make it." She went into the hall and yelled, "Jim! Coffee!" before bustling back to the grinder and getting on.

Clyde sank into a chair, and Martina sat next to him, looking concerned. "I'll go and get Laura," she said, suddenly but firmly. "I've driven the minibus a few times before. Give me the address and her contact number, and I'll sort everything out. You stay here to get things ready and spend the time with Jim."

Clyde looked at her in surprise, then panic, and then, defeated by the fleeting images of all the things that could go wrong with the scheme, passed her his phone.

"I *can* do it, you know." She was serious, seeing how upset he was. "It'll be fine." It was the first time that the reassurance had flowed in this direction, and Clyde was once again aware of the strength in her that was so seldom to the fore. "I'll get onto it now." She rose to go and he wanted to hug her, but still felt that physical contact would be a jar.

"Martina," he said instead.

"Yes?" she turned.

"Thank you."

She smiled shyly in reply and left the room as Jim came in, shouting into his phone to someone at work.

After the coffee break, they all set to – Mattie, Jim and Clyde – to tidy the place up, Jim having committed to being back at work by the time he was on the train that afternoon.

"You and Martina will be coming round for dinner as usual, won't you?" said Clyde to Mattie.

She and Jim exchanged glances. "Well ... we thought you and Laura would want to be alone," she said awkwardly, "so she can, er, settle in."

Clyde was still incredibly nervous and couldn't quite manage a smile, but he was decided. "Thanks," he said, "but no. We're all going to be living here together and the sooner you, Martina and Laura get to know each other, the better. And besides, it will ease the, er, awkward, er, well, you know ..."

They clearly did, and Mattie said reassuringly, "Yes, of course, if that's how you feel. We'd love to come for dinner."

"Great. Pizza, then," said Clyde. "I'll get started on the sauce. Do you need to book a taxi, Jim?"

"Martina says she'll run me to the station once she's dropped Laura off, before she takes the bus back," said his friend. "Just so we overlap to say hello."

"Great," said Clyde shakily.

By four o'clock, Laura was sitting on one of the big sofas in the drawing room with a steaming cup before her. Clyde and Jim had distributed her enormous luggage to appropriate places in the house before Jim's departure. Her smaller cases still stood in the hall.

Clyde had been astonished to see the two women arrive seemingly as friends, quiet but comfortable and smiling. Everything about Laura was soft, warm and lively, very much a contrast to Martina's terrified rigidity; but neither was erroneously chatty, and both were kind and troubled. Perhaps that was as good a foundation for friendship as any.

Laura wore wide jeans and a high-necked cream angora jumper that set off the ashy gold of her cascading waves of hair, and sat cross-legged with her feet on the settee, looking directly at Clyde, who was sitting at the other end as if on prickles. She reached out and took his hand, and turning to look at her, he was totally in the power of her frank gaze; she shuffled closer to him, still face to face, then leaned across to give him a light kiss.

She returned to her cup. "This is delicious tea. I can't remember when I last had any so good. And I love what you've done to this room. The curtains are magnificent."

"I'll show you round the house if you like."

"I'd love to see the changes you've made, but it's all a lot to take in." For the first time, she looked away, down at her cup. "In some ways, I must know it better than you do."

Clyde, transfixed, spilled hot tea in his lap and jumped up. She came hurriedly to the rescue with a napkin, and on sitting down again maintained a supportive physical contact with him, even if it was only a brush of arms. He wanted to take her hand, but she was holding hot tea.

"Tell me about it," he said gently. "About the house, the college. What it was like for you."

"Oh, I thought you'd know."

"I know it was a municipal residential college," said Clyde. "The council got it for a song after the Hassel/Baxter murders because Brian Hassel didn't fancy staying here and no one else wanted it either. The existing college was gradually falling into a mine shaft or something, and so they moved it here."

"The land in and around the city is like a Swiss cheese," said Laura. "Buildings have a habit of developing unrepairable fissures or sinking into the ground."

"Well, when we bought it, there was a lot of drab paint-work and some antiquated pipework left, and that was about it. Everything had been stripped out. There were some concrete foundations at the back that were the remains of an annex, but it had long been demolished."

"Yes, the annex was a cheap block of motel-style rooms and a classroom that ran behind the stable. It was horrible really. I noticed it had gone and I'm glad."

"What about the internal layout of the house?"

"Well, this room was much the same, and the dining area. It wasn't a big place, you know, a couple of long tables were enough for everyone. The entrance and hall are also the same, but the kitchen's different, of course – much less utilitarian – and I haven't really seen the rest yet. There was the library, a classroom and the art studio down here, and upstairs and in the attic, the rooms were divided to sleep two or three, and there were bathrooms. Frances and I had a suite in the attic: a sitting room, two tiny bedrooms and a bathroom next door.

"Am I imagining it, or do people have a lot more bathrooms now? Virtually every bedroom seems to have its own bathroom attached. I suppose it's convenient, but it must involve a lot of plumbing."

"We all expect privacy for our ablutions these days, and shun the unhygienic practice of sharing with strangers," Clyde replied, laughing. "This is all really useful, though, because we're going to have to think about how we'll use the building when we start offering courses again."

"Offering courses?"

"Didn't Martina tell you? It was her idea to open a college again offering courses in art, languages, gardening, local and natural history, and literature. It's a good idea, isn't it?"

It was Laura's turn to be stunned. She stared at him, speechless.

"After all," continued Clyde, getting into his stride away from the subject of their feelings for each other, "you and I are both out of a job and we'll need something to do. And much as I love this house, the more I've rattled about in it on my own, the more I've realised that it is ridiculously big for one, or even two people. It's a stupid expense and responsibility too, cleaning and maintaining it – not to mention keeping it light and warm – just so that I can ponce about like the lord of the manor. Which is a thing I've never wanted to do."

She opened her mouth, and then shut it again. "Could we?" she said at last, brows furrowed.

"I expect so. I daresay it will be fraught with practical problems, but we can only have a go. Of course, we'll have to ..."

She reached over to touch his face with her hand, and he was immediately quiet, terrified once more. But she drew him forward to kiss her, and this time nothing happened to interrupt the natural progress of their passionate attraction.

Some time later, they were sitting cosily by the fire with large glasses of white wine while in the kitchen, the oven was heating for the pizzas.

"Funny Marjorie's not here tonight," said Clyde, and then, "Shit! You don't think they were around, do you? Frances and Marjorie, while we were ..."

Laura laughed and laughed until she slumped flat on her back on the thin pile of the rug. "D'you think I'll get the sack for inappropriate behaviour," she spluttered at last, "in a communal area?"

Clyde laughed too and kissed her, but as he went to check on things in the kitchen, he felt heavily burdened by the many disquieting oddities that remained without explanation.

"I don't understand," he began when he got back, "any of it really. How can you be here, in the flesh, yourself, and yet be part of life years ago?"

"I know nothing about physics and all that, but I'd say we just diverged onto a parallel timeline where the college carried on at its best, and like a little train, we ran along that branch line for a while until one day we came level with the main line, and merged when the points were set right. And as I said before, I think it was you who set the points."

"Me?"

"Yes, you and your wife – she certainly has beautiful taste, by the way, if this room's anything to go by. We carried on – Frances, Marjorie and me; I don't know about Zeno – probably because none of us had any family and our greatest connection was to the college and to what it meant. I think that's why we were sort of *chosen*. And when you came along, we had a kind of connection; you were without family, except for a wife who was about to leave you, and you felt the spirit of the place, even if you didn't know it. You love books and want to learn new things. It's a wonderful idea to run courses in the garden. Something we never thought of in the old days."

"Don't you have any family, then?" Clyde asked, thinking of his Christmas plans.

"No one close. When my parents split up, I stayed in England with my father, but he died not long after I started work at the college. My mother went back to Canada. She came from a big family – I think I mentioned holidays with them when I was young – and of course we kept in touch. But we'd never been close and when I started work, I never visited again."

She paused to consider, and a sad frown crossed her face. "I must really be alone now. They'll all be gone, won't they? They must have ... Oh, I don't understand!"

"I don't know," said Clyde putting his arm round her gently, "but I can't see how they would still be there."

They sat silent for a few moments in the soft light, then Clyde asked nervously, "So are you here to stay? I mean, in this time?"

"I think so. I told you about all the modern stuff I know, and my trunk was all packed and waiting for me, and I can't find the way back to my old life in the college." She smiled and touched his arm. "Hey, I am the one supposed to be freaked out by it all. And I was, but I feel much better now I'm here. See," she kissed him, "I'm quite robust. I think the present – here, now – has always been there for us in a shadowy way, like déjà vu, so perhaps it's not such a shock as I thought it would be."

He still looked worried and uncertain. "C'mon," she said, gently embracing him. "You know that even if I'd been on your timeline my whole life, I could still drop off it at any time. Death is always a possibility in life, even when you're in love. That's one of the things that makes it so scary."

Some moments later, her mood lightened. "I tell you what," she said, "I can't get used to this screen thing." She picked up Clyde's phone, looked at it with distaste and threw it down.

"You'll find life tricky without one."

"I thought you might say that. Funny, isn't it, because they're not really essential for life like, say, air or something. But someone's decided to make a world where you can't live without one. It seems so arbitrary. They could just as easily have made everyone get electric can openers."

Clyde laughed, charmed. "I'd better go and get supper ready," he said. "Coming?" He was at the all-encompassing stage of love where he didn't want to be separated from her much at all. She got up to follow him.

"Do you think all of you are here to stay? I mean Marjorie and Frances too?" He had once found the chic hauteur of the librarian rather attractive, but now he thought her interference officious and didn't want her breaking up his and Laura's intimacy.

"I've no idea really. Have you seen Frances lately?" She was watching him.

"No, and the library interference has stopped. Marjorie

hasn't turned up this evening either. She'd normally be here now."

Laura thought. "I really don't know. Marjorie's quite old and would certainly struggle to adjust. She might just ... well, pass away gracefully. As to Frances, I haven't seen her since the bonfire party." Her brow furrowed in puzzlement. "You know, I think she might move on. She wouldn't like it here if she's no longer a dominant influence." She laughed. "I wouldn't be surprised if she goes on to haunt that pathetic new library they have in town. Have you seen it? Fewer books than the one in the village here stuck in a bit of spare space in an entrance foyer, and the old Central Library standing forlorn and empty behind it. I can just see Frances there as a sort-of orderly poltergeist. She's rather ruthless in some ways."

They arrived in the kitchen just as Mattie and Martina were at the door, and Laura subtly and diplomatically assumed the role of hostess as Clyde set about shaping his dough. A new pattern of life at Valencia House was established, and Jim had been right; the spare bedroom was not required.

Chapter Fifteen

CONTENTED DAYS PASSED. Clyde and Laura, in the intense early stages of their relationship, were glad of the luxury of so much time together, but could still enjoy being part of an active community. Laura began to settle into Lucinda's studio, thrilled by the luxury of it. Clyde fed his Christmas cake with alcohol and made seasonal preparations. Martina ordered the fruit trees and gave some much-needed attention to the old ones. Together with Clyde, she planned the greenhouse and polytunnel.

All of them became involved in helping Mattie prepare the new bookshop. Martina did indeed prove to be adept at shelving and general DIY, and they had fun shopping for what Clyde thought were scary-looking power tools. There ensued much frenzied drilling, sawing and sanding. Laura turned out to be useful at decorating and got Clyde started with emulsion and a roller. He enjoyed himself immensely, watching the fresh new colour grow across the tired walls under his hand, while Laura was working on signs for the shop. He was even more amused to see the snow of paint in his hair and across his face afterwards. At least it was non-toxic.

In the evenings, they sat sociably together at supper, poring over the wholesaler's catalogue and Mattie's potential stocklists and budgets. Clyde, who still remembered her privately as a bit of a drip, found her knowledgeable, well organised and businesslike, though he acknowledged to himself that sadly, that was not enough to guarantee success. On the other hand, overheads were low, and the girls were getting the cottage as part of Martina's job. Housing was the main cost for everyone in the country, and once it was provided, many more things became possible.

Mattie was talking about a particular small publisher. She was enormously enthusiastic about their list, and as Clyde perused it, he too was drawn in by the selection of authors, some vaguely recognisable and others entirely new to him, but all with beguiling stories to tell. She had brought over some of her own copies of their books for him and Laura to see, and he soon felt intoxicated by the burgeoning ideas of the twentieth century in all their rich seriousness of experience and thought. These were works drawn from a deep well of skill and care, even if the subject matters were sometimes dated.

"Do you remember Bungle who runs *The Green Door*?" asked Mattie.

"With the mop of hair? Yes, of course."

"He's been in the book trade a long time, and when he started, booksellers used to buy direct from the publishers. Reps would come round like salesmen with the new titles and you'd decide how many you'd take. Can you imagine publishers selling to us now? Of course, they needed book-shops in those days because there was no internet. Apparently, the staff would do a stock order with most of the big publishers every week in a large shop. They'd never go to a wholesaler unless it was for a special item or a rush order."

"I suppose he remembers the Net Book Agreement." Martina's clear tones broke in unexpectedly.

"I've heard of that," said Mattie, "but I'm not sure what it was."

"On some old books, you'll see the price printed on the jacket with the word 'net' after it. It was a legal agreement by which prices of books were fixed by the publishers."

"Good God, price fixing! You can't believe it was ever legal in this country, can you?" Something of the old Clyde had bubbled up from somewhere. Martina stared at him, the terrifying energy of her mind flickering as its cavernous uncertainty made itself felt once more.

"It's wrong and ridiculous to think everything was better when I was a child," she announced bravely with a quake in her voice, "but it's somehow difficult to bear modern life when you've come from that context."

They all heard the break and saw the tears form. Mattie drew the larger woman to her in a hug. Clyde was all confused apologies. Laura felt that an old-fashioned remedy was called for and without fuss produced a huge pot of scalding strong tea, milk, biscuits, sugar, a small jug of whisky and four of the kind of mug that fitted in the palm like a comforter.

"I advise sugar and whisky," she said, smiling. "They're both revolting, but effective, and strangely soothing." They all added a slosh of the amber liquor and sat imbibing the fumes and taking sips that tasted like alcoholic porridge.

"I've still got a problem," Mattie said at length, clearly referring to a practical rather than an upsetting existential problem, "in that I need another member of staff. I can't be there all the time. I have to eat and use the loo as well as attending to various business things that may crop up. Does anyone know anyone?"

"We can ask around," said Clyde, and then, "What about Michael, the communist library volunteer? He might like some paid work."

"I don't know. Old-school librarians can be very sniffy

about bookshop work, you know. They don't regard it as being part of the same profession at all. I know, I met a few in the shop. Bungle says they had to do fantastically long training – degree plus three years – for about tenpence a week, so they're probably entitled to a bit of hauteur. I mean, that's as long as a doctor!"

Laura laughed. "Yes, Frances Harvey did that kind of training. It certainly gave her superior airs."

"I knew someone too," Martina piped up with a slight smile of recovery. "I think they ended up at some government organisation ..."

"Do you want me to ask Michael?" said Clyde. "I bet he remembers the Net Book Agreement, whatever it was."

"You can," said Mattie, "but I don't think it will turn out well."

Clyde persuaded Michael to come round to the shop and meet Mattie a few days later. He'd counted on the old man's curiosity to lure him in, and was not fooled by the show of reluctance. The first of the books had now arrived and Mattie was unpacking.

"Hello, Michael," she smiled and held out her hand, "nice to meet you."

"You're not a library user, then," he observed sniffily.

"Well, no. I have a lot of books of my own; I've always worked in bookshops."

"I don't believe in the concept of ownership," said Michael bluntly. "You can't own a person's thoughts and ideas. In public libraries, the books belong to the people, and we serve to disseminate those thoughts and ideas that cannot be owned."

This did not bode well, and Mattie looked unsure what to

say. Clyde was ready to step in and tackle the difficult interviewee, but she collected herself rapidly.

"I'm looking for someone to do a few hours in the shop when it opens," she reset the conversation, "and we wondered if you would be interested in the role."

"I'm a *librarian,* a trained professional – for all that matters nowadays! – not a shop girl," said Michael with scorn. "How much and how long for?"

"Probably a morning or afternoon, Tuesday to Saturday, minimum wage."

"I don't think I will," he said moodily. "Bit much at my age, and they need me to keep the library going. I know someone who might, though. Very bright boy, likes books, not troubled by my political principles. Julian Cardwell. He's done a bit of volunteering at the library. Intelligent lad, nice manners. Puts up with me," he added with a twinkle.

"Is he looking for a job?"

"Doesn't know what he's looking for; young people don't these days. He's doing a degree, but he's stuck at home having no fun at all. I remember in my student days ..."

"He won't be able to spare enough time, though, will he? It's not just a vacation job."

"Doesn't seem to have much work to do, and never goes to any lectures. It's all online. Stuck in, staring at a screen full of meaningless jargon all day. Poor sod, do him good to get out. When I think of my young days ..." He chuckled, and then coughed as if his body was reminding him of the effects of those well-remembered excesses. "I could make myself available occasionally to cover time he can't manage," he continued once he'd recovered, "on a voluntary basis. In return for a show of your appreciation that won't affect my tax position." He fixed her with a gimlet eye. "Waitrose vouchers. It's owned by the workers, you know."

"I don't think, I mean ... I have to run everything according to ..."

Clyde interrupted. "I'm sure that can be arranged within the legal framework," he said, giving Mattie a reassuring nod. "Thanks, Michael. Glad to have you on board. You don't have contact details for this Julian lad, do you?"

Michael drew himself up. "There is such a thing as Data Protection Legislation," he said stiffly. "Fortunately for you, though, I don't submit to the controlling forces of the fascist state, so I'll look it up when I go into the library tomorrow." As he walked to the door, he glanced at the piles of history stock that Mattie had started to unpack and shook a finger at her. "I hope you've got some Hobsbawm in there," he said sternly, fishing in the top box, "and something by E. P. Thomson. Get some real intellects on the shelves, instead of all these airbrushed TV personalities."

Mattie gave a big sigh as he shut the door. "It's all very well for you, Clyde," she said pointedly. "It's me that's got to work with him."

"I think his bark will be more annoying than his bite," said Clyde, "and a 'character' could be an asset in a shop like this. Don't worry about the vouchers either. I'll get my accountant to act for you. I'm sure he can come up with a legal way round it. At least, legal on your side. Michael's conscience is not our responsibility, thank goodness."

Julian Cardwell turned out to be a skinny youth with big glasses and a mop of unruly dark hair who looked as if the sun had never touched his surface. He was polite, but very quiet and had a tendency to stare at the floor. He turned up at the shop the following afternoon, saying that Michael had sent him.

"Would you like to work in the bookshop for me?" said Mattie, trying to be encouraging.

"Yes, please," said Julian.

"Are you interested in books?"

"Yeah, I like them."

"Any particular sort that interests you?"

"Not really. I don't read them. But they're good things to be around. I'd like to read them, but I've never got into the habit."

"What are you reading at uni?"

"We don't have books. It's all online."

"I mean, what subject are you studying?"

"Business Studies."

"Oh!"

"Yeah. It's all a load of useless cra ... rubbish, but my mum wanted me to do it. She wants me to get on, you know – money and stuff."

Mattie pulled a face. "And what does your dad think?"

"I don't think he minds as long as I do something and she's happy."

"Ah."

Julian nodded to show that he knew she understood his situation.

Mattie went on to outline the work, the pay and so on, showing him the stock system and till, which was a handsome ancient cash-register that had belonged to the old village grocer. The young man was quick to pick it all up and made a couple of suggestions on improving the stock system.

"I can't show you the layout of the shop itself, yet," said Mattie, "as I haven't finished organising it."

Clyde and Laura were hanging around at the back of the shop, which was on a slightly higher level, fitting some of Laura's new signs. Julian gave them the odd glance, so Mattie introduced them.

"So, Julian, are you going to take the job?" asked Laura, sitting down cross-legged on a crate.

"Yes," said Julian brightly with a little smile, clearly impressed by her. "Thank you."

"Well," said Laura with a glance at Clyde, "I've got an idea that could help you. As a bookseller, you need to know about books; not just organising and displaying them, but what's inside. So as part of your training, you should read one book from each section of the shop." She pointed at the 'History' sign that Clyde had just screwed – slightly off level – to the top of a shelving unit. "You need to be able to advise customers, you see, and help them to choose."

"Oh," said Julian uncertainly, but plainly keen to please this charming woman who was taking an interest in him.

"We all had to start somewhere with reading," Laura went on blithely, hoping hard that Clyde had picked up that he would be paying for this spur-of-the-moment scheme. "You can pick any one you like and you get to keep it," she glanced at Clyde again, and to her relief he gave a barely perceptible nod, "to start your own library."

"Oh!" said Julian, then, "Thank you."

"If you want help picking, you can ask any one of us, or maybe Michael – it's up to you. Will that be okay?"

"Yes," said Julian definitely, raising his head to beam at Laura like a seedling unfurling before the sun. Clyde, who had been similarly bowled over by her powerful attraction, wondered if Julian was going to be alright, and whether Laura was aware of what had happened. Julian wasn't a child ...

He decided to join in and make his presence felt. "You could really help us, Julian, or at least Laura and me," he smiled at Mattie, "by telling us what you think of them when you've read them. And by taking an interest in new publications and the book market generally. We're both out of touch with young people, and you could give us lots of valuable insights."

Julian paused. "I don't really know many," he said at last.

"Books?"

"Young people. Only a couple of friends from school."

"Yes, but you *are* a young person," said Laura delightedly, "and that's just what we need."

Julian went a beautiful shade of China rose at the thought that he could be just what Laura needed. "Okay," he said to the floor.

"And I'm sure you'll have lots more helpful suggestions about the computer and things," she went on, waving a dismissive hand at the IT equipment on the desk. "I'm hopeless at all that stuff."

"I can help you!" A buzz of energy whipped through the limp boy. Clyde rolled his eyes and nudged Laura sharply with an elbow. She just grinned.

"That would be great," she said brightly, "but first, we have to get the shop open for business and put on the launch party. Mattie's got it all planned and Clyde's making the cake."

"Cake?" asked Julian with interest.

"Yes," Mattie resumed control, "Clyde and his assistant Zeno are going to be making cake for the shop. We'll have a few tables at the back, and help-yourself tea and coffee."

Julian's attention was now all for Clyde. "I'd like to try your cake, please."

"I'll bring some in for your first day."

"Great, thanks."

"And now Mattie had better fill you in on the murders, the launch party and the fabulous Melrose Burke."

"*Murders*?"

Mattie explained to a wide-eyed Julian, who was clearly an aficionado of the gruesome like herself. It looked as if they were going to get along well.

205

"Do you know Melrose Burke, the historian?" said Clyde at last.

"Is he the puffy old guy with the mad clothes you see around?"

"That's him."

"Weird."

"Indeed."

After the boy had left, ready to start on Monday, a puzzled Clyde said to Mattie, "I thought kids all spoke in some incomprehensible jargon and everything was 'sick'."

She laughed. "Some of them do in London. But why ask me? I'm at least seven years too old!"

"He's just an intelligent but inexperienced boy," said Laura. "I bet he'll come out of his shell working here."

"You do know that he's already coming out of his shell with you, don't you? And he's not really a boy." Clyde was just a touch sharp as he found himself ridiculously jealous, although also sympathetic to the smitten victim. "You need to be careful."

"Don't worry," said Laura. "He needs encouragement. And I need to get in touch with modern times. It'll be fine."

"Hmm," replied her partner. "Just take care, that's all."

The second week of December brought arctic weather in short days of dim lustre and solid frost. Clyde was worried by the encrusted, wilting plants set in the icy ground, which was as hard as concrete, but Martina assured him that they were all hardy and would simply carry on as normal after the thaw. The weather would delay delivery of the fruit trees, that was all, as they couldn't be dug or planted in the rigid earth.

He marvelled again at the wonders of nature that he had passed so many years unaware of: the tiny birds, puffed out like sponges, milling around the feeders in what seemed a wondrous act of survival; the coppery tinge of a fox glinting at the edge of the shrubbery. He once thought he saw a pine marten popping up its head from the trees like a little bibbed highwayman, but it was probably wishful thinking.

The bookshop was opening on Saturday with the launch event in the afternoon. Clyde was amusing himself by trying to predict Melrose's costume for the occasion, having a bet with Laura that he'd be sporting velvet again. Julian was settling in at the shop with Mattie and had already read *The Adventures of Sherlock Holmes*. He seemed to look forward to dealing with customers as a way of interacting that could be learned and did not depend on personal input, but he was showing general curiosity; questions were becoming a habit. He was not altogether impressed with some of Conan Doyle's scenarios and was keen to point out flaws and alternative explanations, but there was so much in the life of that period he did not understand that he soon exhausted Mattie's knowledge and she referred him to Michael, Melrose or Agnes. He did not see a lot of point in fiction, but he *was* interested in why other people thought there was, and as Clyde said, an interest in something was all you needed in life; it didn't matter if it seemed a really odd point of view to the rest of them.

"Think of all the interests of people we know here," he said. "History, true crime, trainspotting, gardening, cookery, art, literature, theatre, birdwatching, cards, tennis and more – some of these would be boring to a lot of people, but it doesn't matter. You just need to have a connection to something – something which you have a passion to learn, and hence perhaps explain or justify your existence. What is there to life except learning really? Hobbies, challenges and even pain are just that, and I'm fairly sure that if we stop learning, we will be dead. There would be no point in being here at all."

It was a good philosophy for someone about to open a

college, and he hoped it would be enough to see him and Laura through their own learning experience of the many practical and financial challenges ahead.

Laura was nervous about the bookshop opening, which was to be the first social occasion for her since she had 'come through'. She was worried about giving herself away, and about being recognised, in particular by the sharp-eyed Agnes Beresford. How would she explain herself? No one would believe her story, for which she had no scientific evidence, and yet if word of it got out into the wrong circles, it could bring a lot of unwelcome attention and publicity. Clyde did not tell her that this aspect of the situation was even worse than she imagined, as she had no idea of the power and influence of online media.

Clyde considered Agnes Beresford. On the whole, he thought it would be alright. Agnes was far more personally interested in men than women, and he thought that the most she might observe was a vague familiarity about Laura, which would be assuaged by Laura's modern clothes. She had bought some, with some chagrin at the flimsy, cheap quality and the outrageous prices, not to mention the very odd sizing; her old size was about three times too big and everything fitted in all the wrong places. It would seem like a mere coincidence that Laura reminded her of someone who had once taught the same subjects at the college years ago. Wouldn't it? For a practical mind like Agnes's, he thought that it would.

But then he thought of Laura's work. That would be much more of a giveaway. The vagaries of life might be responsible for bringing an art and languages teacher to Burnton who very much resembled one who had been there years ago, but they would *not* be sufficient explanation as to why the new teacher produced artwork identical to the old one. From what Agnes had said, he thought that her keen eye and sharp sense of taste had taken in a good deal more about Laura's art than they had about her person. He knew that art experts could tell if a work was by a particular artist or not, and anyway, Laura's were signed.

He had an urgent conference with Laura. "We can get away with the artwork aspect for now," he said, "as your work's not going to be on display at the shop launch, but I'll have to introduce you and the name may be a problem."

"I think someone told her my name at the bonfire party and she showed no signs of recognition. But then I wasn't being introduced as an art and languages teacher at the college. What d'you think we should do?"

Clyde was still thrilled to hear her say 'we' and not 'I'. He could see she was nervous, and this was precisely the kind of problem that she'd asked him to support her with. He must think of something.

"We could get married!" he blurted out. "Then no one would need to know your maiden name."

She smiled and gave him a playfully condescending kiss. "That's very gallant of you, darling, but we can hardly get married by tomorrow, and anyway, you *are* married already. To Lucinda."

"Oh yes, I'd forgotten."

"That's encouraging." She kissed him again. "Couldn't I just change my surname?"

"It's not that easy nowadays. You'd need a solicitor and deed poll and all kinds of proof."

"Oh! So many things seem to have become so much more fuss for no discernible reason." She thought for a moment, and then took his arms to look him full in the face. "Well, we'll just have to brazen it out and leave the artwork problem for another day. Okay?"

"Okay!" he said. "We'd better brief the others. In a moment or two," he qualified, as she leaned up to kiss him properly this time.

. . .

There was a good turn-out for the opening event; at one stage, it even looked as if it might be too good and not everyone would fit into the small shop. Julian took charge of the refreshment table with Clyde very much his assistant at the urns, and there was soon a buzz of chatter and delighted murmurs through mouths full of cake. People were milling around the shop rather than looking at specific books, but that was only to be expected as there was no room to browse properly.

At the higher end of the shop was a table with a projector and screen, and Clyde's stomach somersaulted in horror as he wondered whether Melrose was going to show the gory crime-scene photos. That would not be a good start! He desperately signalled Laura, who jumped in to cover the hot drinks – much to Julian's delight – and collared Mattie.

"It's alright," she said impatiently, busy entertaining customers. "I told him he mustn't use them tonight."

"Are you sure he won't do it anyway? Or by mistake?"

Mattie excused herself and came close to him, looking annoyed to have her authority questioned. He noticed how capable and masterful a figure she looked in the grass-green patterned maxi dress and sparkly makeup. He felt as if he had never seen her before.

"It's alright!" she repeated. "It's a PowerPoint presentation. You don't think Melrose knows how to do that, do you? I did it. He'll just be pressing the button." And with that, she turned away, a glittering smile plastering her face once more.

Clyde had just sidled back to Laura and Julian when the star of the show stepped out, hands aloft as if to suppress the hysterical excitement at his appearance. He wore dark mustard trousers, yellow shirt and a flowing silk scarf patterned in various shades of orange and gold that floated rather distractingly forwards over his expanse of frontage.

"Where *does* he find the stuff?" said Clyde under his breath, although he had to admit that it was quite a smart ensemble if you liked that sort of thing. He just about let himself wonder if he could carry off something like that, but knew he would never even admit to having thought of it.

Melrose began to squeak and rumble through his talk, pulling faces and waving his arms extravagantly like a technicolour Dr Caligari. Several times he unwittingly moved the slides forward too soon through an enthusiastic gesture. Still, the combined package of his assumed authority, his showmanship, the local connection and the sensational material had the audience hooked, and they shifted a good number of copies of the new book when he'd finished.

He'd wanted to do a signing, but Clyde had persuaded Mattie that close contact with the great author might not be such an encouragement as he fancied it to be, and so she had pleaded lack of space and got him to sign the copies in advance. He still had a good enough time shuffling flamboyantly round the room, greeting his audience in person. Strains of 'my dear boy' and 'on Channel 5 next year' could be heard above the general chitchat.

Michael had popped up at the refreshment table just as Melrose was about to speak, and spent the entire talk guzzling as much cake as he could get away with, washing it down with an occasional slurp of coffee, his back resolutely turned to the speaker. He came up for air just as Melrose stepped down to mingle.

"Tcha! Just look at him," he said scornfully, wiping his fingers on a paper napkin. "The seedy bourgeois in his flashy get-up with his sensationalist story about the death of two useless parasites on society. And they're all lapping it up," he added with disgust, looking over to the till where guests were queuing to pay for their copies. "The proletariat! Tcha! Could I take a bit of this cake home, d'you think?" He produced a plastic freezer bag from his pocket.

Clyde let him take as much as he could cram into the bag, and then said, "Julian's settling in well," watching the young man packing purchases and handing them to customers as Mattie manned the till.

"He's a good boy," said Michael approvingly. "I hear he's been reading books."

"It seemed a prerequisite of the job," said Clyde.

"He can see through that bourgeois rubbish you've given him, though," Michael continued with enthusiasm. "*Sherlock Holmes*, indeed! Class-ridden nonsense. He's very critical of it."

"He was allowed to take any book of his choice," said Clyde. "That was Laura's idea," he added proudly. "And probably the main thing is to get him reading so that, being a bright young man, as you say, he can develop his own taste. Don't you think?"

"A bit of guidance never hurt," replied Michael obstinately, "although the young are never keen to take it, of course. And they have no concept of theory these days; no rigorous framework to their ideas, if they have any. Give him something by Edward Upward. See what he makes of that, instead of puff like *Sherlock Holmes*." And, keen as ever to have the last word, he stalked away clutching his spoils.

Mattie, Martina, Laura and Clyde arrived back home towards dinner time, exhausted. Clyde had left lasagnes ready to go into the oven. The girls went home to rest and clean up, intending to return later to have supper with Clyde and Laura.

"God," said Laura, "I'm tired. And I haven't really done much. I think I'll have a bath, if that's okay."

"I'll be up in a minute myself," replied Clyde. "I'll just

check on the food in the kitchen and get a few things ready. Fancy a glass of wine?"

"Yes, why not." She gave him a weary smile and started up the stairs. He went into the kitchen and had pottered around the counters for a moment before noticing a piece of paper on the table. He picked it up.

'Just got back. Need to rest and recover. Will see you tomorrow, Zeno.'

Clyde stopped in his tracks, for a second reliving all the emotional turmoil of recent times. This was it. This would be the time when everything finally came out and was settled. This would be the end of the beginning of his life at Valencia House and the beginning of all that would go on to happen.

Chapter Sixteen

IT WAS TEATIME the following day when Zeno knocked at the door. He wouldn't usually have done that, of course, but it was a tactful way to ease himself back into life at Valencia House and test the waters. After all, when Zeno had left, Clyde had been in what his Aunty Gwen would have called 'a state', and had not been speaking to his once-valued house-keeping assistant.

Laura said, "Let me go," and Clyde, Mattie and Martina, who were, as usual at that time of day, sitting round the kitchen table with mugs of hot tea, today with the first of the year's mince pies, heard her friendly greeting.

"Hello, Zeno. Have you had a good holiday? Hope your family's well."

"Laura! I'm glad to see you here. Yes, thank you." They approached in the shuffling bustle of removing coats and settling into a new space.

The kitchen became lively with Zeno's arrival. The energetic little man was beset by busy conversation on all sides: Martina had lots to tell him of mutual friends, the drama group, and her new role at Valencia House; Laura had plenty of catching up to do; and Mattie wanted to tell him about her moving onto the property, her new projects and his possible involvement in the bookshop café catering. The girls both asked politely about his family too, and he promised to bring photos to show them next time they were all together.

Only Clyde was quiet, considering and adjusting. Eventually, Zeno, who was sitting opposite him, stopped talking and looked at him with such an intensity that the others soon stopped speaking too. Clyde's gaze was equally unwavering.

"Good to see you, Zeno," said Clyde at last.

"It's good to be back," said Zeno steadily.

"Shall we have it all out now?"

"Yes!"

A frisson of alarm ran around the room at the tension between the two men, like gunfighters about to duel. Laura was braced to intervene if they engaged in combat, but Clyde gave Zeno the floor and he started to speak.

"I'm sure Laura has told you the main part of the story," he said, and at Laura's nod of confirmation, he went on, "So it only remains for me to explain my part in it.

"I was resident caretaker and assistant cook here when I was young, at the time when Laura and Frances Harvey were working here too. I was great friends with Arthur Colclough who lived in the lodge cottage that is now my home, which is why I knew what it had been like years ago. I know that puzzled you," he acknowledged to Clyde.

"Then I met my wife, who had a little money to put together with my savings, so I left the college and we opened a restaurant. It was just at the start of the college's decline, after Arthur had died, and I lost touch with the place. It was about twenty years later, when we divorced and closed the restaurant, that I thought of returning here. I found that the college was sadly rundown and might even close, but there was casual work going, which I was happy to take.

"As soon as I did, things started to drift backwards. Laura and Frances were here, running things very much as they used to be, and I felt rejuvenated. So of course, I stayed on in my residential capacity, but in the new 'old' time. The difference for me was that when I left the college, I came back into current times – I mean the timeline we are on now – and aged correspondingly. It meant that I could keep up with my daughters, who merely thought that I looked very well and happy after separating from their mother. In a way, I think it was easier for me, because both timelines were running simultaneously in my life and I moved from one to the other constantly from the start. And once the timelines began to synchronise again, it was natural for me to get out into the modern world and help the transition, which is why I came to work for you."

"But why," burst out Clyde, who could wait no longer, "didn't you tell me what was going on?"

"I was going to," said Zeno regretfully, "but it's not the easiest thing to explain. I wasn't sure what exactly the result of the time merge would be either. I didn't – and still don't – have all the answers. Also," he added after a pause, "there was the presence of your wife to consider. She was not sensitive to what was happening, I could tell, and would not be open to any explanation I might attempt.

"And then the subject of the murders cropped up. I'd only vaguely heard of them before and I wasn't sure at first if what you were seeing really was connected to them. After all, if there was one time slip, there might have been another for all I knew. It was only when I myself saw the figure in the drawing room the following evening and realised – with relief – that it was Marjorie Barker, that I understood. But the more disturbed by things you became, the harder it seemed to attempt an explanation ...

"And then you had the bonfire party and Laura came along to upset you even more!"

He smiled at Laura, and then watched Clyde anxiously to see how he was going to respond. It took a moment or two for Clyde's pride – subterfuge is never pleasant or easy to swallow – to adjust.

"I would like to stay and keep working for you, if you could see your way to it," Zeno said at last. "Not only is this my home, but I *like* working with you. I felt we had become friends."

"So did I," said Clyde cautiously. "Yes, I'd like you to stay, Zeno, but no more lies by omission. On every other subject, you've always been, I believe, frank with me, and I accept that this was a difficult situation for you. But it must never happen again. If we can surmount the oddities of recent events, then there will be nothing that we can't discuss in the future. Clear?"

"Clear!" replied Zeno, looking Clyde straight in the face. "I apologise to you all, because in hindsight, I could have handled the situation much better."

"It's settled, then," pronounced Clyde, and brought his assistant up to date on everything that had happened in his absence.

"Zeno, it does sound as if this ridiculous paranormal investigator Anthony Lill was right," he said at length. "What do you think?"

"I have read a couple of his books, and I think that his explanations fit my experience – all our experiences – very well. There isn't any robust scientific evidence to back up his theories – the 'physics' he does is all nonsense – but that doesn't mean that someone won't do some proper research on it one day. Until then, it seems a useful way of understanding and referring to what we've lived through." He looked at Laura, who nodded.

"So," Clyde clarified, "you all ran off the mainline of time at a discontinuity and carried on a parallel branch line – except Zeno, who was able to change from one train to another at the station; this house. Then eventually your branch line re-joined the mainline further down the track, before which we could see each other sometimes as we got nearer, and now here we all are. It's not a very sound analogy, and not at all rigorous, but it does make a sort of intuitive sense."

He considered. "To be honest, I don't find the situation anywhere near as hard to believe as the idea that Anthony Lill might know what he's on about."

"From what you've said," replied Zeno thoughtfully, "the man is vain, shallow and rude, but that doesn't mean he's without abilities. You know life's not that simple. Perhaps he senses something, consciously or subconsciously, and filled in the gaps with the spurious science to build it up in a convincingly marketable way. Or perhaps it's a complete fabrication and just a fantastic coincidence that it fits with our experience. Who knows?"

"Well, we do, sort of," said Clyde. "And now it's time to think of the future. We're all travelling on the same train, and it's supercharged by this strange, rich variety of experience. So let's go somewhere! Martina, why don't you tell Zeno about your college idea?"

They all rushed into an animated discussion that lasted for so long that Clyde, at the approach of evening, rustled up his quick vegetable biryani to feed everyone. Eventually, they decided to have a dinner-party-cum-meeting and invite Melrose Burke and Agnes Beresford. They debated whether to ask Mr Lemon, agreeing that his memories of the old college days and legal knowledge might be useful. Clyde considered inviting some of Lucinda's local art-scene contacts, but decided that at this stage, they might not be supportive, seeing the new college as competing for funds with their own ventures.

Mattie suggested including Julian, to represent the under-25s – "Do they eat dinner?" asked Clyde, who thought of modern youth as strange aliens. "I don't know, but I bet if Laura asks him, he'll come," replied Mattie with a twinkle – and Zeno suggested Michael. No one else, especially Mattie, was keen on this idea, but Zeno pointed out that they might need a librarian, Frances Harvey seeming to have abandoned them, and that Michael was very well-read and knowledgeable in his fields.

"It's true," said Clyde, "that if we are going to include politics and economics, or even geography, we'll need to bring in all the very significant theories and practices of recent times that have been so well airbrushed from the collective consciousness. Anyway, Michael certainly won't refuse a free meal. Melrose, Michael and Marjorie are always eating huge quantities at others' expense," he observed drily.

"What's happened to Marjorie?" asked Zeno. "Does anyone know?" He looked at Laura.

"No," she said, sadly, "she hasn't been seen since I moved in. I can't see why that would have put her off. I wondered if … I mean, she was old, and just because you're on a different, more elongated timeline doesn't mean that you can cheat death altogether."

"You can never cheat death," said Zeno solemnly. "It comes to us all in the end."

There was a silence. "Poor old Marjorie," said Laura at last with a sigh. "I suppose we might never know. But without us, who will be at her funeral?"

Zeno, with uncharacteristic familiarity, patted her hand. "I don't think there's anything we can do, my dear," he said gently.

Laura sniffed. "I know," she said. "And she had a good

run, queening it round the place." She was smiling again at the recollection. "What about Frances?"

"I thought she might have moved on elsewhere."

"Yes, I thought so too. I suppose we *might* hear something of her ..."

"You think so?"

"Yes," said Laura. "If we keep a look out for the right kind of strange happening, we'll know when we see it."

Zeno considered. "Hmm. You might be right."

As Clyde served fruit salad, the discussion turned to accommodation for students, privacy for Clyde and Laura, and all kinds of conditions for their ambitious scheme.

"I still can't get over how keen people are on bathrooms these days," said Laura. "As if they have to have one per person. It seems like a waste of useful space to me. I like showers, though, so much more refreshing and easy than a bath."

"I suppose you like your bathrooms in bright colours too," teased Clyde, "like pink, primrose and avocado."

"Some of them could look good," said Laura defensively. "I certainly don't like the endless shades of grey that are in fashion now. It's like washing inside a galvanised tank or something. You can scoff," she dug him playfully in the ribs, and they both giggled, "being all modern and superior, but there's a lot to be said for colour in life. It's expressive, responsive, alive, and I love it!" She pulled a face at Clyde.

"I tell you what is *amazing*, though," she said at length, sucking a morsel of pineapple, "the food! You're the most fantastic cook, Clyde – nearly as good as Zeno," she winked affectionately at the little man. "So much flavour, and different tastes and ingredients ... it's all very exotic and overwhelming, and delicious. I think I've put weight on."

"Does it make up for the lack of maroon bathroom suites?" asked Clyde, delighted.

"I know you're joking, but actually," she paused to swallow another mouthful of dessert, "it does feel rather as if you've swapped one sense for another. All this vibrancy of taste and nothing for your eyes to feast on.

"In fairness, that's not true in this house," she admitted with consideration, still eating. "The library in particular has the most opulent colour scheme."

"I hope you are going to get all your library stock through me," said Mattie, picking up the book-related reference.

"Naturally. I'm not sure how we're going to pay for it yet, though. None of our contacts is an expert on funding, as far as I know. With budgets so violently slashed everywhere, what we really need is a billionaire philanthropist."

"You are joking about the *billionaire* bit, aren't you?" said Laura, surprised. "I mean, surely no one could be that rich?"

"There's a whole class of them these days," replied Clyde. "And it's growing by the hour.

"There is also the problem of a name for the college," he went on. "I don't want to reopen as the Samuel Shaftacre Memorial College; too many links with the past, Greater Blocton Council etc. And the Shaftacre name isn't as universally well known as it was. If we call it simply Burnton College, it sounds too much like state education."

"How about the Berenia Hassel Memorial College?" said Mattie.

"No." Clyde was firm. "No bringing the murders into it. And anyway, Berenia wasn't the only one who died."

"I think we should get away from the 'memorial' thing altogether, if possible," put in Laura. "It's not very forward-looking."

"May I make a suggestion?" Zeno spoke slowly and carefully. Clyde looked across at the man, who had adopted his most inscrutable Jeeves-like expression, with just a glint of cunning in those bright eyes.

They all waited.

"How about 'The Jason Deaville Foundation, President Lucinda Lowe'?" He glanced at Clyde. "If you could bear it," he added.

"Er, yes," said Clyde, astonished, "but …"

"I don't think," interrupted Zeno, "that Mrs Tranter is going to find it quite as easy as she believes to renege on her commitments under the Regional Funding Plan. And Mr Deaville has just had some very unsavoury publicity about his financial probity and tax avoidance. Before *that* was his divorce from that well-known newsreader. Funding an educational foundation here would kill two birds with one stone: make him look like he spends his excess money considerately at home, rather than laundering it in the Cayman Islands, or whatever such people actually do, and make it clear that his new wife's divorce was entirely civilised and amicable. He could spare a million or two without even noticing it."

Clyde was not convinced. "I don't see him going for it. Men like that don't like giving money away, and neither does Lucinda."

"It's not giving money away," insisted Zeno. "It's an investment in cover and positive publicity. I don't think he'll give it to you if you ask him, but that's not what we're going to do."

They all stared and waited.

"I know someone on the Regional Funding Council," whispered Zeno as if he were planning a daring escape. "I can have a word and suggest that they shouldn't give in easily to Mrs Tranter's demands; after all, why should they? They have paid for services they haven't received. Mattie has press contacts who could drop in a story – quite mild and entirely truthful – about your divorce and Lucinda 'moving on' from the Midlands to foreign parts. They can also," he gestured to Clyde, "let it slip that you are looking to start a college here and want to make it a charitable foundation. Then we'll let Jason Deaville put two and two together and make the offer to you."

"It's very far-fetched," said Clyde. "I don't think he'll do it. A man like that isn't so easily manoeuvred. We're not in a fairy story, you know."

"Aren't we?" said Zeno, blinking quizzically. "Are you sure?"

Clyde wondered once more about his housekeeping assistant and who he really was. Perhaps he'd come to Burnton through the magic portal in Ridgley.

"It sounds dishonest," said Clyde. "I won't tell lies, and I won't engage in smears and abuse. Not of anyone."

"There's no need," said Zeno comfortingly. "We'll just be getting on with trying to establish the college in an honest and straightforward way. Let's see what happens."

"Okay," said Clyde at last. "That's what we'll do."

Clyde spoke to all the prospective dinner guests to give them some idea of what he and his friends had in mind about the college. This proved to be wise, as though enthusiastic in principle, some of them were concerned at the financial rashness of such a project. Still, a dinner invitation at Valencia House was too good to miss, and they were all keen to hear what Clyde had in mind.

It was certainly an occasion for the long table in the formal dining area, and Clyde began to give some thought to the food. As it was mid-December, the spectre of Christmas dinner hovered and rather eclipsed any other celebratory roast that might be offered. It needed to be something special and slightly formal with a vegetarian option. He considered a pie or two, but that did not fit the mood of the occasion.

Then he had it; Indian food! He and Zeno could have fun preparing a selection of the many different snack foods from that most varied of culinary regions, which would make the perfect first course to encourage conversation. Chicken korma, butter paneer and mounds of snowy steamed basmati rice next, followed by a fresh mango and yogurt dessert, finishing with a selection of homemade biscuits favouring cardamom, butter and nuts to be served with coffee. He rushed off to consult Zeno, who offered a recipe for chapli kebabs given to him by a friend years ago, and insistently recommended a non-vintage champagne.

On the day of the dinner, the delicious background aroma of oil and spices seemed to have penetrated the fabric of the house. Laura embellished it with fragrant incense until the depth of olfactory experience was a special occasion in itself. She also set about decorating the table with greenery and candles, the former gathered by Martina, who had collected armfuls of seasonal foliage from the grounds. Mattie, surprisingly, produced a pair of beautiful antique silver candlesticks that had belonged to her grandmother, which she and Martina filled with hand-dipped beeswax candles from the farmers' market. Zeno polished and placed the crystal glassware and firmly-pressed linen napkins on the table. Clyde had rashly purchased sufficient Shaftacre plates and bowls for the guests to eat from, at a somewhat eye-watering cost; he hoped none of them got broken. The dazzling purity of the white china under the soft wetness of its glaze, encircled by a deep band of embossed ultramarine and heavy gold, gave the dining room a hint of the mogul's palace.

"If only we had silver serving dishes," said Clyde with a
's they all admired the table. "Something fancy –
say." Looking at Mattie's candlesticks, he felt

suddenly aware of how few family pieces he had – furniture, pictures, ornaments or tableware – and regretted it. It would have been lovely to have had a stack of old-fashioned and unnecessary serving dishes that could suddenly drop into use for an occasion like this. One of the luxuries of being able to afford a large property was that there was room to keep all the family things that one didn't really need, but liked too much to part with. He sighed again for the connections he did not have.

Zeno, of course, was the one to come to the rescue, not with fabulous silver, but with a selection of ornate metal serving dishes borrowed from a restauranteur friend.

The guests arrived to be greeted by Laura, looking both relaxed and stunning in a long black and gold dress of empire line, her hair loosely up, and a single diamond pendant – bought for her by Clyde for the occasion and costing considerably less than the tableware – gracing her neck and chest. Inwardly, she was still nervous of meeting Agnes Beresford, but was determined to carry it off.

Agnes herself looked very elegant in a gold and cream brocade dress and arrived accompanied by Neville Lemon, his limbs held loosely together by a superlatively well-tailored dinner suit. Mattie also wore her black evening suit with a striking red silk shirt beneath the jacket, and Martina looked defiantly handsome in emerald green and black, her dark hair piled above her long white face and neck in regal style. Melrose Burke sported the full maroon velvet suit and frilled shirt, his enormous gold watch flashing from beneath the cuff, and even Michael, who was dressed in his everyday style, seemed to have picked his most colourful clothes. Julian too was dressed much as usual, although with an indefinable sense of being especially smart for the occasion.

"I don't understand youth fashion," Clyde whispered to Laura in a quiet moment. "I'm sure they spend money on their clothes, but they never look like they're wearing anything."

"Like the Emperor?" said Laura, laughing.

He laughed too. "No, but the clothes are invisible in a way. I mean, it's impossible to notice them. All that remains is an impression of a body that's covered up. They don't seem have any discernible colour or style."

"Like modern bathrooms," said his partner with a smile.

Having mingled briefly with champagne, the guests and their hosts were soon all seated, exploring dishes of pastries, fritters, kebabs, fried vegetables, salads and chutneys with animation. It was just as Clyde had hoped. As the first course drew to a close, the platters with only crumbs remaining and conversation ebbing, he rose and refilled all the glasses before returning to the head of the table.

"Thank you all very much for joining us this evening," he began, looking round his guests. "We're so happy to welcome you to our home," he smiled at Laura, "some of you for the first time. We are particularly hoping for your help and advice in opening out this house," he paused to let the right words come, "to some of our fellow students in life, so that we may share our knowledge and skills; and our belief that life is nothing if it is not a journey of learning and expansion.

"Before we discuss the project in more detail, I want to remember some former residents of this house: four people who lost their lives through violence here – Berenia Hassel, Sheila Cope, Janet Baxter and Alf Baxter – and three more whose lives were irrevocably changed – Brian Hassel and the two young Baxters, Keith and Eileen. This tragic event was almost certainly a belated consequence of earlier widespread violence and destruction across swathes of our species on an ...cedented scale. Who knows why people behave in such a ... to let these things occur? Who understands the ... between the great goods and great evils, the works of genius and acts of madness of which human beings are capable? If there were a Divine plan, how could it be so?

"We cannot know. But we can know that from the terrible slayings here in this house and grounds came an opening for something good, happy and constructive; a manifestation of life, the college. And we do know that it was those past events, the murders and the running of the college, that have led all our paths to cross and brought us together. So I say, let the sacrifice of those lives once again lead on to something good, constructive and meaningful. Let us make this house a place of learning, love and life."

He raised his glass, and Zeno quickly proposed a toast: "The college!"

"The college!" everyone echoed, slightly choked. Then it was time for the main course, and the bustle of eating and conversation gradually resumed.

Epilogue

AND SO, the new college at Valencia House began to take shape the following year, and some small experimental courses were running within twelve months. Mattie's bookshop established itself successfully as a place to visit for browsing and refreshments before a walk on the heath and a visit to the Shaftacre Museum on the factory site.

Melrose Burke's book on the Burnton murders was a great success and did indeed spawn a documentary on Channel 5, but was not, of course, as lucrative as Anthony Lill's autobiographical international bestseller. Still, it generated useful publicity for the new college, and also inspired the Greater Blocton Museum and Art Gallery to mount a permanent exhibition about the history of Valencia House, including the story of the murders and its time as a college. With the assistance of Neville Lemon, Clyde arranged for Berenia Hassel's jewellery to become part of the display, along with the length of lead piping, which he happened to have kept, and the 'P Hutchinson' name plate. Despite the interest in Melrose's well-developed theories, no additional evidence to support Brian Hassel's – or anyone else's – involvement in the murders came to light, and so the full facts of the crimes at Valencia House remained a mystery, with Alf Baxter still officially responsible.

Laura found her art practice was dramatically changed by the bizarre life experience from which she had emerged. Her long grounding in the past followed by the burgeoning expansion into modern times gave her work new scope and power. She became particularly interested in exploring media that were new to her, and under the gracious patronage of Lucinda Lowe, after whose charity foundation the college was named, had a couple of moderately successful exhibitions.

Clyde had occasional dealings with Lucinda and even Jason Deaville over the financing of the college, which came about much as Zeno had prophesied, although once the foundation was established they had very little personal involvement. He looked back on his relationship with Lucinda with such detachment that it was almost as if it had happened to someone else. If he ever wondered about the genesis of his ex-wife's relationship with the great impresario, it was only with a passing idle curiosity and no powerful emotion.

Martina's garden flourished so much that she soon needed further assistance, and she and Clyde were able to sell surplus produce to the pub and at the farmers' market. Her relationship with Mattie blossomed and rooted too, and the girls were planning to get married in the old village church, now a civil weddings venue. Martina still had time, though, to help Julian when he decided to abandon the dreaded business studies for geography.

Julian never quite got over his adoration of Laura, and hence developed a taste for art. He eventually became a confident and enthusiastic bookseller whilst working for his new degree, and a selective, highly critical reader who began to hold his own in heated discussions with Michael.

Neville Lemon retired to his dahlias, and became a regular

companion of Agnes Beresford. Agnes herself was, of course, very much involved in the running of the college, providing support and advice to Clyde, who relied on the friendship of someone so much older and more experienced than himself all the more from having no surviving family. She did give him a few moments of disquiet, though: first she borrowed his copy of Wells' *The Time Machine*, then Zeno's acting edition of Priestley's *I Have Been Here Before*; next, he found her in the bookshop ordering *Time Travel: A History* and *The Order of Time*.

Finally, she remarked to him quite pointedly at one of Laura's exhibitions, "I do admire Laura's work. But then, I always did." He knew then that it was time for him and Laura to take Agnes into their confidence about the parallel histories at Valencia House.

Marjorie Barker was not seen or heard of again until the day of the rehearsal for Martina and Mattie's wedding. As they were waiting outside the village church, Laura suddenly called Clyde over.

"Clyde, come here! Look at this."

Before her was a polished headstone with gold letters:

George Barker 1900–1975
beloved husband of
Marjorie
1907–1990
who also lies here

Laura took Clyde's hand and squeezed it "So now we know," she said.

Meanwhile, in town, the conversion of the old Blocton

City Central Library and Archives to investment flats had not been a success. No one would stay there long. People would come home and find their belongings had been moved, tidied and reorganised while they were out. Piles of books appeared overnight, swamping furniture and kitchens, and beds disappeared, leaving metal shelving units in their place. Spookily, the word 'SILENCE' was written in large black letters across any available wall space, and no matter how many times it was washed off, it always came back. But most unbearable, and costly, to the residents was the vandalism of any electronic device that produced sound: televisions, speakers and Alexa hubs would all be found dismantled, smashed or otherwise disabled. Eventually, insurers refused to cover contents in the building.

Frances Harvey may have been lost to Valencia House, but Laura saw the news and felt sure she knew where her former flatmate's branch line was now crossing.

About the Author

Emily Tellwright was born in Stoke-on-Trent, UK and read mathematics at Christ Church, Oxford and science, society and technology at the University of East London, later studying cello at the Royal Welsh College of Music and Drama. She has worked, amongst other things, as a bookseller, an accountant, a musician, a tutor and a carer. She lives with her partner in Stoke-on-Trent writing, studying art, cooking, gardening and running Castle Sefton Press.

Ghost Train is her first book.

To find out more about Emily and her work:
https://www.emilytellwright.co.uk

Eco Giving

If you enjoyed this book and are reading a second-hand or borrowed copy...

... that's great! Here at Castle Sefton Press, we too love second-hand books. And we are very aware of the need to reduce consumption of physical resources and make the best use of every book printed.

But...

... without new books, there would be no second-hand ones to enjoy. So much goes in to the creation of a new book: months, or even years, of work by the author giving of their unique experience, inspiration and talent; copyediting and proofreading by skilled professionals; typesetting; original artistic design combining a wide range of practical skills; printing and the associated costs; marketing and publicity to help readers find the book; and distribution so that they can buy one.

We are a tiny business with just a handful of people to perform all these functions vital to bringing our books to you, the reader, and if you have enjoyed this book second-hand, sadly you have made no contribution to the costs of that process at all.

The good news is...

...that you can now support our work producing original new books and still enjoy eco-friendly second-hand copies. By going to www. castleseftonpress.co.uk/eco-giving *or scanning the QR code, you can make a small donation to Castle Sefton Press to reflect the enjoyment you have had from one of our products. Less than the price of a coffee would make a big difference to us!*

Thank you for your support, but please only donate if you can afford to do so without causing yourself hardship.

Castle Sefton Press

We are a tiny craft publisher based in Stoke-on-Trent, UK.

*Find out more about our publications, authors, associated merchandise and latest news at **www.castleseftonpress.co.uk** or contact us at **contact@castleseftonpress.co.uk**.*